LOVE AND OHANA DRAMA

A Romantic Comedy

MELISSA BALDWIN

Formatted by The Letterers Collective

Print ISBN: 9781697688917

Version: 10-09-2019

Books by Melissa Baldwin

Cozy Mystery

Movie Scripts & Madness (The Madness and Murder Mysteries #1)

Room Service & Murder (The Madness and Murder Mysteries #2)

Romantic Comedy & Chick Lit

Love and Ohana Drama

On the Road to Love (Love in the City #1)

All You Need is Love (Love in the City #2)

From Runway to Love (Love in the City #3)

Pushing Up Daisies Collection (Love in the City short story)

One Way Ticket (written with Kate O'Keeffe)

Friends ForNever (From Gemma Halliday Publishing)

An Event to Remember (Event to Remember #1)

Wedding Haters (Event to Remember #2)

Not Quite Sheer Happiness (Event to Remember #3)

See You Soon Broadway (Broadway #1)

See You Later Broadway (Broadway #2)

About Love and Ohana Drama

Love and Ohana Drama **is a romantic comedy that explores the challenges of family dynamics and reminds readers that there is always hope for a second chance. Sometimes the most challenging situations bring the most happiness...**

Twenty-something Cora Fletcher is a book-loving public relations executive who lives with her overly Zen best friend and attention-loving cat. Newly single and focusing on her exciting career, she feels like she's in a good place. She's even been invited on an all-expenses-paid Hawaiian vacation! The only catch—it's a family reunion . . . and her family can be a lot to handle.

Cora vows to not let that get in the way, but even before the family has boarded the plane, the *ohana* drama begins. As usual, there's the sister-in-law who is bent on causing friction, the self-centered cousins, and the aunt who loves to party a bit too much. Her mother has filled the itinerary with endless activities, and she's even invited Cora's ex-boyfriend in an attempt to get them back together.

Although she feels overwhelmed, Cora gets a blast from her past that could impact her life forever. This is one welcome reunion she did not expect . . .

Will Cora make it through a week of family togetherness? And will she be able to say *aloha* to someone she thought was out of her life forever?

I dedicate this book to the Parente Ohana.
I know Grandpa and Grandma are smiling down on us!

Chapter One

Why does the idea of a family reunion cause every cell in my body to beg for a Xanax? You would think the reunion being in Hawaii would soften the blow, but alas, not even a tropical paradise can make this event any less painful. At this moment I'd rather hang out with a bunch of terrifying clowns than go on this vacation.

∾

I close my laptop and lean back in my chair. *Why?* Why did I check my emails this morning? I had a feeling, call it a premonition, that I would regret it. As soon as I saw my mother's email address in all its glory, I should've walked away or deleted it, accidentally of course. *Come on, Cora, that was a total rookie mistake.*

And where was Kiwi in my time of need? Of all days for my cat to avoid parking herself on my laptop. Why does she only do that when I'm working or shopping online? Where's the loyalty? Some people say cats aren't as loyal as dogs. Maybe it's true?

The cold hard truth is that receiving emails from my mother is the equivalent of waking up on the wrong side of the bed, only eighty thousand times worse. Her emails start a domino effect: she makes a snarky comment about my love life, I get frustrated, and the remainder of my day is ruined. Most of the time she forwards me quotes or stories with a not-so-subtle message about finding true love or giving my ex-boyfriend a second chance, but not today. No, today she unleashed the bomb that my parents are planning their fortieth wedding anniversary celebration in Hawaii and we're all invited.

Okay, I know this sounds like a pretty sweet deal. Hawaii, the land of coconuts, pineapples, and pristine beaches. A place I've only dreamed of visiting, and on top of that, all expenses paid. I should be ecstatic. And if I were going to celebrate with friends or, let's say, Chris Hemsworth, then this trip would be a dream come true. Unfortunately, this isn't a vacation with an Australian superhero, it's a vacation with my family.

It's a proven fact that I don't fit in with the Fletcher clan. If I didn't look like a carbon copy of my father, I would question whether or not I really am a Fletcher. I was blessed with my dad's sparkling blue eyes, defined cheek bones, and much to my mother's dismay, his dry sense of humor. You'd think she would appreciate this about me since she's been married to my father for almost forty years. He's extremely laid back and lets my mother dominate most situations. We've all learned it's easier on everyone to let her take charge.

My brother Shawn is a mama's boy; he'll do and say whatever he has to in order to manipulate both my parents. And my sister is exactly like my mother; they both crave drama and expect to get their way all the time. If you look up the quintessential middle child, you might see my picture.

Kiwi saunters over casually and rubs against my leg. Now she wants some attention. *Where was she five minutes ago?*

She's a good pet, well, usually, and she has great instincts. I should've trusted her the first time she hissed at my ex-boyfriend Jackson. Supposedly cats are very intuitive. I'm sure Kiwi knew we were weren't compatible from the start. Jackson isn't a bad guy, but Kiwi definitely didn't like him.

I still don't know why I didn't go with my gut and say no to my sister, Maya. It was her brilliant idea to set me up with her husband's friend, and against my better judgement, I went along with it. Honestly, I'm a matchmaker's worst nightmare, or as my mother says, I'm too picky for my own good. She's convinced I've sabotaged relationships with the best of the best. She was really upset when I ended things with Jackson, whom she thinks of as another son.

"Okay, tell me what happened," a voice whispers.

I look up to see my roommate, Fran, staring at me with her hands folded in prayer position at her chest, I think it's one of the *chakras*. I can't remember which one.

"Your aura is completely compromised," she adds.

I snort. This isn't the first time she's accused me of having a compromised aura, whatever that means.

I tell her about the fateful email.

She pushes her long black hair behind her shoulder. "Cora Fletcher, this is an incredible opportunity. A chance to travel to a beautiful island, immerse yourself in the rich Polynesian culture, and become one with the land. If you don't want to go, I'll gladly take your place."

I give her a wistful look. "You sure about that? A week with my entire family—Maya and her husband, Hunter, my parents, Shawn and Brynn …"

Fran raises her eyebrows at the mention of my brother's wife.

Brynn, Fran, and I go way back, and not in a good way. Never in a million years did I think my older brother would marry the most horrible girl in my sorority. Brynn was the ultimate mean girl, and she hasn't changed the older she's gotten. My brother Shawn went to a university with a five-girls-to-one-guy ratio, but he still ended up marrying my worst nightmare of potential sisters-in-law.

Fran begins to wave her hands around me and chant something under her breath.

"Cora, bring it back to the present."

I nod absently.

"I'm here. Just thinking about being stuck with Brynn for the week." I make a gagging sound. "Why couldn't my brother marry you?"

Fran shakes her head. "Nah, if the universe had wanted us to be together, it would've happened."

I purse my lips.

There's a bit of a backstory there, and whether she wants to admit it or not, she had a thing for my brother during our sophomore year when she came to my parents' house for Thanksgiving. I saw the sparks fly between Shawn and Fran. Everyone did. They talked to each other most of the evening, and Shawn even said he'd been thinking about coming to visit me at college, which was news to me. Fran was definitely interested, because she was asking a lot of questions about him after dinner. I have no doubt that if we hadn't been at my parents' house, they would've hooked up. Sadly, nothing ever came from their attraction. I think they spoke on the phone a few times, but the timing was never right. And because the universe hates me, Shawn met Brynn at a charity event, and the rest is history.

"Oh well, you just have to avoid her," Fran says, dragging me out of my memory. "Because you're going to Hawaii." She grabs her bag from the counter and hurries out the door before I can protest.

I slowly run my hand over Kiwi's back. She's made herself very comfortable next to me while I slowly open my laptop as if it's attached to an explosive. I click on my mother's email and read through her message again and again.

> *Dearest family and friends,*
>
> *As you know, in September Warner and I are celebrating a blissful forty years of marriage. After much discussion, we've decided we want to commemorate this momentous occasion with a week in the Hawaiian Islands. The only thing that would make this celebration more perfect would be to have our ohana (family) there with us—our treat. We can't wait to see you soon!*
>
> *Mahalo,*
> *Leann and Warner*

I press on my temples as I try to process what's about to go down. Other than holidays, I haven't spent a lot of time with my family in several years, and Jackson was with me this last Christmas. Although he spent most of the holiday talking to my brother-in-law, Hunter, about a potential business venture and their hiking trip through the Appalachian Mountains. My mother and sister spent the weekend shopping online with Brynn close by.

Like my brother, Brynn knows how to work my parents and work them good. She'll go out of her way to be helpful when we're all together, and she's the one who will search out the perfect gift for my mother to win her over.

Shortly after she and my brother were engaged, my mother told her a story about a special Christmas ornament that broke. Apparently it was the first ornament my father had ever given her, and it was a collector's item. Lo and behold, guess what was hanging on the tree the following year? Somehow Brynn managed to search it out and ordered it from a tiny little shop in Germany.

She'll do thoughtful things like that, but at the same time she'll try to undermine me and Maya (mostly me) when it comes to our mother.

Brynn has Mom completely snowed, and I still can't gauge what the rest of my family really thinks of her. She and my brother have been married for two years, but I blocked out the first year entirely.

Anyway, I spent most of the holiday curled up on my favorite window seat, reading, while my brother and dad argued fantasy football. It was a typical Fletcher family event with me on the sidelines.

The only good part of that visit was spending time with my grandfather, the greatest man on the planet. He told me all about his girlfriend and how she makes him feel like a young man again. It was TMI, but I didn't want to hurt his feelings, so I listened and threw up in my mouth a little.

I'm kidding. It was very sweet.

He used to refer to my grandmother as his beautiful bride, even when they were in their later years. He told everyone he met that she was much too good for him and he was the luckiest man alive. He treated her like a queen, and she adored him just as much. When I was young I remember my grandmother cooking and Peepaw would walk up to her, take her by the hands, and twirl her around. They'd dance and sing around the kitchen together. My father has told me on many occasions that his parents acted like this as long as he can remember. If I can find a man who talks about me the way Peepaw spoke about my grandmother, and now his new girlfriend, then I'll be a very lucky lady.

A girl can dream.

I sigh and click *Reply*.

I'M IN.

This is really happening. It's time to stock up on Xanax and wine. Oh, and lose at least five pounds. I can totally do this in three months.

I click *Send* before I lose my nerve then quickly close my laptop. I did it —I agreed to go on vacation with my family. My stomach is already twisting into knots.

Maybe I'm completely overreacting. This isn't about me—this is a celebration for my parents. I probably have nothing to worry about.

Chapter Two

Okay, so I know I agreed to go on this trip with my family, but admittedly I've spent the last week trying to come up with a good enough reason to skip it. The best and only excuse I have is work. Unfortunately, right now I don't have anything pressing the week of the Hawaii trip. I've thought of everything, including making up a huge project and writing an imaginary business proposal. I've also considered asking my boss to draft a letter saying I'll get fired if I take off that week. Thankfully, I come to my senses before I drag my boss into my messy life. I have a good thing going here, and the last thing I want to do is jeopardize it by doing something stupid.

I really enjoy my job, something most people can't say. I work for a public relations firm which affords me the opportunity to have incredible experiences. I've been able to visit different cities and meet interesting people in the last three years. I've stayed at some of the grandest hotels in New York City; Washington, D.C.; Miami; and Nashville. I've attended dinners at the finest restaurants and been to some of the most lavish parties with private concerts featuring Panic at the Disco, Flo-Rida, and One Republic.

I could tell my parents I have a huge work-related event that same week as the Hawaii vacation—it's a legit possibility because things pop up all the time. The only problem is I'm sure the guilt will eventually eat away at me, and my siblings will never let me live it down. Or at least my sister, Maya, will never let me live it down. With my luck she'll somehow find a way to figure out the truth. My brother probably won't notice if I'm there or not because Brynn completely monopolizes his time.

As of now I'm still going on the trip.

It's Monday, and I've been busy working on a social media account launch all morning. Mondays don't bother me. In fact I kind of like them. I like the feeling of starting a fresh new week being busy. My job has been my whole life for a while now. Fran and I go out to dinner once a week, and I attend a book club once a month, but that's basically it.

Ever since I ended things with Jackson shortly after the holidays, my weekends haven't been full, so by Sunday night I'm anxious to get back to work. The good news is since I've been single, I've caught up on my to-be-read list. So, there's a positive.

I didn't get a lot of reading done when Jackson and I were together because we were always on the go. Don't get me wrong. I loved being with him. But sometimes I wanted to stay home and curl up on the couch.

My phone rings from somewhere on my desk, so I shift some things around to find it. I groan when I see it's my sister calling. It surprises me it took her this long to reach out. I was expecting to hear from her as soon as my mother's invitation hit our inboxes. I could let it go to voice mail, but I might as well rip off the Band-Aid now.

"Hey, Maya."

"Hi. What do you think about Mom and Dad's anniversary? Isn't it so exciting? It's going to be an epic vacation."

I grit my teeth. "Yeah, it sounds great." I run my finger across my laptop keyboard. "Although, I'm surprised they want us all to come along. I'd think they'd want to celebrate such an important event with only each other."

She snorts. "Are you crazy? They're alone all the time. And don't go putting any ideas into their heads. They're paying for us to go. This is what they want, and why should we upset them by acting ungrateful?"

Typical Maya. She's all about the freebies. She's the baby of the Fletcher family and milks it for all it's worth. She's thought the world revolves around her ever since she was a little girl, and she married a man who thinks the same way. The two of them together are quite a pair. My brother-in-law has an entrepreneurial spirit. Lucky for them he's one of those people who makes it happen. It's great for my sister and really annoying at the same time.

"I'm just saying it's a major milestone in their marriage," I answer. "Having five other people tagging along could cramp their style."

"Five?"

Yes, five. Wait, is someone not coming? I almost fall down on my knees and pray that it's Brynn. Or maybe it's more than five? I wouldn't mind if Peepaw and his new lady friend joined us. A vacation with Peepaw would be a blast.

"Um, yeah. The five of us—you, me, Hunter, Shawn, and Brynn."

I scowl at the thought of Brynn.

"Cora, didn't you see the invite list?"

List?

"No. I only read the message. I didn't pay attention to who it went to. Who else is on the list other than us?"

I wait for Maya to finish yelling at another driver to move out of her way.

"Everyone."

Seriously? Could she be any more vague?

"Who's everyone?" I ask, rolling my eyes.

"All of us, and the whole extended family. Peepaw, Uncle Sterling, Aunt DeeDee, our cousins..."

I quickly reopen my mother's email. So, when she addressed the email to family, she meant extended family, too. And friends? How did I not catch this? I guess I was still reeling enough from the whole idea I didn't realize they invited so many people. The Sterling Fletcher (my dad's brother) family are a lot to take. And I thought dealing with Brynn was bad enough.

"Wait, I just realized Mom addressed the email to family and friends. Who else did she invite?" I chew on my fingernail.

"Oh, yeah. Ken and Alaina are coming, too," Maya says.

Finally, some good news.

Ken and Alaina Webber have been my parents' best friends as long as I can remember. I guess they really do want to celebrate with *everyone.* And holy crap, did they win the lottery?

"Has everyone responded? That's a lot of people to pay for." I try to wrap my head around the total cost, but my brain doesn't do numbers.

"I think almost everyone is coming. Although I'm not sure about Tara."

Our cousin Tara is a professional ballroom dancer. She's not our favorite person, but she's still better than Brynn … at least I think so.

"I certainly won't lose any sleep if she doesn't make it," Maya adds.

Maya feels about Tara the way I feel about Brynn. They've been in competition since birth. Tara is one day older than Maya, and I think their love-hate relationship began that day. Tara came into this world twenty-four hours before my sister, and she's been trying to catch up ever since.

Things really went downhill between them when Maya and my cousins attended summer camp together. The story goes that Maya was hanging out with a guy at a dance and Tara swooped in and stole him away. It seems kind of pointless now that Maya is happily married, but I suspect she's never gotten over it.

"Anyway, I'm pretty sure everyone else will be there," she adds, dragging me out of my thoughts. "No one is stupid enough to turn down such a generous offer."

Except me.

I think again about the list of possible excuses I could use to not attend (yes, I've made a list). I might as well throw it out there now, in case I decide to bail at the last second.

I clear my throat. "Speaking of that, there's a small chance I might have a work conflict that week."

My sister doesn't say anything for a few seconds.

"Maya?"

"I'm here," she says flatly. "I'm just trying to understand you skipping our parents' anniversary. Is your job more important than our parents? Are you really that selfish?"

Cue the guilt trip.

"I'm not planning on it. But things do come up, and I usually request time off well in advance."

She lets out a judgmental sigh. "Cora, it's only a few days off. Plus it's over the holiday weekend. And considering you never go anywhere or do anything, I'm sure you have plenty of time off."

I groan. She's right.

"It's too bad things didn't work out with you and Jackson. We'd have a blast together on this trip."

I close my eyes at her mention of my ex. This is a subject we rarely talk about. Let's just say she wasn't happy with me when I broke things off with him shortly after the holidays. You would've thought she'd be loyal to her own sister over some random friend of Hunter's, but no. I believe she said something like, *"you'll regret it someday,"* and, *"you're making the biggest mistake of your life."* Honestly, I tuned her out as she went on and on about what a stand-up guy Jackson was and that I would be lucky to find someone else as great as him. Ouch!

She's right about one thing—he is a good person. He just wasn't right for me—*at all.*

"Maya—"

"I know. I was just stating a fact."

Sure she was.

"While we're on the subject, is there anyone you'd want to bring?"

I start to choke on my water. "To Hawaii? Um, no. Well, other than Fran."

Hmm ... now there's an idea. Holy crap, I'd give anything to see the look on Brynn's face if Fran showed up. That would be freaking amazing.

"I'm talking about a man," she scolds.

"I know you are, and the answer is still no. And please don't try to set me up with anyone else."

"Oh, you don't have to worry about that. I told you I'd never set you up with anyone again, and I meant it. This is your life, and if you want to keep wasting time, that's on you."

I roll my eyes.

"I have another call," she says. "I'll talk to you soon."

Luckily, she hurries off the phone. Talk about perfect timing. I don't need any more reminders about my mistakes and how I'm not getting any younger from my little sister. I'm nearly thirty. I have plenty of time to find my soul mate, despite what my family thinks.

Speaking of family, it sounds like this anniversary trip has turned into a full-blown family reunion with a few welcome additions. While I'm not thrilled about some of my extended family being there, my parents' friends Ken and Alaina are great. The truth is I always felt I fit in better with their family than my own. They are much more laid-back, and Alaina and I have similar interests, including reading, music, and cats.

And then there's Owen.

Owen is their son, and he was my first love ... only he didn't know it. When our families would get together, he'd always hang out with my brother, even though he was my age, and I'd admire him from afar. I'd watch them play whiffle ball in Owen's large backyard and take them lemonade. I remember becoming completely giddy when Owen would ask me to join the game. Keep in mind I'm the least athletic person on earth, so I'd always decline his generous invitation. Instead I'd sit on the deck, pretending to read a book while I watched Owen catch line drives and hit home runs over the fence. I still remember the way he ran his fingers through his wavy brown hair. And his smile, wow, it always lit up the room.

Anyway, time went on, and we grew up. We stopped going to those family get-togethers, and he went away to college on a baseball scholarship. And that's where he met Alyssa, his beautiful wife. My whole family attended their destination wedding in St. Thomas, but I was conveniently unable to go because of work. My mom sent me all the pictures of the ultimate dream wedding, which reminded me how glad I was not to be there to witness it in person.

This reminds me that I haven't seen Ken and Alaina in quite a while, and the fact they're coming makes the trip a tiny bit more bearable, especially now that more Fletchers will be there.

Maya was definitely right about certain people not being stupid enough to pass up this trip. I'm sure my cousins jumped at the chance to have an all-expense-paid vacation. I know my cousin Tara will join us if her schedule allows, but the last I heard she was trying to get on one of those reality dance shows. She's always been very into herself. In fact, she's the person who's been absent from most family get-togethers, including Peepaw's birthday parties. She's always been more into her friends and her career. Maintaining extended family relationships has never been a priority.

Her sister, Ashley, has supposedly done everything and been everywhere. I just don't know how. She hasn't been on this earth enough years to have accomplished all she says. The last I heard, she had gotten her master's degree, climbed Machu Picchu, and became engaged to a guy who was the heir to a massive fortune. I think they're still engaged, but who knows. I can't keep up. I've heard there were other engagements, lots of them.

Anyway, other than seeing Alaina and Ken again, I'm most excited about spending time with my Peepaw. I always leave our visits inspired because he shares a random piece of wisdom with me. And I don't know how, but it's usually something I need to hear even if I don't realize it yet. Then sometimes it's silly, like during our last conversation when he told me not to cross a rope bridge without a rope. Clever, right?

One thing's for sure, I have a feeling this will be a vacation I'll never forget. I'm just not sure if that's a good thing or not.

Chapter Three

I just learned you can't bring fruit from the mainland into Hawaii. Who knew? I admit, after a lot of back a forth on whether I should go, I'm finally getting excited about this trip. Mostly because I'm going to visit places I've always dreamed of seeing. I've pulled a page out of my ex-boyfriend Jackson's book and been researching the must-do spots on the island of Oahu. He was always good about finding the best places to go. I've joined several vacation and travel websites, and now my inbox is full of emails. I also watched a video online about how to pack for a two-week vacation in a carry-on suitcase. It's mind-boggling, but these people are truly masters of their craft. I'm now convinced that packing light is an art form. I even practiced packing a small suitcase a few times. Sadly that's the extent of my life right now. Maybe I really do need a vacation...

I love history, so I'm the most excited about going to the Pearl Harbor Memorial. I also want to climb to the top of Diamond Head, visit Waimea Falls, take Polynesian dance lessons, visit the North Shore, drink from a real coconut, and read lots of books while lying on the beach.

My parents have planned a few adventures for us as a group, including a family picture, and my mother wants everyone to wear matching outfits. *Sigh.* I'm scared to see what attire she'll choose. She says she's still narrowing down her choices. And twinning with Brynn is not at the top of my list of things I want to do on this vacation or ever.

It's very annoying that most of my mother's emails lately begin with the words, "Brynn has suggested." Brynn is very good at working my parents. My brother has taught her well. The only good thing about Brynn trying to take control is she could have some influence over what we wear for the family picture, and although it sucks she has that kind of power, she's still a safer bet than my mother making a selection on her own.

"You need to go kayaking, maybe cliff diving, oh, and swim with the sharks," Fran says excitedly. "They have divers take you out there and tell you exactly what you need to do."

I grit my teeth. Sharks? Fran has been my best friend for years; she should know that me swimming with sharks is not going to happen.

Normally I'd start twitching at the idea of such death-defying excursions. Purposely jumping off a cliff and swimming with the ocean's predators are daring enough. However, a week with the Fletcher clan is also adventurous, and potentially dangerous.

"Very funny, Fran. Are you forgetting who you're talking to? None of those things are going to happen. Besides, my to-do list is already pretty long, and I haven't even accounted for the fun-filled stuff my mother is expecting us to do. According to her, Brynn has been helping her with the itinerary, so who knows what that entails."

Fran sits at the kitchen table and puts her feet up on the chair across from herself. "Don't let Brynn get in your head. You have more important things to focus on. Just worry about enjoying yourself and maybe even leave time open for some romance."

I snort. "Romance? Yeah, right. With whom?"

She shrugs innocently. "You never know, maybe some hot islander who can crack a coconut with one hand, or maybe some other poor soul who's also stuck with his family in paradise." She grins. "Cora Ann, I have a strong feeling that something big will happen for you on this trip."

Ahhh, leave it to Fran to fill my head with a million possible scenarios. The crazy thing is, her feelings are usually accurate. Granted, something big could be I'll be sitting next to Justin Timberlake on the plane, which works for me. Or it could be that I'll fall into a volcano. You never know. Regardless, she's always had a sense about these things, so I'm not ruling anything out.

"Are you sure you don't want to come?" I ask her for the hundredth time. "I promise it won't be a boring family reunion." I've spent hours trying to convince her to join me, but despite being offered a free trip, she's turned me down. "I know my parents wouldn't mind, and they're already footing the bill for half the population."

She frowns. "You have no idea how much I wish I could go, but with all these new clients, I need to be here." Fran is an amazing massage therapist, and she's thinking about continuing her education and going to acupuncture school. She should go for it because she has a true passion for helping others. She could also become a therapist because she gives really good advice. Either way, she has a natural way of putting people at ease, and that's a great quality to have.

I pull Kiwi into my lap and stroke her fur. She purrs softly. "I understand, but it would be so much fun if you could come."

I think there's more to why she doesn't want to go, and it has to do with my brother. Of course, she'd never admit it. Anytime I mention this to her, she gives me her standard "if the universe had wanted us to be together it would've happened" answer. Honestly, I don't understand why she thinks the universe gets to make all the decisions.

She points at me. "Remember, even though I won't be there with you physically, I'll be there in spirit. And I expect you to text me a day-by-day detailed report."

I don't know whether I should be happy or worried she thinks I'll have lots of details to share. Right now, the most exciting thing that could happen is for Brynn to suddenly come down with a plague and bail on the trip. Wishful thinking? I guarantee the only thing that would keep Brynn from a luxurious vacation would be a coma, and even then it's questionable.

"I'm not sure I'll have much to report, but I'll definitely keep you posted on my adventures, and during my downtime, I plan on finding a quiet spot on the beach to read."

She smiles. "And avoid all that Fletcher family fun."

"Exactly."

The truth is, my family isn't as bad as I'm making them sound. There are far worse out there, but they aren't the easiest to deal with. Fran comes from a huge family, and while they have their squabbles, they sincerely love each other. She has two sisters and a brother who are all married, five adorable nieces, and her mother is the sweetest. She's the doting kind who will have breakfast waiting for you when you wake up, and she's patient and unconditional. She actually reminds me a lot of Alaina. If their family was having a reunion, I would be there in a heartbeat.

I stare out my office window, trying to concentrate on work. My sister and I have been messaging about contributing to an anniversary gift for my parents. As usual, no one can agree on what to get them, and it doesn't help that Brynn shoots down every idea except her own. I'm not sure why my sister included Shawn and Brynn. They could've gotten a gift on their own.

I read the message from Maya.

HUNTER SAYS WE SHOULD GET THEM A DIGITAL PICTURE FRAME.

My brother-in-law is so cheap. There are five of us contributing to this gift, and our parents are taking all of us to Hawaii. The least we can do is get them something really nice.

I type a response.

NO WAY!
MAYBE WE SHOULD GET THEM BALLROOM DANCE LESSONS. WE CAN ASK TARA FOR SOME RECOMMENDATIONS. ☺

I smile while I wait for my sister to respond.

HELL, NO.

I laugh.

Just then my boss appears in my doorway.

"Hey, Cora. I noticed you requested some time off. Good for you. I can't remember the last time you used any of your vacation days."

Lydia is the best boss ever, and she's a really good person. She's worked in public relations for over thirty years and has a wealth of knowledge. She's so inspiring. I'm not surprised she approved my vacation time without a second thought.

"Thanks, Lydia."

"So where are you off to?"

"Hawaii."

Her eyes light up. "Now we're talking. I always say if you're going to do the vacation, do it up right."

I give a her a sheepish smile. "Yeah."

She frowns. "Wait a second. Why do I get the feeling you're not as excited about this trip as you should be? Have you ever been to Hawaii? Which islands are you visiting?"

I sigh. "We're just going to Oahu. And believe me, I'm looking forward to going there. I'm just not thrilled about my travel companions."

She sits in the chair across from my desk. Her black hair is in a bun on top of her head, with a few loose pieces hanging down on the sides. As usual, she has a pen over her ear, and she's dressed in head-to-toe couture.

"What's going on?"

I sigh and tell her about my impending family reunion. I even tell her how I considered asking her to write a letter stating I couldn't have the time off. I know it isn't the best idea to unload personal issues on your boss, but Lydia is different. She's all business when she needs to be, but she also understands we have lives outside of this building.

"I sound like a terrible, ungrateful person, don't I?" I ask, putting my hand to my forehead. "Unfortunately, my relationship with my family is complicated."

She purses her lips. "You're entitled to your feelings, but maybe it won't be as bad as you think."

I nod. "That's what I'm hoping. It's completely possible it will be an enjoyable vacation without any drama."

If only I really believed that.

"Anyway, thanks, Lydia. Sorry to bring this into the office."

She waves her hand. "Oh, please. I've heard far worse than issues with a dysfunctional family. But, it definitely sounds like you're in for quite the adventure, and you're going to fall in love with the islands."

I continue by telling her about my plans of relaxing on the beach with a book, and she suggests a few must-dos. Talking to her gets me feeling excited, and she says something that really hits home. She tells me how much she wishes she was able to spend time with her parents again since they've both passed away.

It occurs to me I should be feeling grateful for this time with them. How many people get an amazing opportunity like this? I need a better attitude and to stop being such a pain in the ass. Really, why should I let Brynn ruin this for me? I won't let her. It also occurs to me Peepaw isn't getting any younger, so I'll use this opportunity to soak up as much time with him as I can, and I'll meet this new girlfriend he adores.

"I appreciate you letting me take the time off."

She laughs. "It's yours to take. We can handle things around here while you're gone. Just don't go falling in love and staying there. It's difficult to leave once you're there, believe me."

I laugh. "There's a slim chance of that happening—falling in love, I mean. Honestly, I'd be more excited if I didn't have to spend a week with my sister-in-law."

She laughs. "You have one of those too, huh?"

I grit my teeth.

"Do I ever. She also happens to be my sorority sister."

She gives me a funny look.

"So, you set your brother up with a girl from your sorority?"

I gasp in horror. "Absolutely not. They happened to meet by chance. I tried to warn him about her, but he fell hard and fast."

Lydia pushes her glasses up with her finger. "So, what makes your sis-in-law so bad?"

A dozen different memories flip through my mind. But one moment in particular stands out.

"Brynn and I rushed together, and at first she was extremely nice, but that all changed very quickly. She wanted to stand out and make a name for herself. She didn't care who she hurt in the process. After we joined, I became good friends with our chapter president. Brynn didn't like that, so she began to sabotage me behind my back. It wasn't until my best friend Fran caught her in the act that I found out the type of person Brynn really is." I pause when I realize how immature I must sound. "It seems trivial now, but imagine that type of person becoming part of your family. It's very difficult to trust her."

Lydia nods sympathetically. "Well, my advice to you is try to enjoy your trip and not worry about her. And I should add that I *had* one of those sisters-in-law."

"Had?"

She gives me a wicked smile. "Yep, she showed her true colors when she was caught with the guy who cleaned their pool."

I sit up straight in my chair. "Oh, snap."

She laughs. "My brother finally got a clue. So, if this girl is as bad as you say, everyone else will figure it out at some point. In the meantime, don't let her steal your joy."

She's right.

"You never know, maybe a trip together will help you finally mend your friendship," she suggests.

It's doubtful, but stranger things have happened. And I don't see Brynn getting caught with the pool guy or anyone else. I think she loves my brother—in her own bossy, controlling sort of way.

Lydia looks at her phone and stands up. "I'd better get back to work."

"Thanks for the advice."

"Any time." She walks toward the door and stops. "I almost forgot. You need to visit the Dole Plantation and get some chocolate-covered pineapple. It's so good, you'll be addicted."

"It sounds divine, I can't wait to try it."

She smiles. "You won't regret it, and you're welcome to pick up a box for your favorite boss."

I laugh. "Will do."

Lydia waves over her shoulder, leaving me to think about our conversation. Maybe this vacation is the bonding experience the Fletcher family needs.

Chapter Four

I sit down with a bowl of veggie pasta, when my phone rings from the bag on the couch. I hurry to the living room and see it's my mother calling.

"Hi, Mom," I say cheerfully. After my conversation with Lydia, I'm determined to embrace this family reunion and all it entails. Even Brynn—*gag!*

"Hello, Cora Ann."

My mother always uses my full name. Usually that happens when kids are in trouble with their parents, but not in my case. "Did you see my email? I sent the picture of the outfits we're wearing for the family picture. I know it's a bit outrageous, but this is a once-in-a-lifetime opportunity."

I abandon my dinner to get to my laptop because I'm anxious to see what she's chosen. I open the attachment and gasp ... and not in an *OMG, these outfits are stunning* kind of way. More like an *I want to curl up and die* kind of way.

She's kidding right? She has to be.

"Well, what do you think?" she asks eagerly. I check my emails to see if she sent a *ha ha, I was joking* follow-up email. Unfortunately, this is it.

"Um, Mom, this is a coconut bra and a grass skirt."

I don't want to hurt her feelings, but I'm wondering if she's lost her damn mind. I immediately know Brynn has something to do with this. She's willing to do almost anything to draw attention to herself, even at the expense of everyone else.

"Yes, isn't it fantastic? I thought it would be fun for us to wear traditional outfits for the picture. It would be something we'd never forget."

She's got that right. I know I'll never forget it. In fact I'll probably have nightmares about this outfit for years to come. Instead of being naked in my dreams, I'll be wearing a coconut bra.

I shudder at what she wants the men to wear. Never mind the coconut bra, this is so much worse. The image of my father and grandfather in something that resembles a loincloth flashes through my mind. Peepaw will probably get a kick out of it. My father, not so much.

"Has Dad seen this?"

She laughs. "Yes, he has. He's not thrilled, but I told him it's my one request for our anniversary and of everyone, especially since we're bringing you all along. I don't want any gifts. I just want a nice family picture for my Christmas cards and to hang up over the fireplace."

Christmas cards? This is getting worse by the second. She wants to send a picture of her half-naked family to her correspondence list. And

I know my mom—that list is long. I should tell her this is not the way to send holiday greetings or cheer.

I have to give her credit though, it's very smart of her to use the fact they are paying for this vacation to her advantage. Really, what are we supposed to say?

"I don't know what your father is fussing about. He has great legs, strong and muscular. I think they are very sexy. He should want to show them off."

What? Why? Gag me. I can't help but wonder if I'm dreaming this entire conversation. I lightly pinch my arm and hope at any moment I'll wake up in my bedroom and this conversation would've never happened. Or perhaps I'll find another email with a photo of a gorgeous, flowing dress to wear for our family photo. Hell, at this point I'd be happy with tacky Hawaiian shirts or gaudy polyester dresses.

"You just have to pick the color of your skirt," she continues. "The selection is at the bottom of the picture, and then respond with your cup size. And don't worry, honey, they make them in all sizes, even for girls who are smaller on top."

I cringe because this conversation has gone from bad to worse. I'm the one Fletcher girl who's missing the curves on top. Brynn and my cousins have purchased their curves, so they should fill out the coconut bras nicely.

"Gee, thanks, Mom," I reply glumly.

"Cora Ann, it's nothing to be ashamed of. You're perfect just the way you are," she insists. "And Jackson certainly didn't mind that you aren't as endowed on top as other women."

"Mom!"

"I'm just saying ..."

She had to go there. It's no secret my mother liked Jackson. A lot. He said all the right things and knew how to overdo the compliments. He won her over the first day they met. It's possible she may never forgive me for breaking up with him. I get that parents want the best for their children, but she's going overboard about Jackson. The truth is I never felt like I could be myself when I was with him. Don't get me wrong, the physical attraction was there, and he did treat me well, but something was missing. I ignored my feelings for a while in hopes I was just overthinking. And it was nice he got along so well with my family. The crazy thing is when we were together, I actually felt like I fit in with the Fletchers.

Maya was the first to find out that I had broken up with him. I guess that's to be expected since her husband is Jackson's best friend. I'll never forget the phone call I got from her. She had the nerve to demand I reconsider and give our relationship another chance. And when I say demand, she actually used that word. I hung up on her, and we didn't speak for several weeks.

My mother expressed her disappointment in a different way. She basically called me in hysterics and told me I had destroyed my life forever. She didn't say those exact words, but that's what she was implying.

Anyway, I don't want to get into another discussion about Jackson, so I decide to change the subject.

"I'll take the blue skirt," I say flatly. Giving into her madness is better than listening to her remind me about her disappointment yet again.

"Oh yes, I was going to suggest blue for you. It will match your eyes perfectly. Brynn thinks so, too."

Ugh. I knew it.

"Mom, has Brynn been involved in the planning of everything?"

She hesitates. "No, not everything, but she is very helpful because she knows how important this trip is to me."

That's it. I'm done with this conversation. I end the call before any more mention of Brynn, the size of my chest, Jackson, or the latter two topics combined. There are just some conversations that you shouldn't have with your mother.

While I finish my dinner, I think about this family picture. I open the email and look at the photos of the outfits again. The skirts are basically see-through, so we'll need to wear shorts or something underneath. The men really do have it worse—it's basically a colorful Speedo with a small piece of fabric over it. Wow, there's going to be a lot of bare skin showing. Hopefully the photographer will be a world-renowned expert in editing and photoshop.

I went into this knowing that something like this was bound to happen. It's one picture, and hopefully that's the extent of the discomfort I'll have to endure. Maybe I can get away with hiding behind someone in the picture. I already know Brynn and my cousins will look fantastic. And both Hunter and my brother are in good shape, so they should be fine.

Admittedly, Jackson would've looked good in traditional Polynesian attire. He's a former college football player who's probably in better shape now in his late twenties than when he was in college.

I exhale slowly.

I know my family still doesn't understand why I broke up with him. I tried to explain it didn't feel right and I was tired of forcing it. We were just too different. He would've been happy to be out every night of the week or have guests over for dinner. Don't get me wrong, I love being with friends, but I'm also content to spend quiet evenings at home with a movie, games, and takeout. I can't count how many times he'd call me at work and tell me we were meeting up with people for dinner or drinks. There was one point when we did this for ten nights straight, and honestly, I was over it.

Jackson was also much more adventurous than me. He was always up to do something crazy. I remember waking up on Saturday mornings hoping for a nice quiet day, and he would want to go on a ten-mile hike or drive up and down the California coast. Again, once in a while this was fine, but not every weekend.

No doubt Jackson would go cliff diving or swim with sharks in a heartbeat. I felt being with me would eventually hold him back, even though he told me he didn't care. He said he loved our differences because we balanced each other out. I agreed but at the same time wondered if he'd eventually get bored with me. After way too many doubts, I chose to end things. Needless to say, Maya and my mother were disappointed, but I'm pretty sure my brother-in-law was devastated, probably more devastated than Jackson himself. He still hasn't said more than two words to me since it happened over seven months ago.

Jackson was visibly upset, but I think deep down he knew it was coming.

Anyway, it's been several months, so everyone should be getting over their heartbreak by now, even though they all like to bring it up from time to time.

And who knows, maybe Fran's feeling is right and something big will happen to me on this vacation. I'm definitely open to meeting someone, if he's right for me. Either way, I'm determined to enjoy my vacation. Coconut bra and all.

～

"Let's make a toast," Fran says, holding up her wine glass. "Here's to tropical paradise, magical moments, and an unforgettable journey for Cora Ann."

I giggle. Fran loves to make up toasts, and they usually have some deep hidden meaning. This morning she told me that she had a dream about a handsome stranger in Hawaii. I tried to use it to help my case and convince her to come with me, but no luck. And she likes to tease me about Cora Ann since my mother always uses my full name.

"You keep saying something big is going to happen on this trip. Maybe that's the universe trying to tell you that you need to be there."

Hah! It's about time I used this universe thing to my advantage.

"I'm being serious. What if this something big is supposed to happen to you? You're the one who had a dream about a man, *Francesca*."

She shakes her head. "Nope—this isn't about me. Besides, I have a feeling someday you'll help lead me to my soul mate anyway."

Fran has said this for years. In the beginning I thought she could've been talking about Shawn, but obviously nothing ever came from that.

"I can't believe we leave in a few days," I say, swirling my wine glass.

"Has Leann dropped anymore bombshells?" she asks.

"No, and please don't jinx me. The horrendous family picture outfit is enough."

She shakes her head. "I have to hand it to her. Leann Fletcher is a woman who knows what she wants."

I snort. "Hell yeah, she does. And she'll remind you what it is every time she talks to you. You still have time to change your mind. Hawaii could hold magic for both of us."

She takes another sip of her wine. "You never know, maybe in the long run it will turn out that way."

I have no idea what she's talking about, but hopefully this is another one of those times her feelings are right.

Chapter Five

*I*t's been a whirlwind leading up to the big day, and it's finally here. The Fletchers are heading to Oahu. The poor island doesn't know what's about to transpire. I was feeling pretty good about the trip until last night. I started getting anxious, so I almost called my parents to cancel. My finger was on the call button, and then I thought about how upset they would be and stopped myself. I keep remembering what Lydia said: this is about my parents, not me.

Before I leave for the airport, I give Fran very specific instructions for Kiwi, even though she knows exactly what to do. Kiwi is very easy to care for, but she does require a lot of attention. When I go to retrieve my laptop, Kiwi has conveniently positioned herself on top of it. She must know I'm leaving, so I pull her into my arms and give her a big hug good-bye.

I arrive at the airport exactly two hours before the flight. None of my family has arrived yet, which doesn't shock me. I'm by far the most punctual. My immediate family all lives within an hour of each other and within an hour of the Santa Barbara airport.

Our extended family, including Peepaw, lives farther south, so they'll be flying out of different airports, and we'll meet up in Honolulu. At least the plane ride should be mostly peaceful, as long as I'm not sitting next to Brynn.

A few nights ago, I sent my mother a text asking for details about who was sitting next to each other on the plane and whose hotel rooms were near each other. She sent me a response a few hours later telling me she didn't have time to send out all the specifics. She said not to worry because we'd all be together.

That's exactly why I wanted to know. I will happily pay any amount of money to upgrade to first class if I'm not satisfied with my seat. It is a five-and-a-half-hour flight.

I breeze through security despite the other passengers around me. It baffles me that some people who travel can't follow simple directions. I mean, unless you've been living under a rock, it's common knowledge you need to take off your belt and shoes, empty your pockets, and throw away water bottles. Why can't people do this right the first time? The couple in front of me has to walk through the security scanner three times. The first time the man left his belt on, the second time he had change in his pocket, and the third time his wife had not one, but two water bottles in her bag. Never mind that the agent was repeating the instructions over and over again during the ten minutes we were standing in line.

After I finally get through the security madness, I find a comfortable seat in the corner near my gate and put on my headphones. I check my emails and send Lydia a few notes I've been working on for an upcoming project.

I almost jump ten feet into the air when someone grabs my shoulders. I turn around to see my father in a loud Hawaiian shirt and a huge woven hat with a wide brim that screams, "I'm going to Hawaii!" He's also wearing sandals with socks. Typical. Despite his choice in travel attire, my dad is pretty cool.

"Hey, Dad," I say, standing up to give him a big hug.

"How's my favorite girl?"

I laugh. He says the same thing to my mother and my sister. I've called him on it a few times, but he insists I'm really his favorite. Sometimes I think I am, but he has good relationships with both my siblings, and parents aren't supposed to pick favorites, right? Thankfully, he didn't have much to say after I broke up with Jackson. He did say I had a good head on my shoulders. I didn't ask him what he meant, but I don't think he cared either way. He does have to live with my mom though, so maybe it's easier for him not to have an opinion on my relationship or my breakup.

"I'm doing good. Where's Mom?"

He places his bag on the chair next to mine. "She's in the shop getting magazines and souvenirs."

Souvenirs? Only my mother would buy souvenirs from our hometown. Her favorite thing about travel is getting something from every place she visits. She even decorates an entire Christmas tree with ornaments from every city and country she has been to. Still, I'm not sure what she's buying here considering we live in California. Not to mention she's going to drag her trinkets all the way to Hawaii and back.

"Is everyone else on their way? Hopefully no one misses the flight."

In other words, I hope Brynn misses the flight.

"Everyone is en route," he says, putting his glasses on to look at his phone.

"Oh, good," I say unconvincingly.

He peers at me over his phone, and I give him an innocent shrug.

"Everyone will be arriving in Honolulu within a few hours of each other," he adds. "We're going to have a motley crew, aren't we?"

I groan under my breath.

He takes his glasses off and places his phone down on top of his duffle bag. All of a sudden he stretches his arms over his head and starts doing toe touches and side bends. Then he begins jogging in place, in all his sandals-and-socks glory.

What's happening? I quickly look around for the nearest exit. Maybe I should just sit and pretend I don't know him.

"Dad?"

"We have a long flight ahead, need to keep the circulation going," he says through his huffing.

Oh wow, I need a drink.

"Warner, what on earth?" I turn to my right to see my mother with two large shopping bags in her hands. I can only imagine what's in those bags. My mom looks adorable, as usual. She's wearing a pair of white capri pants and a pale pink T-shirt with a white denim jacket. Her brown hair is freshly cut in a perfectly coifed bob that frames her face.

"Hey, Mom."

She lets out an exasperated sigh as she watches my father continue his calisthenics. He's now doing something that reminds me of a Richard Simmons aerobic routine.

"Hello, honey," she finally answers me. "As you can see, your father is really taking his exercise seriously."

"Darling, you know how these long flights can take their toll on the circulatory system," he says as he does lunges. I rub my forehead while other travelers in the gate area start pointing and whispering. Then something unexpected happens—two other people stand up and begin following my father. My mother and I stare at each other in disbelief. I certainly didn't expect my father to lead an airport aerobics class, but here we are.

I quickly snap a picture and text it to Fran.

> So, this is happening. Warner is holding a Jazzercize class here in the terminal. Please say this isn't a sign of things to come on this vacation. Give Kiwi a hug for me.

"What the hell?" a voice shrieks. "Dad, what are you doing?"

My sister and Hunter have arrived and are now watching as two more people have joined my father. The five of them are squatting and breathing heavily.

"Maya, watch your language in public," my mother yells.

The Fletchers aren't known for being quiet. And now it appears we're about to become airport famous, or infamous.

"Dad has started an exercise flash mob," I tell them nonchalantly. A few other people are now recording it. *I wonder how many views it's gotten on YouTube so far.* I'd be surprised if it hasn't been posted yet.

We all continue to watch as my father shouts out instructions to his impromptu students.

"Four, three, two, one. Done. Great job, everyone," he says as he gives high fives to the other passengers. Everyone in the terminal begins cheering, and a few ask where he teaches classes. I wonder if I'm imaging all of this.

He sits in the chair next to me and opens a bottle of water. None of us say anything for a few seconds. Maybe we're in shock that this just happened.

"My Maya, when did you get here?" he asks, when he notices her. She still looks like she wants to find a place to hide.

"Daddy, what was that?" she asks, a look of horror still on her face.

He launches into his explanation about wanting to be healthier and how he's lost five pounds for this vacation.

"Haven't you heard about how flying can affect circulation? It's very good to get the body moving before such a long trip."

My mother nods her head proudly. "Doesn't your father look fantastic? He's worked very hard to get in better shape. I'm so proud of him."

My mom leans over and kisses his cheek.

"And just wait until you see him in his outfit for the picture. Whoo hoo, he's too hot to handle." She begins fanning herself with her hand, and I suddenly want to jump off the gangway.

Hunter finally looks up from his phone. He's been typing something since they arrived.

"I think it's great that you've been working so hard, Warner. You're the man." He holds out his hand and gives him a high five.

I roll my eyes.

My phone chimes. I laugh as I read the response from Fran.

OOH, I'M SORRY I MISSED THAT. DON'T GET TOO DISCOURAGED.
COULD BE WORSE.

She's right. It could be worse. My father could've been doing lunges in the outfit my mother chose for our family picture.

I quickly type her a response letting her know she might be able to see the workout on YouTube.

"There's my sweet boy," Mom gushes, throwing her arms around my brother who's finally arrived. I suddenly feel like a dark cloud has moved over me—in other words, Brynn is here.

I look at Shawn. His hair has grown out a bit on top. I don't doubt he's used an entire bottle of styling product in it. He looks like he's ready to audition for a boy band. And then there's Brynn, stunning as usual with long, wavy dark brown hair and perfect makeup. She's wearing a cropped yellow shirt, flared jeans, and wedges. I look down at my T-shirt that says *Yay—Vacay* and yoga leggings. I think I look cute and practical for a five-hour flight. I watch as my family greets each other with excited hugs and handshakes. Everyone is excitedly discussing the hotel and the planned events for the week ahead. I remain quiet as I watch from the sidelines, a familiar spot for me.

"Hey, sis," Shawn says putting his arm around my shoulders and squeezing.

"Hi, bro."

I love my brother. He just has terrible taste in women. Brynn and I are now facing each other. The greeting is always the most uncomfortable part. I never know what to say to her, and I'm sure she feels the same way. We usually go through the motions to save face around everyone else, but it's not a secret how we really feel about one another. Cue the fakeness.

"Cora, I love your shirt," she says holding out her arms. We give each other the obligatory awkward hug. "It's good to see you. Is it true you almost had to work this week?" she asks, after we quickly let go of our forced hug. "I told Shawn you would never miss such an important event for your parents. Isn't that right?"

I glance at Maya, who's purposely ignoring my gaze. I'm sure she ran straight to tell Shawn about our conversation and then he opened his big mouth and told his wife. Typical Maya behavior—the girl lives for gossip. "At first I thought I might have to work because we're so busy right now, but I got it handled," I say with a shrug. I won't give Brynn the satisfaction of baiting me. She doesn't need to know I have nothing going on at work right now.

"You guys arrived at the right time. Dad just led a fitness class right here in the middle of the terminal," Maya says, changing the subject.

"What do you mean he *led* a fitness class?" Shawn asks with a laugh.

Maya recounts what we just witnessed. Of course, she makes it sounds worse than it was. She tends to exaggerate, a trait she learned from our mother. Dad was not "inviting everyone to join," nor was he "practically flexing for the cameras."

"Well, sorry I missed that, Dad," he lies, patting him on the shoulder.

"Babe, let's go grab a few things for the plane," Brynn says, taking Shawn's hand in hers.

Hunter looks up from his phone. "Um, I'll walk with you guys."

A few seconds later, Hunter, Shawn, and Brynn wander off to the shops, leaving me alone with my parents and my sister.

"Where are Ken and Alaina?" I ask. I'm hoping they will show up soon to break up the vibe of this big happy occasion. Actually, other than Dad becoming a YouTube sensation, everything seems to be going smoothly. My awkward interaction with Brynn is to be expected.

"They fly in later tonight," Mom says, scrolling through her phone. "Ken had a meeting this morning."

I clasp my hands together. "Great. So, we're all here."

I notice my parents and Maya exchange funny looks.

"Well, almost ..." Mom says.

Judging by their expressions, I know I'm not going to like this. A feeling of dread comes over me, and I feel sick to my stomach. Who else is coming? I mentally run through a list of people who could be joining us. Maybe it's some other long-lost family member?

"What do you mean, 'almost'?"

"Cora Ann, please don't be upset," my mother says softly. "You know we extended this invitation to family and friends who are important to us."

"I have nothing to do with this," Dad chimes in as he folds his arms against his chest.

My mother shoots him a dirty look as I stare her down. She turns her attention to Maya who shrugs. Obviously they're having some kind of nonverbal conversation. My mother and Maya are so tight they have a way of speaking without saying anything out loud.

"Okay, well, someone tell me what's going on," I snap.

Maya looks behind me and points. I turn around and suck in a breath when I realize what they've been talking about.

I should've known.

Hunter is slowly walking through the terminal, and he's not alone. My ex-boyfriend Jackson is with him. My heart sinks because I know right away what's happening. He's coming to Hawaii with us.

Chapter Six

I think it would be so cool to have access to a time machine. There are a few things in my life that I would go back and change if one suddenly became available. First of all, I wouldn't have quit taking dance classes before high school. I was so burned out I took a break. Unfortunately, when I was ready to go back, it was too late. Second, I never would've dated this guy named Giovanni. Talk about a big waste of time. The last I heard he wasn't doing much of anything. I think he plays in a band and lives in an apartment with five roommates. I really dodged a bullet there. And lastly, I would've gone with my gut and not come on this vacation.

I've just been blindsided by my family, the very people I should be able to count on. Seeing Jackson here reminds me they don't listen to me. I know they want me to settle down and be happy, but I specifically told them things with Jackson weren't going to work out. And what do they do? They ignore my feelings and invite him to come along on our week-long reunion in Hawaii.

I'm not naïve as to the purpose of this secret plan. I know they're hoping that being in a romantic tropical destination will help us reconnect, but I don't see it happening. This all makes sense now. Every time I asked my mother for more information about the flight seating chart and the hotel rooms, she told me she didn't have time to give me the details. Has she been planning this all along? I don't remember seeing Jackson on the original email.

And what about Maya? She made that comment about how much fun it would be if Jackson came with us. Did she already know he was coming when we had that conversation? I have so many questions right now I don't know where to begin.

"Hey, Cora ..." Jackson says, giving me a sheepish smile. "Can I talk to you a sec?"

I nod slowly as I follow him away from my family. *Ugh.* I'm so frustrated with them right now I could scream.

"I wanted to tell you that I don't want things to be weird between us," he says over his shoulder. "Didn't we say we were going to stay friends after we broke up?"

We did say that.

"Yes."

He puts his hands in his pockets. "You know I think your family's awesome, and Hunter's my best friend. When the invite for this trip came, it was hard to pass up. I wanted to call and talk to you first, but Maya told me not to."

Figures.

"I hope you're not upset with me," he adds. "I really feel bad now, though. I should've told you I was joining the party. I'm sure it's a shock seeing me here."

I know this isn't his fault. Like Maya said, no one is stupid enough to turn down an offer for an all-expense-paid trip. And like he said, we did agree to be friends, so his coming along shouldn't matter. Except that it does, because my family kept it from me until the very last second.

"I'm not upset with *you*."

Although he kept it from me too, my family members have had plenty of opportunity to tell me since my parents invited everyone.

The corner of his mouth curls into a smile. "That's a relief. So, we're cool."

I nod quickly. "Yes, we're cool."

As we make our way back to my family members, they all pretend like they weren't watching.

Really? They can't even own up to their behavior.

"I can't say the same for some people, though," I add, glaring at my sister.

"All right, all right—let's go to Hawaii," Jackson announces.

I don't say a word to anyone and excuse myself to go to the restroom so I can collect my thoughts in peace. The truth is, I'm not upset with Jackson, and I don't feel weird around him. I'm bothered that my sister and my mother didn't take my feelings into consideration. Sure, they could say they acted out of love, but I don't see it that way. I see them trying to force something because it's easy and it's what they want. And yes, Jackson does fit in with my family, and it's seamless and comfortable.

When I get into the bathroom, I wipe a bit of smudged mascara from under my eye.

"Hey, Cora, are you doing okay? I can't believe what just went down."

I turn around to find Brynn standing behind me. *Lovely.* She's the last person I want to be discussing this situation with. And this gets me thinking. Wasn't she super involved in the planning process of this trip? I wonder if she really did know, and what if she encouraged my mother to include Jackson? It wouldn't surprise me at all.

I focus my attention on my reflection. "You must be talking about Jackson being here. Did my mom tell you she invited him? She said you were very helpful with the planning."

She joins me in front of the mirror and checks her reflection. Her makeup is applied so perfectly it looks like she isn't wearing any. "She didn't say a word to me. I helped organize some of the events, but I had no idea your ex-boyfriend was coming along."

Hmmm ... either she's an excellent liar or she really didn't know. Regardless, I refuse to give Brynn the satisfaction of knowing how frustrated I am with my mother and sister.

I shrug. "Oh well, it is what it is, and there's nothing I can do about it now."

She clears her throat. "You could speak up. Tell them you feel it was wrong of them to include your ex on our family reunion trip without consulting you."

I give her a side glance. *Sorry, Brynn, I'm not going to let you stir up drama on my behalf.*

"I could, but what good is that going to do? We're about to board a plane, and I'd rather not get into a heated discussion right before our vacation."

She leans against the wall. I'm sure my non-reaction is driving her crazy, and I'm loving it.

"I know Leann's worried about you, Cora. We all are."

I fight the urge to make a snarky comment. Instead, I add a layer of gloss to my lips and drop the tube back into my bag. She seems to forget that other than my brother, I'm the person who has known her the longest. I know how manipulative she can be in order to get what she wants.

"There's no reason for anyone to be worried about me. I'm totally fine. I'm great actually, and I can't wait to get to Hawaii. I'll see you later."

I pick up my bag and make my way back to our gate with Brynn at my heels.

Brynn joins my brother, who immediately puts his arm around her. My parents have their heads together looking at something on my father's phone. Hunter and Jackson aren't in sight, and my sister is watching me carefully.

Without saying a word to her, I put my headphones over my ears. Sometimes no response is the best response.

When it's finally time to board, I'm expecting Jackson to be seated next to me, especially since my mother wouldn't give me the details about the seating chart, but surprisingly he's not. Instead I'm in the window seat with Brynn and Shawn next to me, which is worse than sitting next to my ex-boyfriend. Cue the drink service for this five-hour flight. I overhear Brynn tell my brother she's already taken her Ambien. Thank goodness for small favors. A silent and sedated Brynn is a good Brynn. Jackson, Maya, and Hunter sit in the row directly in front of us.

Just as I put my headphones back on, Brynn and Shawn switch places so he can be next to me. *Hallelujah!* Shawn motions for me to take them off. They haven't even finished boarding the plane, and he's already annoying me.

"What's up?" I ask, lifting one speaker off my ear.

He leans his head into me so he can whisper in my ear.

"I wanted you to know Brynn and I were not in on that plan to bring Jackson. We knew nothing about it." Brynn leans over to listen to our conversation. I swear, I can't even talk to my brother without her being a part of it.

"Fine." I go to move the speaker back over my ear.

"We want you to know Brynn and I want you to be happy. Jackson's really cool, but we totally understand what it feels like to find your soul mate. You would know if he was the one for you. Just like I knew Brynn was the one." He blows Brynn a kiss, and she pretends to catch it.

I look in the seat-back pocket for the airline sickness bag. We aren't even moving yet, and I'm already nauseated.

"Thanks. I appreciate your support," I say. I replace my headphone and lean my head against the seat.

I close my eyes and think about what Shawn said. I love my brother; but I wish I could trust his wife. It's not that I haven't tried. There's always a feeling that she has an ulterior motive. My issues don't stem from the past. There have been a number of times she's undermined me with my family. She knows my mother and I have a complicated relationship, and she purposely tries to exploit that, always claiming innocence.

There was one time I made the mistake of complaining about something my mother said to me. It wasn't anything major, but not even an hour went by before Mom called me on it. I finally learned my lesson not to voice my frustrations to my brother either because it always gets back to Brynn. It's disappointing I can't vent to my own family, but it is what it is.

My thoughts are interrupted by the announcement that we're getting ready for takeoff. I take a few deep breaths. Despite the unexpected vacation crasher, I'm looking forward to this. In just a few short hours, we'll land. Hawaii, here I come.

Chapter Seven

I'm jolted from my sleep when I feel the plane drop several feet. I grip the arm rests, causing my fingers to turn white and then look out the window to see nothing but the dark blue water below me. Different thoughts swirl in my head. Is this the end? Am I meant to die in a plane crash over the Pacific? Where are those oxygen masks again? Why didn't I pay better attention when the flight attendant was doing her presentation? I hope Fran will take good care of Kiwi. I wonder if Kiwi would feel abandoned (probably not). I can't believe one of the last faces I'll see is Brynn's.

Damn. What a crappy way to go.

Next to me Shawn and Brynn are blissfully sleeping with their heads together. It's really odd, but they look posed. They do make an attractive couple, and as much as it pains me to admit it, my brother does seem happy.

The plane drops again, and so does my stomach. I gasp loudly, causing Jackson, in the seat in front of me, to turn around.

"You good back there? Pretty wild ride, huh?"

I scowl. Like I said, I'm not a daredevil at all. The last thing I want is a crazy plane ride with nothing but deep water below me for thousands of miles.

"I'm okay," I say unconvincingly. I don't think he can tell that my fingers are going numb from holding on so tightly.

"Those two don't seem to be phased by the turbulence," he says pointing at Shawn and Brynn.

I shake my head. "Only because they're loaded up on Ambien," I joke, but I probably should've asked Brynn for one. I could be peacefully sleeping right now, too. Instead, I'm staring death in the face. Maybe I should review the safety brochure that's in the seat-back pocket.

He nods knowingly.

"It'll be fine. Only three hours to go," he says.

Great. "Thanks."

Jackson turns back around, and I try to relax. The plane is now moving smoothly through the air again, so I let go of the armrests. My parents are sitting in first class, which they deserve considering it's their anniversary. It occurs to me I still haven't thanked them for this vacation. And even though I'm frustrated with my mother and her actions, I'm also incredibly grateful.

More crazy thoughts swirl in my head, so I quickly send them both a text letting them know how much I appreciate and love them. I'd go tell them in person, but the stupid seat belt sign is lit. Not that I would get up now with the way the plane keeps dropping. There have been several announcements warning us passengers to stay in our seats due to rough air. And more importantly, I don't want to take the risk of waking Brynn up. I don't need anything else to stress me out on this flight.

There are some conversations I prefer not to be a part of. With a little over an hour to go, everyone has awoken from their restful slumber. The turbulence has stopped, and the exhilaration over our arrival in Hawaii is creeping in.

The excitement is brought to a temporary halt when my siblings and their spouses begin discussing the mile-high club. Thankfully, most of the passengers around us are either sleeping or have headphones on.

Leave it to my brother to question if our parents have become members yet. *Why?* Then of course, Hunter begins to drop little hints to Jackson about a flight attendant he used to date. It doesn't bother me at all, but seriously? Hunter is annoying, but I would take him any day over Brynn.

"I don't think you want to start bringing up the past," Jackson says with a laugh.

Maya looks at Hunter and raises her eyebrows.

"Good point," Hunter says nervously. He turns around in his seat and peers directly at me. "What about you, Cora? Any wild escapades you want to share?"

Ugh. I'm not surprised he wants to call me out. It's obvious he hasn't gotten over the fact that I dumped his best friend. I know he resents me, although we didn't have much of a relationship before that anyway.

"Nothing I'd share with you," I say sarcastically.

He gives me a wicked grin. "Ouch. Come on, sister. We know there's more going on behind all those books you read. They say the girls who read all the time are the wildest."

I scowl. He's trying hard to push my buttons.

"There were some crazy times back in college, right, Cora?" Brynn chimes in.

Crap.

"I'm not sure what you're referring too, Brynn," I say pointedly.

She has a mischievous gleam in her eye.

Honestly, I'm surprised she's waited this long to blab about our sorority days. We do have a sisterhood bond, but I never believed Brynn took that seriously anyway. She probably should've been kicked out of the sorority; she broke more rules than I can count.

"I knew it. Everyone's got something good to share from their past," Hunter insists. "Even you, Cora Ann."

Jackson is watching our conversation intently. He knows all about my history with Brynn, so this is nothing new to him. For the most part Jackson loves my family, but I know for a fact he's not a Brynn fan. He's been around long enough to see her in action. There was one incident at a family dinner when Jackson actually said something about her behavior. She got all bent out of shape and cried to Shawn about it. He defended her, of course, telling us she'd had a bad day and hadn't meant to offend me. My poor brother is going to be making excuses for her for years to come.

Seriously, though? What is with Hunter and Brynn? I can't count how many times I've wondered what my siblings saw in the two of them. The good news is I have a lot more dirt on Brynn than she has on me.

"Okay, Brynn, you really want to tell college stories?" I ask, raising my eyebrows.

Her smile begins to fade at my suggestion.

"Let's do this," I add sarcastically. "Where should we start?"

I'm totally calling her bluff, knowing that she'll back down.

And because luck always seems to be on Brynn's side, the pilot announces our final decent. I couldn't have asked for a better interruption, and I'm sure Brynn is thinking the same thing. I know this conversation will be brought up again at some point; good thing I'm armed and ready if I need to be, and Fran has plenty to add.

Everyone begins checking their seat belts, and I hear Brynn breathe a sigh of relief.

"Hey, guys, one more thing," Maya says, turning around in her seat. "Can we all make a pact we'll stick together on this trip? Especially since the *Gone with the Wind* girls are coming."

I smile to myself. I haven't thought about that nickname in years. My mom says my aunt DeeDee used to be obsessed with the classic Margaret Mitchell novel. Coincidently, my cousins' names are Tara and Ashley. The funniest thing is when Aunt DeeDee gets excited or fired up about something, a fake Southern drawl starts to come out.

"You never know what kind of drama they're going to bring with them," she adds. "We shouldn't have to worry about that on our vacation."

Is she serious? I look at Jackson. Hmmm ... no more drama than her inviting my ex-boyfriend to come along. I stop myself before saying it out loud.

I stare out the window at the approaching land. The sun is shining, and the ocean is a stunning shade of turquoise. I can't believe it. We're about to touch down in Hawaii. Let the fun begin.

The Honolulu airport is so much different than any other airport I've been in. There are long open-air breezeways that connect the different terminals, and the fresh air feels glorious after such a long journey. The first chance I get, I separate from my family members. I snap a few pictures of the beautiful airport landscaping. Then I wander in a few stores and take my time before dealing with my family again.

When I finally get to the baggage claim, there are drivers holding signs with our names on them. I feel so VIP right now. I'm beginning to wonder if my parents inherited some long-lost relative's fortune. I haven't come out and asked yet, but I'm planning on it. I know my father had quite a bit of stock. Obviously they either got some huge windfall or racked up massive credit card debt. Regardless, this is how they wanted to spend their anniversary, so it's not my place to judge.

As we begin our journey to the resort, I feel like I'm in a dream world. I look out the window at the lush green mountains surrounding us and see the ocean just beyond them. It's such a surreal feeling to be on a tiny island in the middle of the Pacific Ocean. I can't wait to soak up everything Oahu has to offer.

I shoot Fran a text letting her know we're arrived and check on my cat. It's a good thing Kiwi likes Fran. Although not a cat person, if there's anyone I would trust in this world to look out for Kiwi, it's Fran. She responds with lots of questions.

> How was the flight? How's the fam? Is it weird with
> Jackson being there?

I sigh. This is exactly why I wanted her to come with me.

"Are you planning on staying mad at me this whole vacation?" Maya whispers, interrupting my thoughts. The men and our parents are in other cars, and Brynn has her headphones on. Although she probably isn't listening to music. I have no doubt she's eavesdropping on our conversation.

"I haven't decided," I whisper back. She has a worried look on her face.

Not only are my mother and sister super close, but Maya is the spitting image of our mother, so much that sometimes I feel like I'm talking to a younger version of her. They have the same brown eyes and the same smile. And since I look exactly like our father, we don't look like sisters. Shawn is definitely a combination of our parents, so he looks like both of us.

She huffs. "Cora, is it that big of a deal? You said yourself you hoped you two would stay friends."

I sigh loudly. "Yes, I did say that, and I meant it. The issue is you continue to do whatever you want, and you didn't have the decency to tell me he was coming. You could've at least given me a warning instead of a straight-up blindside. How many conversations have we had since Mom sent the initial email?"

Maya looks away because she knows I'm right.

I look over at Brynn, who now has her eyes closed. She still has her headphones on, but I guarantee she's listening.

Maya chews her lip and finally responds. "You're right, and I was going to tell you the first time we talked about the trip, until you mentioned something about not coming because of work. I was afraid if you knew about Jackson being invited you definitely wouldn't come."

She has a point, and my decision would've been completely justified. I could've used the fact that my family, the very people who are supposed to support me no matter what, didn't have any regard for my feelings. My mother could've asked if I'd be okay with her inviting Jackson, but she knew I wouldn't be happy about it, which is why she felt it was better to surprise me right before we got on the plane and then deal with it.

"Whatever, Maya. It's done now, but don't expect me to get over your betrayal instantly. You all need to start considering my feelings. Jackson and I are in a good place, but we're not getting back together, and forcing us to take a vacation together isn't going to change that."

"I know you're not." She pauses. "But can you just pretend to be over it for now? You can be mad at me after we get home. We need a united front on this trip. The *Gone with the Wind* girls have a way of sucking the joy out of everything. I don't need to be worried about you hating me, too."

I crack a smile. "I don't hate you, and I'm willing to put it aside for now so we can deal with the cousins. Don't think I'm over it, though. I'm sure I'll still be mad at you when this vacation is over."

She breathes a sigh of relief. "Fine with me."

A few seconds later we pull into a long circular drive and toward a covered entryway. The Grand Oahu Resort stands tall and majestic, the lobby a large open area that looks out into a valley of pools, shops, and restaurants. And just beyond that is the white sand beach and the Pacific Ocean.

I draw in a breath as I overlook my home for the next week. At this very moment, I'm so thankful I didn't stay at work. As I step out of the car and feel the ocean breeze against my skin, the family drama seems to melt away. This reminds me of what Lydia said—it will be difficult to leave this paradise behind.

"Hi. Hellllooo," a voice shouts.

I'd know that high-pitched, fake Southern drawl anywhere. My aunt DeeDee is rushing toward us. She's wearing a yellow flower-printed dress with long yellow and white beads, which totally reminds me of Mrs. Roper from that old TV show, *Three's Company*. She has a martini glass in her hand, and she's swaying. Ah, I wonder how many beverages she's consumed so far, and with the time change, the day on Hawaii time just started.

"My loves are all here," she announces. "Hot damn, this is a good day."

My parents and aunt start discussing their travels. She tells them my uncle's sciatica is bothering him, so he's already in the spa.

"Cora, sweetheart. I'm so glad you could make it," she says pulling me in for a hug. She smells like a combination of liquor and baby powder.

"Thanks, you, too," I say, trying not to gag from her overpowering scent. "Where are the girls?"

She takes a sip of her drink. "Ash is down by the pool, and Tara should be arriving in a few hours. They are looking forward to seeing you. They are happier than pigs in mud."

Is that a Southern term? The interesting thing is my aunt is from Southern California and to my knowledge hasn't spent any time on a plantation in Georgia.

I look at Maya, who frowns. After the day I've had, the cousins are the least of my worries.

"Where's Peepaw?" I ask. He's the only family member I care to see anyway. Naturally, I don't say this out loud.

"He and Evelyn are napping."

Ah yes, the famous Evelyn. I'm so curious to meet her.

"She's such a sweet thing," she says, taking a sip of her drink. "He's very smitten with her, and they are just precious together."

Our conversation is interrupted when the hotel concierge approaches us. She introduces herself as Kalaina. She's holding several leis and talking a mile a minute.

She begins draping the sweet orchids over our heads. I take a long whiff of the glorious floral scent wafting from around my neck. This is everything I expected and more.

Kalaina continues to point in different directions as she explains the luxurious hotel amenities, and then she produces a stack of folders. According to her, all of our rooms are in one hallway, and some are adjoining. We follow Kalaina through the lobby toward the elevator. She begins calling out our names and handing us a folder with our keys and important information for the week. I admit I'm impressed with how organized this seems. It can't be easy to coordinate so many people.

I'm grateful I ended up with my own room. The thought crossed my mind I would somehow end up sharing a room with one of my cousins or even Jackson. I wouldn't put it past my mother to book us in a room together in the hopes it would magically reconnect us. Thankfully, she hasn't completely lost her mind … although the coconut bra and grass skirt family picture has me questioning.

Kalaina leaves us, and we make our way to the fifteenth floor. I'm not surprised to learn my room is squeezed in between Jackson's and Shawn and Brynn's. I may not be sharing a room, but the location is almost as bad.

"You may want to wear your headphones, little sis," Shawn says with a laugh as he opens his door.

Gross!

Brynn playfully hits him on the arm while he picks her up and carries her over the threshold and into their room.

"We'll try to be as quiet as possible," he calls before shutting the door.

"Thanks for the warning," I say with a groan. Oh well, I'm sure I won't be spending much time in my room anyway. I have a whole island to explore.

When I enter my room, which has to be a suite, a huge smile spreads across my face. Not even details of Shawn and Brynn's private life are going to steal the joy of this moment.

Two large french doors open out onto the balcony. I close my eyes and listen as the waves crash over the shore. Despite the long flight and dealing with my family, I suddenly feel re-energized.

"Pretty awesome, huh?"

I look over to see Jackson also standing on his balcony and looking at the ocean. I guess we had the same idea when we entered our rooms and headed straight for the balconies.

"It really is," I reply.

He lets out a deep breath. "I'm going to chill for a while. See ya at dinner?"

"See you then," I call as I continue to stare out at the ocean.

I'm enjoying this moment too much to be phased by him being in the room next to me.

"Shawnnn."

I cringe when I hear Brynn's voice and her giggling. Yep, that definitely ruined my serene moment. Maybe I should try to switch rooms with someone, although I can guarantee no one else will want to be next door to those two. I need to suck it up, and thankfully I know Brynn will pop a few Ambien at some point.

I hurry back inside my room to get settled before I set out to do some exploring of this gorgeous resort. It's time to get my vacation started.

Chapter Eight

The Grand Oahu Resort is huge. I stop in to see Kalaina, the concierge, to get all the must-know details and information about this part of the island. My parents set up a few family excursions, but I'm excited to get out on my own. Not to mention, I hope to ignore most of my family as much as possible.

I walk through the massive pool area which they call the Hau'oli Valley. There are several pools, a lazy river, and a big slide that looks like a volcano. Closer to the beach, there are three endless hot tubs overlooking the ocean. This place is absolutely magical. After my walk, I sit in a comfortable chair and order a piña colada at the beach-side bar called the *Hula Hula*. I know there are a million drinks I could order, but for some reason I feel having a piña colada on the beach in Hawaii is mandatory.

I lean back in my chair and look around and notice a few women taking a dance lesson down the beach. My mother requested that all us girls take a class together, which is fine because I wanted to take a lesson anyway.

A few people are heading into the water on kayaks, and some families play in the sand. A light breeze and Hawaiian music plays in the background. As surreal as it feels being here, it's everything I hoped it would be and more.

As I scan the beach, someone catches my eye. The very attractive someone is emerging from the ocean. He runs his fingers through his wet hair, and I can't help but notice his shoulder muscles tighten. There's something very familiar about him ...

Suddenly I remember Fran's dream about the handsome stranger. Could this be—

"Corrraaaaa."

I jump up in the air when I feel two arms close in tightly around my neck, almost choking me.

"I'm sooooo happy to see you."

I look over my shoulder to see my cousin Ashley standing behind me.

She's wearing a light pink romper and a huge woven hat. Her blonde shoulder-length bob is styled in perfect beach waves. Our cousins have the best hair no matter what the climate is.

"Hi, Ash, good to see you, too," I reply.

She sits in the chair next to me and orders a mojito. "This is unbelievable," she says, grabbing my hand. "The fact that we're here together right now—it's fantastic."

When I turn back to face the beach, the attractive man is gone. I do a quick scan of the area, but he's nowhere to be seen. I frown. *Thanks a lot, Ashley.*

"When I heard Uncle Warner and Aunt Leann wanted all of us to come, I started crying. I've been looking forward to this reunion, haven't you?"

Um, not really. Of course, I don't say that out loud. Instead, I nod and take a sip of my drink.

"How are you doing?" she asks. "Mom told me you were seeing someone, Maya and Hunter's friend, right? That sounds like fun. Do you guys double a lot?"

I force a smile. The four of us did go out together quite often, which was fun sometimes. Although I can only take Hunter in small doses.

"I *was* seeing Hunter's friend, but it didn't work out."

And he's here, in the hotel room next to mine, but whatever.

"Oh, I'm sorry," she says, patting my arm. "I totally know the feeling. Stephan and I are no longer together, either. Breakups are wretched."

I give her a sympathetic look, even though I suspect she isn't that heartbroken. "I'm sorry to hear it."

She frowns. "We were just beginning to discuss wedding plans, and then he had a trip to London, and I went to Santorini with some girlfriends. Anyway, we both met other people while we were traveling, and well, you know how it goes. I felt really bad after it happened, and I actually wasn't going to tell Stephan because I didn't want to hurt him."

I raise my eyebrows as she continues her story. I feel like I'm watching an episode of *Days of Our Lives*.

"When we returned home, a woman called his phone, and I answered. He told me about being with her in London, and I told him about my twenty-four hours with Mauricio."

Wow, so basically both Ashley and her fiancé cheated on each other while they were on vacation. Sadly, this isn't that surprising. She has always been into herself, and I don't think she wants to be tied down. That's why her relationships don't seem to last. As soon as my mother told me about her whirlwind engagement, I suspected it was doomed. I can't be sure, but I think she's been engaged at least two other times. Maybe engagement is her thing? Like Ross from *Friends*. His thing was getting married. Ashley's thing is getting engaged. That just proves we're all different.

"Anyway, since we're both here and single, we should make the most of it. I've been to the islands before, of course, so I know some the best places for the nightlife scene."

Hmm ... I'm not sure I'm up for hitting the *scene* with Ashley. I've seen pictures of her escapades online, and I'm pretty sure I can't hang. If I go out with her, I may wake up tomorrow in some hut in Bora Bora, although there are worse things. And I'd rather spend time with Ashley than Brynn any day of the week.

"Erm, maybe. I'll think about it."

She frowns. "What do you mean 'think about it'? We're young, single, and in Hawaii. It's time for us to live it up a little. There's nothing to *think* about."

"So, what else have you been up to besides—" *Cheating on your fiancé?* Crap. I can't say that. "Um ... besides your travels."

One thing I know is the *Gone with the Wind* girls love to talk about themselves.

She takes my bait and launches into a story about being on the boards of some hospital charities and learning to speak Mandarin Chinese.

Does this girl ever sleep?

I take another sip of my beverage. "Ash, I'm dying to ask you something."

She smirks. "Okay, shoot. You know you can ask me anything. I'm an open book."

Well, that's one way to describe her.

"Do you sleep? Because for the life of me I can't figure out how you do so much. I mean, you're always traveling or working or ..." I almost say getting engaged, but I stop myself in the nick of time.

She laughs. "I sleep about five hours a night on average. Even if I try to get to bed earlier, I lie awake and toss and turn."

Five hours? *Ugh*, I wouldn't be able to function.

"A few years ago, I met with an Eastern medicine guru, and he told me my body rhythm doesn't require as much sleep as the average person. Our bodies require ten hours a day of rest, but we can spend that time doing whatever meets our individual needs. Sleep is not at the top of my list, but I do a lot of meditation, and that benefits me."

Bummer for her. My body rhythm loves to sleep.

"Do you meditate?" she asks.

I shake my head. "No, but I love to read, so that relaxes me."

She nods and sips her drink. "Good for you."

I glance at the beach to see if the handsome stranger has reappeared. Unfortunately, I don't see him.

"Have you seen Peepaw yet?" she asks.

"No. But I can't wait."

"It's so cute seeing him with his new love, Evelyn. Have you met her?"

I shake my head.

"You'll like her a lot. She's good for Peepaw."

We talk for a few more minutes before Ashley looks at her phone and jumps off her chair.

"Oh, I better start getting ready for dinner."

I glance at the time. It's only three o'clock, but whatever. Maybe that's why she always looks so good, but four hours is a lot of time to get ready.

"See you later. I'm excited to get out and have some fun with you."

"Me, too," I reply unconvincingly.

I stay at the bar a while, hoping to get another glimpse of the gorgeous man from the beach. Unfortunately, he's gone. And for all I know, he's here with his wife and kids anyway.

After I finish my piña colada, I'm feeling great, like I can finally relax on my vacation. I'm not a big drinker, so one cocktail is usually perfect for me. I leave the Hula Hula bar and take a stroll around the hotel gardens to get a better look at all the gorgeous tropical foliage and the traditional Hawaiian décor. I'm not sure I'm ready to go back to my room yet, especially after Shawn's warning to wear my headphones. *Ew.* The thought of having to listen to Brynn in an intimate moment makes me nauseated. Anyway, just in case, I'll let them get it out of their systems and take my time. Unlike my cousin Ashley, I don't need four hours to get ready for dinner.

As I climb the stairs toward the grand lobby, I hear a familiar jovial laugh. A smile spreads across my face, and I race up the last few steps.

At the top of the stairs, there's a balcony overlooking the resort. Sure enough, Peepaw is sitting with a petite woman and my parents.

"Peepaw!" I shout excitedly.

He turns around and gives me a warm smile. "There she is, Miss America," he announces.

I rush toward him as he stands up to greet me, and of course at 6'3" he towers over me. His blue eyes sparkle under his white eyebrows.

He takes my face in his weathered hands and gives me a kiss on my forehead.

"It's so good to see you," I tell him as I wrap my arms around him.

"It is, isn't it," he replies with a chuckle.

We all laugh. That's a classic Peepaw answer.

I notice my dad has his nose buried in a resort guide, and Mom is sipping on a bright pink cocktail. I look behind Peepaw at the woman I'm assuming is his new girlfriend.

"You must be Evelyn. I'm Cora."

She holds out her pale, thin hand. "Yes. I'm happy to meet you."

I slide a chair next to Peepaw and Evelyn and ask them about their flight.

"It was very good," Evelyn answers. "It's such a lovely place, and how terrific that the family can be here together. I've heard so much about all of you."

Terrific? That's not exactly a word I'd use to describe us being together, but I don't disagree.

"So, what do you do, Cara?" she asks.

"Cora," I correct her.

She giggles. "Yes, yes."

"I work in public relations and love my job."

My mother chimes in about the time I met Tom Hanks and when I was in the same building as Oprah. She gets more excited about the perks of my job than I do.

"How wonderful," Evelyn exclaims.

I ask her about herself and her family.

I learn she was a nurse and has one son and one grandson. Other than mentioning them, she's rather vague about her life.

"I've been single and alone for a very long time, so meeting Louie has brought me back to life again," she says, blushing.

"Louie," I'm assuming, is short for Louis. I've never heard anyone call my grandfather *Louie*.

"Well, Peepaw is the best," I tell her.

She smiles fondly at him, and he pats her hand gently. Their interaction is very sweet.

"And what about you? Do you have a special someone in your life right now?" Evelyn asks me.

Ugh, I hate this question. Especially with my mother being here. Why does there always have to be a "special someone"? What's wrong with being a strong, independent, single woman?

I plaster a big cheesy grin on my face. "I'm between special someones at the moment."

"Good for you. Give 'em hell," Peepaw announces. "My granddaughter should never settle, no matter what anyone tells her."

And this is only one of the many reasons I adore him. He makes me feel he's in my corner no matter what decisions I make. With him I never feel like I'm a disappointment or like there was a mix up at the hospital on that beautiful April afternoon I was born.

"Thanks, Peepaw."

I glance at my mother who looks like she wants to say something. I make a quick decision to mention Jackson before she does. Her version of my relationship and breakup is bound to be different than mine.

"My last relationship ended earlier this year. He's a good person, but we weren't right for each other. We've remained friends, and believe it or not, he came on this trip with us."

Evelyn looks confused, and why wouldn't she be. I just told her my relationship ended and that the man came on vacation with us.

I turn to my mother, who I know is dying to add her take on this juicy piece of gossip.

"He's our son-in-law's best friend, and we consider him a part of our family, so he joined us," Mom continues. Clearly she's trying to justify her reasons for inviting Jackson to come with us.

My father peers over the resort guide he's reading and rolls his eyes. I still wish he would've taken more of a stand when this not-so-brilliant plan was in the works.

"Oh, well, that's nice that your relationship ended peacefully and that he could still join you on vacation," Evelyn says.

I watch my mother drain her glass. Hah! Maybe she's finally feeling a little awkward about her sneaky plan.

"Exactly," Mom agrees, raising her voice. "Warner and I wanted to share this special occasion with everyone important to us."

"Speaking of which. Are Ken and Alaina here yet?" I ask, changing the subject. Other than Peepaw, they're the only people I'm looking forward to seeing.

"Anytime now," Mom says excitedly. "Ken and Alaina are our oldest and dearest friends." She begins explaining to Evelyn how they met Ken and Alaina.

This is one of my favorite stories. Mom had taken Shawn and me to the beach when we were young. Alaina was also there with Owen. Alaina and Mom started talking about motherhood. They really hit it off, so they made plans to get together with Ken and my father, and the rest is history.

"Hey, you," Peepaw whispers. He motions me to lean in closer to him. "You sure you're okay with that boy being here?" he asks, cupping his mouth with his hand so my mother can't see.

I shrug. Peepaw has always been very observant, I'm not surprised he's picked up on my frustration with the situation.

"I mean, I'm not thrilled, but I'm not going to let it ruin my whole vacation. I can't exactly do anything about it now anyway."

I tell him how I found out Jackson was joining us only minutes before boarding the plane.

He shakes his head. "My daughter-in-law means well, even though she has an odd way of showing it."

I look at my mother, who's talking a mile a minute to Evelyn.

"I know," I agree. "I just wish she'd back off a little."

He pats me on the shoulder.

"We're hoping for some grandchildren soon," my mother says. "Both Maya and Shawn have wonderful spouses. They'll give me some beautiful grandbabies."

I look at Peepaw who gives me a wink.

"So, what are you most excited about doing while you're here?" I ask Evelyn. I don't have anything to add to the grandchildren conversation, and I'm perfectly okay with that.

"I'm really looking forward to seeing all the tropical landscaping. Gardening is my hobby."

"You should see her backyard," Peepaw chimes in.

Evelyn gives him a warm smile.

We stay another twenty minutes, and then Evelyn, Peepaw, and I walk to the elevator.

"I'm going to relax a little while before dinner," I tell them. "It was great meeting you," I say to Evelyn. "I look forward to talking with you more."

She smiles. "It was lovely meeting you too, Cara."

Ugh. I feel bad correcting her again. I'm sure she'll get my name right eventually.

"Rest up, sweetheart," Peepaw says. In other words, get ready because the whole gang will be here tonight.

"See you at dinner."

I walk to my room, and thankfully there aren't any cringeworthy sounds coming from Shawn and Brynn's room. Hopefully the worst is over and it's smooth sailing from this moment on. I can't help but wonder if I'll see the man from the beach again.

Chapter Nine

I open my eyes to the sun streaming into my room. *Where am I?* I lie still for a few minutes until I remember I'm at a resort in Hawaii. I stretch out on the glorious king-size bed. I need to thank my parents for this room. Even though the location of my room isn't ideal, I can overlook that for this huge comfy bed and the soft feather pillows.

I reach for my phone on the nightstand and quickly sit up. I have three texts from my mother and a missed call from my sister. I look at the time. I'm late for dinner. Crap! Maybe Ashley had the right idea? Four hours to get ready would've been better than four minutes. I jump out of bed and run to the bathroom to make myself presentable.

After I returned from visiting with Peepaw and Evelyn, I sat down on the bed and turned on the TV. I shouldn't have lain down. I guess jet lag and a piña colada don't mix.

I throw on a turquoise maxi dress and new wedges. I run a brush through my hair and touch up my makeup. I don't look terrible, but you can definitely tell I just woke up. Oh well, it's as good as it's going to get for now. And it's not like it's a super formal dinner anyway. The big anniversary celebration isn't until the last night of the vacation.

I grab my room key and race down to the restaurant. I hate being late for things. And now that I'm late, I won't get to choose who I sit next to—and with this group, the good options are very limited.

When I walk into the restaurant, I hear Peepaw's laugh coming from the back room. I make my way through tables as if I'm heading for a lion's den. Too bad there isn't any dramatic music playing in the background.

I pause when I walk into the private room and see everyone sitting at a long table. I'm trying to process what's happening, but maybe I'm still not fully awake, or maybe I'm dreaming.

"Cora Ann, there you are," Mom exclaims. "I was starting to get concerned."

Unfortunately, I can't move or speak or anything. Everyone is here—my parents, Peepaw and Evelyn, my siblings and their spouses, my aunt and uncle, Ashley, Tara, Jackson, Ken and Alaina, and … Owen.

I'm hallucinating, right?

"Where were you?" Maya asks. "We were about to send out a search party. I was beginning to wonder if you were kidnapped by the Volturi." Normally I would laugh at the *Twilight* reference, but I still can't move or speak. All I can think about is that Owen is here, in Hawaii, sitting at the dinner table with my entire family.

Say something, Cora!

It was him—the handsome man from the beach. I knew there was something familiar about him. Wait, was he the handsome stranger from Fran's dream? I need to send her a picture of him, stat.

"I'm sorry. I-I fell asleep," I stutter, as I try to keep my gaze off Owen.

Everyone at the table is watching me right now. I need to get it together.

"Cora, it's so good to see you, honey," Alaina exclaims. She stands up and gives me a hug.

I could always count on Alaina to save me from completely embarrassing myself.

"Hi, Alaina, Ken."

Ken stands up and pats me on the top of my head. "Little Cora is all grown up. I still remember when you wore that Little Mermaid dress everywhere you went."

The whole table starts laughing.

"She wouldn't take that thing off. I think Mom had to bribe her with candy so she could wash it. It started to smell pretty bad, right, Mom?" Shawn says with a laugh. "Do you still have it? That thing needs to be bronzed."

Seriously? How did my favorite childhood dress become the topic of dinner conversation?

Owen stands up and turns toward me.

"Hey, Cora. Long time no see."

It occurs to me everyone is still watching, so I refuse to say or do anything stupid.

"It has been. Hi, Owen."

He gives me a hug, and every cell in my body tingles at his touch. This can't be a normal reaction. *Pull yourself together, Cora.*

"I didn't know you were coming," I say, quickly moving away from his arms when he lets go of me. Clearly I was left out of the loop on a lot of the guest list.

He chuckles. "I wasn't at first, but I was able to get some time off work at the last minute. How often do you get offered a trip to paradise with a great family?"

I glance around the table. "Yeah, good point."

Everyone else returns to their prior conversations. I see there is one empty chair, which happens to be between Aunt DeeDee and Brynn, basically the worst seat in the house. That's what I get for being late. I will never take another nap again.

I sit down in the chair and take a long sip of the water that's already at my seat. I purposely try not to stare across the table. I must be feeling groggy from my unexpectedly long nap, or maybe I'm still in shock Owen is really here right now. I down the entire glass of water and place it on the table. I feel like time has stood still; Owen hasn't changed at all. *Is it warm in here?*

"I'm sorry, Cora. If I'd known you were asleep, I would've woken you up," Brynn says sweetly. "I think we all needed a good nap after our long flight."

She obviously has her party manners on.

I shrug. "Don't worry about it."

"Are you all right? You know with—" She motions toward her left where Jackson is sitting next to my cousin Tara at the end of the table. They seem to be engaged in a private conversation. Although she did stop talking to Jackson long enough to wave at me when I arrived.

I look over at Maya, who gives me a horrified look. I know she's watching Tara and Jackson very closely. It would serve her right for being so deceptive by inviting him behind my back.

"I'm doing great," I tell Brynn.

My father clinks the top of his water glass with his fork. "Excuse me, everyone."

The conversations come to a halt as we all turn toward him. My dad is a great public speaker. I just hope he's not planning to bust out another exercise routine.

"Leann and I wanted to thank you for being here. We're looking forward to spending time with all of you and strengthening our family bonds."

Everyone cheers, even me. I don't want to be the only one with a bad attitude.

"No, we should be thanking you, brother," my uncle yells, holding up his beer. "Thanks for footing the bill."

I suspect he and Aunt DeeDee have been drinking since they boarded the plane to fly here, maybe even before that, and the night is still young.

"I'm so happy to have my family and dearest friends here to celebrate with us," my mom chimes in as she dabs the corners of her eyes with a napkin. My father puts his arm around her and pulls her in for a sweet kiss. There are more cheers and whistles.

After my father's speech I sit back in my chair and scan the table. Brynn and Shawn are practically sitting on top of each other. Seriously? I want to yell, "Get a room." Can't they save it for later? We're sitting in a restaurant.

Tara and Jackson are leaning into each other, looking at the wine list.

Okay, so maybe that's a little weird. I let out a sigh. The fact he's even here is just wrong.

Maya is frantically whispering to Hunter, who looks worried. I don't doubt she's warning him about a possible Jackson and Tara hookup. That would be her biggest nightmare.

Ashley is flirtatiously flipping her hair as she runs her eyes over Owen. Not that I blame her. Too bad she's wasting her time. Maybe someone should tell her he's married. Not that it would make a difference to her, based on what she told me about how her engagement ended.

Ken and Alaina are talking to Peepaw and Evelyn, my aunt and uncle are ordering more drinks—big surprise there—and my parents, well, I can't remember the last time they looked so happy.

"I'm feeling a lot of love in this room," my uncle says a few minutes later. "My big brother and his bride of forty years are a great example to us all."

My parents look at each other and smile.

He holds up his beer. "Tell us how you keep the magic alive. And now we're all adults, you can give us the dirty details."

He starts to move his body in a way that makes me want to laugh and throw up at the same time.

Thankfully, we are rescued by the servers who come to take our orders. By the time they are finished, Uncle Sterling has moved on.

The rest of the evening is mostly uneventful except for a few inappropriate jokes which make sweet Evelyn raise her eyebrows. She needs to get used to that if she wants to hang around with the Fletcher clan. After we finish dinner, everyone makes their way to the Hula

Hula bar and fire pit, except Peepaw and Evelyn, who announce they're up way past their bedtime.

I find a comfortable lounge chair facing the water and sit down.

"You have to do something," Maya snaps, sitting on the edge of my chair. "Tara and Jackson have been talking all night. Hunter is no help because he thinks Jackson deserves some TLC. I'm so frustrated with him right now."

I fold my arms. "Me? What is it you think I need to do? You invited Jackson here."

She scowls. "I didn't invite him here to hook up with our miserable cousin."

I shrug, clearly letting her know this has nothing to do with me. I admit it feels good to see her sweating now that her big sneaky plan is backfiring. Karma is a good thing sometimes.

"Really, Cora? This doesn't bother you at all? What if he and Tara hook up? He's your ex-boyfriend."

I hold my hands up in the air.

"Exactly, he's my *ex*. And they're just talking, Maya. He can talk to anyone he wants."

She lets out a frustrated sigh and storms off.

What exactly does she expect from me? I don't have any right to tell Jackson he can't talk to another woman, including Tara. I gave up the right when I broke up with him.

Alaina walks toward me and sits down on the lounge chair next to mine.

"Is she okay?" she asks, pointing to where Maya ran off.

I laugh. "You know how my sister is. She doesn't like not getting her way."

She nods. "So, tell me about life. What are you reading right now? I just finished a great book you would love."

This is exactly why I was so excited to visit with Alaina. There isn't another person here who I could discuss books with.

"I'm on a romantic comedy kick right now," I say excitedly. "Tell me about your book."

We discuss our latest reads, and I tell her about my job and Kiwi. Alaina is a cat person like me.

"I was really happy when I heard you guys were coming," I say. I take a peek behind me, just to make sure there aren't other ears listening to our conversation. "Can I be honest with you?"

She gives me a wink. "Always."

I already knew this.

"I thought about skipping this happy family reunion," I say, lowering my voice. "I was trying to come up with a good enough excuse that would be believable."

She gives me an understanding nod. "And what about the ex-boyfriend?"

I scowl.

"For the record, I told Leann I thought it was a bad idea to invite him," she adds.

"Clearly she didn't listen to you. I found out he was joining us at the airport this morning," I add with a sigh. "They obviously knew I wasn't going to be happy about it, or they wouldn't have kept it a secret."

She chews on her fingernail. "You know I love my best friend. She really just wants the best for her daughter, and she was hoping—"

"She was hoping a magical vacation would help Jackson and me rekindle our romance," I interject. "I know exactly what she has up her sleeve."

Alaina nods in agreement.

"Did you know she even put us in rooms next to each other?" I tell her. "What was that about? Not to mention it's gross that my mother would purposely encourage us to … well, you know."

As much as I adore Alaina, I don't want to discuss the specific details about my private life with her.

She puts her hands to her forehead. "You poor thing."

I glance behind me to see Jackson and Tara now sitting at the bar talking to each other.

"Yeah, well, as much as it sucks, I'm not going to let it ruin this vacation."

She smiles. "That's the Cora I remember; you've always been able to take things in stride."

I know exactly what she means. Alaina has been around long enough to know the dynamics of my family.

"Do you think Jackson was hoping he'd have another chance with you?"

I shrug. "I'm not sure, maybe a little. Honestly, I think he saw a free trip and jumped on it."

She smiles. "Ken and I weren't going to come either because of that. We didn't feel right about your parents paying for us. Ken and Warner actually got into an argument about it, and finally they let us make a compromise. We paid for our flights, but they insisted on paying for the hotel since they had the big group discount."

Ahh—a group discount makes more sense. That probably cut a big chunk of the cost.

"I was wondering how they were paying for everyone."

She smiles. "It's so generous of them. Your mom told me they didn't want anyone to have an excuse not to come, the cost obviously being a huge factor."

I think about how happy my parents looked at dinner. They wanted this week to be special for all of us. I start to feel guilty for having such a bad attitude.

"Lainey."

She looks up when she hears Ken calling. "Coming, dear."

She leans over and gives me a hug. "Let's catch up more this week. Maybe breakfast?" she says with a gleam in her eye.

"You remember?"

She leans her head to the side. "Of course I remember breakfast is your favorite. Both you and my Owen would eat pancakes for every meal if we let you."

The mention of Owen sends a jolt through my body. I'm about to casually ask her about him when Ken calls her again.

She leaves to join him, my parents, and aunt and uncle.

I lean my head against the back of the lounge chair.

Shawn and Brynn have disappeared. I'm assuming they've returned to their room for the evening. That's one good thing about getting a nap in—I won't need to go back to my room for a while.

Hunter and Maya are now sitting with Jackson and Tara. I try to hide my smile because I know where Maya is going to be spending her week now. She looks kind of miserable. Admittedly, this brings me quite a bit of joy, despite the fact that my cousin and ex-boyfriend really seem to be hitting it off.

A few seconds later I get up from the chair and walk out onto the sand toward the water. The moon is casting a glow on the ocean, and it's absolutely breathtaking.

I take off my wedges and let the water lap over my feet.

"It's nice, isn't it?"

I turn to see Owen standing next to me. I suck in a breath as I look up at him. He looks the same as I remember him. Same wavy brown hair, warm hazel eyes, and his smile—it's like I've gone back in time.

Chapter Ten

I quickly collect myself now that Owen has joined me on the beach. I need to forget about some silly childhood crush and carry on a normal conversation. I'm no longer the awkward Cora Fletcher who's secretly drooling over baseball hero and family friend, Owen Webber.

"It's breathtaking. I think I'm still in denial I'm really here," I tell him.

And that you're here.

He continues to stare out at the ocean. "I know the feeling."

I move my feet through the sand while I try to think of something else to say.

"So, how's life been treating you?" he asks. "I was trying to remember the last time we saw each other."

I clear my throat. "It's been several years, probably before you left for college. And I'm sorry I missed your wedding. We had some big projects going on at work, so I wasn't able to get away."

He shrugs. "Totally understandable."

Neither of us says anything for another few seconds.

"How about you? Is your job going well?"

He scratches his forehead. "Work is busy. I wasn't sure I'd be able to come. My firm is really doing well, which is a good thing. I'm crossing my fingers I'm close to making partner."

"That's amazing," I gush. My voice has suddenly gone up a few octaves.

Tone it down, Cora.

"Congrats," I add calmly.

"Thanks. It's been quite a ride."

The tide comes up a bit higher, and I take a few quick steps back to avoid the rush of water when I almost trip on the bottom of my dress. Owen catches me like a true knight in shining armor. I tightly grab on to his arms to balance myself, feeling his muscles flex against my fingers.

We lock our gazes, and I quickly let go of him.

"Thanks for saving me from the embarrassment of walking through the hotel soaking wet. My family enjoys getting a few laughs at my expense. I don't need to give them any more material to work with."

He gives me a playful smile. "I'm glad I could be of service."

We're interrupted by loud cheering coming from the bar.

I hear my aunt offer to dance on the bar, and Ashley yells something about her mom being the coolest mother ever.

I groan. "The Fletchers have officially invaded Oahu. This resort and this island will never be the same. It's quite possible we won't be allowed to ever return here after this week."

He laughs. "Your family is great. I've always loved hanging out with them."

I snort. "For the most part, yes. I'm just a little frustrated with a few of them right now."

He makes a face. "Yeah, I heard about the ex-boyfriend saga. That was kind of messed up."

"Kind of messed up?" I repeat. "Yeah, you could say that."

There's more loud cheering, and my aunt and uncle are now singing "Bennie and the Jets" by Elton John at the top of their lungs. Those two have certainly made their mark on this place.

Owen puts his hands in his pockets and cringes. "You want to take a walk?"

My heart starts beating a little quicker at his request. "Um—sure."

We start walking slowly down the beach and away from the crazy shenanigans that are going down at the Hula Hula.

"So, what happened between you and Jackson?" he asks. "I only spoke to him for a few minutes, but he seems cool. He's Hunter's best friend, right?"

"Yes. I ended the relationship, not because of anything he did. I just didn't feel like we were right for each other. The truth is I should've never let my sister set me up in the first place."

He shakes his head. "Yeah, I was never a fan of being set up."

At least he's lucky he doesn't have to worry about that anymore.

"My family was obviously very upset by my decision. Especially Maya and Hunter. They were counting on Jackson and me getting married and us being one big happy family. And then there's my mother ... I think my decision broke her heart."

Owen listens intently. "And that's why he's here."

I sigh. "Yep. They came up with this grand plan to bring us here to reconcile. His room is next to mine, too. So, I'm stuck with him on one side and Brynn and Shawn on the other."

Owen throws his head back in laughter. "Whoa, you did get screwed."

I laugh. "Totally screwed."

"Well if it makes you feel any better, I'm next to my parents, and our rooms are adjoining."

"Aww, how sweet. Wanna switch?"

He gives me a thoughtful look.

"Normally I'd say yes. But I'm not sure about being next to Shawn and his wife. Although it might be worse next to my parents. Sometimes they hint around about their sex life and, well, there are some things a son should never hear."

I giggle.

We walk a few more steps in silence. I finally feel at ease talking to him. I remember how nervous I used to get around him.

"Breakups are difficult," he continues. "And you made the right decision by getting out of that relationship when you knew it wasn't right. Some people stay because they think they can fix everything wrong in their relationship. The important thing is you feel good about your decision and you're happy."

He's right.

"Thanks. Now if you could tell that to my mother, I'd appreciate it. Maybe she'll listen to you because she sure as hell doesn't want to listen to me."

He laughs. "I will. I'm not sure it will do any good, but I totally have your back."

I feel a spike in my pulse when Owen tells me he has my back. *Ugh.* Why am I doing this to myself? It's been over a decade since this man made my heart flutter, and now it's completely inappropriate for me to have these kinds of feelings.

As we continue to walk, I decide to rip off the Band-Aid by bringing up his wife.

"So, Alyssa wasn't able to make it? That must've been hard for her to skip this vacation." I find it hard to believe my parents didn't extend the invite to Owen's wife as well.

Owen stops walking.

"Alyssa? Cora, didn't you know? I would've thought Leann told you. I know how much she likes to—"

He stops talking, but I already know what he was going to say about my mother. I'm still stuck on what he's referring to.

"You thought she would've told me what?" I ask. "And yes, my mother lives for gossip, but our communication has been minimal the past few months since I broke up with Jackson."

He gives me an understanding nod. "Alyssa and I are divorced."

Owen is divorced. All of a sudden I feel as if a weight has been lifted off my shoulders. I'm so glad it's dark outside so he can't see my expression.

"Oh, I'm sorry to hear that." I pause as I try to collect my thoughts. "But you were only—" I cover my mouth to stop myself from saying the wrong thing. Not to mention, I feel like the most horrible person in the world right now. What kind of a person is happy to hear someone got divorced?

"We were married for thirteen months," he tells me as he folds his arms. "But we only lived together for three. That's what I meant when I said you made the right decision about ending things with Jackson. I ignored my doubts and got married when I shouldn't have. I kept telling myself all relationships had their issues." He sighs. "Anyway, I know we made the right decision to end our marriage."

The breeze picks up, causing me to get a chill. I run my hands over my bare arms.

Owen must notice because he removes his jacket and puts it around my shoulders.

"Thanks," I say with a nervous laugh. "I was in such a rush to get to dinner I forgot my sweater."

Owen starts laughing. "I just remembered something."

"What?"

He shakes his head. "It's totally random."

I pull his jacket tighter around me and breathe in the rich masculine scent lingering on the fabric. "Random or not, you have to tell me now."

He scratches his forehead. "Fine. Do you remember when we were at your parents' house and your friend was setting you up on a blind date? We must've been sixteen at the time."

My thoughts begin to swirl as I relive that night. I can't believe he remembers it.

"That is a random memory," I say. "But I remember—it's one of those embarrassing moments you don't forget. That guy showed up at the house with a single rose, and my mother made a huge deal out of it and made me take pictures holding it. You guys were all teasing me about it."

I feel heat rise to my cheeks as I cover my face with my hands.

"Did you end up going out with him?"

I undercover my eyes to see Owen watching me.

"Wow. It feels like a million years ago. But I did go out with him, a few times, actually."

We both grow quiet again.

"Anyway, I'm sorry about you and Alyssa," I tell him.

He nods. "Sometimes things don't work out the way we plan, but it was better we ended things sooner instead of years down the road."

"I agree." I yawn widely. I guess my nap wasn't long enough after all.

"You ready to head back?" he asks.

No.

"Um ... yeah. It's pretty late."

We turn around and head back to the hotel. Neither of us says anything as we walk, but the silence between us isn't uncomfortable at all. The sound of the ocean seems to add to the mood. When we return to the hotel, we find the Hula Hula empty.

"Ah, the coast is clear," he says with a laugh.

I giggle. "I was thinking the same thing. I'm assuming the Fletchers closed the place down."

He shrugs. "Maybe the bartender cut them off?"

"Oh, that wouldn't shock me one bit," I exclaim. "Regardless, it's the first night of our big happy reunion. Things are just heating up."

The corner of his mouth curls up. "I'm interested to see what happens this week."

As we make our way toward to the elevator door, I notice a couple holding hands and swinging their arms back and forth. I usually don't get all swoony over romance, but there's something about the way these two people are looking at each other. They may as well be shouting from the rooftop of the hotel that they're in love. The man twirls her around and kisses the tip of her nose.

"I guess we're going to the same floor," Owen says, dragging my attention away from the lovebirds.

"Yep, my parents wanted us all to be together," I pause, thinking about Jackson being in the room right next door to mine. "Are you sure you don't want to switch rooms with me? My room has an amazing view of the ocean."

He leans up against the wall of the elevator and stares at me. "Now that's tempting. My view is of the gardens, and while they are beautiful, I don't think they can compare to my view tonight."

My pulse picks up as we arrive at our floor, and I step out. *He's talking about the moonlight shining on the ocean, right?*

"Oh, I know. The ocean with the moonlight, there's nothing like it."

We arrive at my room first, as his is at the end of the hall. "This is me.

And right there is Shawn and Brynn's room," I say, pointing to the door next to mine. "Hopefully all is quiet," I add, cringing.

He laughs.

"I hope so for your sake," he says. "Luckily, my parents should already be fast asleep and snoring heavily."

I clear my throat and step toward my door. "Thanks again for the walk."

"No, thank you." He pauses. "Good night, Cora."

He gives me a half-wave as he takes off down the hall.

I'm about to open my door when I look down and notice I still have his jacket.

"Owen, wait."

He turns around as I rush toward him.

"Your jacket." I hold it out to him while he takes it. "Thanks for letting me borrow it."

He gives me a nod as I turn around to head back to my room. "Hey, Cora. For the record, I wasn't only referring to the ocean being beautiful."

I open my mouth to say something when I'm startled by a hotel room door opening. My aunt DeeDee sticks her head out.

"Oh, it's you, Cora. I was hoping you were room service," she slurs. "I'm waiting on my nachos."

Owen and I look at each other, and I cover my mouth to keep from laughing.

"Sorry, Aunt DeeDee. It's just me."

The elevator doors opens, and a server with a tray steps off.

"There they are. Honey, you bring those goodies right over here," she says excitedly, practically attacking the poor delivery guy. She's wearing the hotel robe, and clearly she doesn't have a bra on underneath it.

"Have you ever had nachos from room service?" she asks, scribbling her name on the receipt. "It's a necessity after a few drinks. You two should come in and have some." She sticks her head back into the room. "Sterling, put your pants on. We're having company."

I grit my teeth. A *few* drinks? More like a few bottles.

Both Owen and I are quick to decline her offer.

"Thanks for the invite, Aunt DeeDee, but I'd better get to bed. Mom has a very busy day planned for us tomorrow."

"Yeah, I think I saw something about waterfalls on the itinerary," Owen chimes in. "I'll see you tomorrow, Cora."

"Good night. Night, Aunt DeeDee."

"You rest up, sweetie," she says as she pulls me in for a hug. I gag at how much she reeks of alcohol.

As I walk back to my room, my mind is spinning with thoughts about my time with Owen. The thoughts are swirling about our walk on the beach, the news of his divorce, and then his comment about the ocean not being the only beautiful thing he saw tonight. As tired as I am, I don't know how I'm going to be able to fall asleep.

Chapter Eleven

*a*s soon as I get back to my room, I throw my pajamas on and wash my face. I walk out onto the balcony and look out at the sand where Owen and I just were. I lean on the railing to gather my thoughts.

I can't help but think about what Owen said before my aunt interrupted us. I don't want to read too much into it, but did we have a moment? And what made him think of the night the rose-guy showed up at my parents' house. We were sixteen years old. Even I haven't thought about it in years. Of course, the biggest surprise is he's divorced, and my mother never told me. I'm not sure I know who she is anymore. Between this and the Jackson blindside, she's not my favorite person at the moment.

I finally crawl into bed and shoot Fran a text asking about Kiwi and casually mentioning Owen being here. I'm expecting quite a few messages from her in the morning. I'm especially curious to find out if Owen was the handsome man from her dream.

As expected, the events of the evening and my unexpectedly long nap from earlier have interrupted my sleep schedule, and I lie awake for what feels like hours.

I take a trip down memory lane as I remember countless times I was around Owen growing up. Like Alaina said, we were always the first two awake and ready for breakfast. I also remember when he got his driver's license and drove Shawn and me to Taco Bell in his new car. Shawn made me sit in the back even though I called shotgun, but I didn't care. I was excited to be in Owen's car, even thought my stupid brother was there, too. It's crazy to think of how many of my childhood memories include Owen, and I always believed he thought of me like a sister.

My eyes finally start to feel heavy, and I pull the covers tightly around me before drifting off.

Aren't you supposed to sleep in when you're on vacation? Isn't it a rule or something? I look at my phone, it's only six o'clock in the morning. I don't think I fell asleep until after one, so of course I'm exhausted. I try to fall back to sleep but to no avail, which makes me frustrated, so I hobble out of bed and walk out onto the balcony. The sun is beginning to come up, and there's no sound other than the waves crashing and a few birds chirping. This view is absolutely breathtaking, and to think I almost didn't come on this trip. I would've missed out on waking up to this view, and on seeing Owen.

Suddenly the moments of last night flood back to me. The walk on the beach, the jacket, the trip down memory lane. Is it still possible for me to have feelings for him after all these years?

Gah ... you need to stop, Cora.

I look at my phone and notice a message from Fran to call her. It's three hours later in California, so she'll be wide awake.

"What are you doing up? You're on vacation."

"I know. Believe me, I wish I were still sleeping," I say as I sit in the chair and put my feet up on the balcony railing. "How's my little Kiwi?"

"She's fine, and so am I. Thanks for asking," she says sarcastically. "I saw your message. The one and only Owen showed up, huh? What's it like seeing him after all these years?"

I get a shiver when I think about how good he looked last night.

Fran has never met Owen, but I've talked about him on several occasions, so she knows everything there is to know about him.

"It's surreal. He looks exactly the same. And, I have some news." I stretch my arms over my head and breath in the ocean air. "Owen isn't married anymore, and my mother never told me."

There's silence on the other end of the phone.

"Fran, you still there?"

"Yes, I'm here. I was thinking about how ironic it is that your first love, the one you believed you lost forever, is divorced. Isn't it coincidental your very beautiful and intelligent best friend encouraged you to go on this trip? She even had a dream of a handsome man. It had to be Owen."

"Are you sure?"

"Well, it's kind of fuzzy now, but my gut is saying yes, and you know I have a good sense about this stuff."

I can't disagree because she does. I tell her about Owen mentioning the blind date—rose-guy from when we were sixteen.

"Cora, this is happening for a reason. He mentioned that night on purpose. There are reasons we remember certain experiences."

"What do you mean?"

She launches into some theory about Owen feeling jealous that night, and that's why he brought it up. I admit, I trust some of Fran's ideas because she's wise beyond her years, but I'm not sure about this one.

"So, you're still attracted to him?"

I close my eyes and picture his smile. "One hundred percent. I feel like a teenager again when I'm around him."

She laughs. "Mmmhmm ..."

"What are you trying to say?" I ask her.

"I told you I had a feeling something big was coming while you were there."

I blow out a puff of air. "Yeah, well a lot of stuff is happening here. That doesn't necessarily mean your *feeling* was because of Owen."

"Oh, my client's here. Let's talk later." She rushes off the phone before I can say good-bye.

I sit for a few minutes and listen to the waves crashing against the shore. Fran may be right about something happening for me, but like I told her, that doesn't mean it includes Owen. Regardless, I promised myself I'd have fun, and if that includes spending time with Owen again, fine with me.

Since there's no way I'm going back to bed now, I decide to get my day started, and there's no better way to do it than with breakfast. My parents planned a big day at Waimea Falls, and we have a luau tonight.

I'm sure today will be interesting, and waffles sound like a good way to kick it off.

~

When I arrive downstairs for breakfast, I immediately wish I had been able to sleep in. As soon as I walk into the restaurant, I see Jackson, Tara, Ashley, and Owen having breakfast together. There are so many things wrong with this picture I don't even know where to begin. Maybe I should've just ordered room service.

"Cora? What are you doing up so early? Sit here," Ashley says, pointing to the seat next to her.

Owen is typing something on his phone but looks up to give me a warm smile.

"Good morning," I say. "I didn't think anyone else would be up this early."

"Ash and I did the sunrise yoga practice," Tara says, taking a sip of her tea. "You should come out tomorrow. It was so enchanting. And then we ran into Jackson after he did his morning run."

Jackson holds up his coffee cup. "I needed the run to sweat out the alcohol and jet lag."

I nod knowingly. Jackson loves his morning runs. He used to ask me to join him. I went a few times, but getting up super early in the morning to run definitely isn't my thing.

"And I'm here because I wanted breakfast," Owen interjects. "These guys were already here when I came down."

I giggle. This makes me feel a little better. At least the foursome didn't plan to meet this morning. Being the fifth wheel is not ideal, especially in this crowd.

"That's why I'm here," I say. "Breakfast is the only reason to wake up this early on vacation."

"You got that right," he agrees.

Ashley eyes me curiously. "Well, the buffet is divine. You have to try the poached salmon."

Owen makes a face.

"Thanks for the tip, Ash. Maybe I'll give it a shot," I lie as I pour myself a cup of coffee and make my way toward the buffet.

I stand back and stare at all the glorious breakfast foods.

"It looks like heaven on earth to me," Owen whispers in my ear. His breath tickles my neck, which gives me the chills. I nod my head slowly while I try to recover from his close proximity.

Thankfully, he doesn't notice I've gone weak in the knees.

"Where should we start?" he asks, handing me a plate. "And don't say the poached salmon."

"You don't have to worry," I insist. "My cousin always has to be so fancy. She can have all the poached salmon. I'll take all the carbs."

He holds his hand up to give me a high five. "Good for you. It's refreshing to hear a woman admit to loving carbs."

I hold up my hand to his. "I figure there's no point in trying to fight it. Waffles, pancakes, french toast—I'm here for it all."

"I love it. Let's dive in," he exclaims.

I begin to peruse the unlimited amount of choices. I admit I'm feeling extra proud of myself for keeping calm after Owen was whispering in my ear. Breakfast plus Owen is the perfect combination ... well, almost perfect. *Simmer down, Cora.*

I fill my plate with many delicious goodies and return to the table where Ashley is the only one left.

She eyes my plate with a longing gaze. I guess the poached salmon and half a grapefruit didn't satisfy her this morning. I'm about to offer her a pastry, when she brings up Owen.

"Tell me everything you know about him," she whispers excitedly. "He's so gorgeous."

I stir my coffee. "What do you want to know? I'm not sure how much help I'll be, though, because I haven't been around him in years."

She gives me a coy smile. "Yeah, but you basically grew up with the guy, so tell me everything you can. I heard he's single."

I feel a twinge of jealousy at her interest in Owen. I noticed her eyeing him last night at dinner, but at the time I thought he was still happily married. Now I know he's single, this isn't a conversation I want to have with my cousin.

"Yeah, he's recently divorced," I say ripping off a piece of a danish and putting it into my mouth. I'm hoping this will make her take a few steps back, but I doubt it.

"Ah ... so he's probably in need of some TLC. I think I can handle it."

Oh, hell no.

I'm about to object when Owen returns to the table.

She casually sits back in her chair, but she's clearly ready to put her plan in motion. She doesn't waste a second before striking up a conversation with him.

I quietly eat my breakfast as I listen to her ask him a million different questions. She doesn't miss a beat. She even asks him what his ideal date would include.

Slowly but surely, all the Fletchers join us for breakfast. As soon as Peepaw arrives, I excuse myself to sit with him. I did say I would take advantage of every second I could with him. And I don't think I can take any more listening to the many amazing adventures of Ashley's life.

"Good morning, Cara," Evelyn says.

Why does she keep calling me Cara?

"*Cora*," I correct her, again.

She shakes her head and hits her forehead with the palm of her hand. "Yes, yes. Silly me."

"How did you sleep last night?" I ask them.

"Better than an owl at two a.m.," Peepaw says flatly.

I giggle. Another typical response from him. "I'm glad to hear it."

"Are you serious?" Ashley yells from the next table. She playfully punches Owen on the arm and then runs her hand over it, which causes another wave of jealousy to wash over me.

Owen is still eating his breakfast and laughing at something.

I swallow the lump that's forming in my throat.

"Are you distracted by something, or maybe someone?" Peepaw asks, raising his eyebrows.

I chew on my lip. I could try to lie, but he would see right through me.

"I don't know. Maybe a little?"

He looks at me over the top rim of his glasses.

"Don't try to swim after the boat leaves the dock. You won't catch it."

I give him a confused look. I'm about to ask him to explain when once again Ashley takes over.

"Good morning, Peepaw," she calls.

"Morning, my dear," he answers, giving me a wink.

I know Peepaw loves all his grandchildren, but I've always felt like I was secretly his favorite. I think he recognizes I've never felt like I fit in with our family.

I take one more sip of my coffee and stand up from the table. "I better get ready for the day."

I give my grandfather a kiss on the check and say good-bye to Evelyn. Ashley is still talking a mile a minute, and Owen seems to be listening intently to her. I quickly slip out before I have to watch any more of her over-the-top behavior. I may not be as direct as she is, but I have a long history with Owen. That's something she can't compete with.

Chapter Twelve

*T*his is probably one of the most beautiful places I've ever been.

I swim out into the Waimea Falls and let the cool, refreshing water fall over me. I close my eyes and concentrate on the sound of the rushing water. Fran would be so proud I'm immersing myself in nature.

When I open my eyes, I notice Jackson is swimming toward me. "This is unreal," he says.

"I was thinking the same thing," I say running my hands through my hair.

"Did you know these are healing waters?" he asks, holding on to his life jacket. "I did some research on the history of the Waimea Valley before we came."

I laugh. "Of course you did."

As usual, Jackson is a pro at doing his research. I think it's part of his adventurous spirit. It always seemed like the more he researched, the more he wanted to get out and try new things. He would look up every detail about every new restaurant we tried. He knew the menus before we even got there, and yes, sometimes it got on my nerves.

He throws his head back into the water. "Don't start."

I shrug and splash him. "Don't start what? Teasing you about your research? Let me guess, you can tell me about every flower and tree here?"

"Ha-ha," he says as he splashes me back. "As a matter of fact, I can tell you a few facts about the foliage. And the water goes down about thirty feet deep right here. How's that for research?"

Before I know it, we're playing around in the water, splashing each other and laughing. When we finally stop, I notice my sister watching us with a huge smile on her face.

I shake my head at her. Jackson and I agreed to be friends, and what am I supposed to do, ignore him when he talks to me? This is all her fault anyway.

Hunter swims over to us and starts talking to Jackson, and I take the opportunity to sneak away and head back to the shore where my cousins are still sitting.

"Why aren't you two getting in?" I ask. "The water feels magical."

"The water is *freezing*," Tara replies.

Hmmm … I don't believe the temperature of the water is her reason for not getting in. I know for a fact Tara loves doing adventurous things. I think she'd rather pose on the rocks in her tiny bikini. Not that I blame her though. All the ballroom dancing has paid off, she looks incredible. What's kind of funny is she looks like she's getting ready to do a professional photo shoot, only without the photographer.

"It's not bad once you get in." I pull myself out of the water and squeeze out my hair.

"Ash and I were just talking about going out tonight after the luau. Are you in?"

I make a face. "I don't know."

"Seriously, Cora? You're on vacation. Why don't you let yourself have a little bit of fun?"

"I am having fun," I say, raising my voice.

"What are we talking about?" Owen interrupts.

I haven't had a chance to talk to him since we were at the buffet this morning. And I purposely looked away when he took off his shirt to go swimming in the falls. Let's just say Owen hasn't missed many workouts in the years I haven't seen him. I've tried extra hard to keep from staring at his very toned physique.

"We're talking about going out tonight after the luau," Ashley tells him. "The resort next to us has a great rooftop bar called The Volcano, and we can walk over from our hotel. What do you think, want to join us?" She shakes her hair out, and her beach waves fall down her back. The two of them look like they just walked off a Victoria's Secret fashion show runway.

Owen turns to me. "Sounds fun. Let's go."

He's looking right at me, so that must mean he's asking me to go. This certainly makes a difference, getting an invitation from him rather than my cousins.

"I'm not sure she's going to make it. It might be past Cora's bedtime," Tara teases.

I make a face, although it's kind of true. But since it's at the resort next door and I can leave at any time, I agree to go with them. Before I know it, the plan to go to The Volcano is in motion, and Ashley is still talking.

Owen and I exchange a few glances, and every time he looks at me, my pulse picks up. I'm starting to get a little self-conscious that other people are picking up on my attraction to him.

I notice my mother and Alaina sitting on the other side of the rocks with their feet in the water, so I excuse myself and wade over to them.

"There she is," Alaina says. "Are you having fun, honey?"

I look around and hold my arms up in the air. "Yes, I think it would be impossible not to have fun here in the Waimea Valley."

"Does that mean you're no longer upset with me?" Mom asks, getting a serious look on her face.

Alaina looks at me and raises her eyebrows.

"Mom, can you understand why I'm so frustrated?"

She sighs loudly. "Honey, I invited Jackson because we consider him a part of our family. He's Hunter's oldest friend, and I'm genuinely afraid you're going to miss out on something really great. Sometimes we don't realize what's truly good for us in the moment," she says, patting me on the shoulder. "Often it takes losing something wonderful before we know what a good thing it was, and by then it might be too late."

I press my lips together because I know a lecture is coming, and sure enough she continues talking.

"I've never told you this, but I broke up with your father after we started dating. It took a friend giving me unsolicited advice to bring us back together, and if I hadn't listened to my friend, we wouldn't be here right now. Thankfully, your father welcomed me back, but not everyone gets that lucky."

Is she serious? This is why she invited my ex-boyfriend on our family vacation?

"I was younger than you are, of course, but much like you, I had a few silly doubts, and I panicked," she continues.

I look at Alaina, who doesn't appear to be surprised by this story.

So, what she's trying to say is because my parents broke up and still ended up being married for forty years, she believes Jackson and I belong together. Never mind the fact that she thinks my doubts are *silly*.

"Mom, I appreciate you sharing your story and wanting me to be happy," I tell her as I run my hands through the water. "I know you consider Jackson part of the family, but that doesn't mean he and I are right for each other."

"You don't know that," she interjects.

I look to Alaina for help.

"Leann, I think Cora trusts herself enough to make the right decision."

My dad comes along and drags my mother into the water. I watch as they splash and play before he puts his arm around her, kissing her forehead, and as frustrating as this situation is, I have a better understanding of why she's so adamant I give Jackson a second chance.

When we return to the hotel from the falls, I feel like a new person.

Maybe what Jackson said about them being healing waters is true. I feel refreshed and energized for the first time since we arrived in Hawaii.

I'm relaxing on one of the soft couches in the lobby when Brynn sits down next to me. We've managed to avoid each other for most of the vacation so far, and it's been great, until now.

"Hey, Brynn."

She has a gleam in her eye, and I can tell she wants to say something.

"Is there something you need?" I ask, using all my willpower not to sound annoyed.

"What's the deal with you and Owen?"

I sit up straight and turn toward her. Of all people to pick up on my attraction to him, why did it have to be her?

"What are you talking about?" I ask, trying to act surprised by her outrageous question.

She leans into me. "I heard you talking on the balcony this morning."

I fold my arms tightly against my chest and frown. "You were listening to my phone conversation?"

She shakes her head. "No. I mean, I didn't hear the whole thing. I walked outside to watch the sunrise, and you were being really loud. Honestly, I wasn't trying to listen."

Sure you weren't.

I narrow my eyes at her. "I'm not sure what you think you heard, but there's nothing with me and Owen, other than the fact we've known each other since birth."

She gives me a skeptical look. "Right. Don't worry. I'm not going to say anything to anyone."

Which means she's going to tell my brother, and he's going to make a big deal out it.

I shrug nonchalantly. "There's *nothing* to say."

She gets up from the couch but pauses and looks at me.

"Whatever you say, but maybe you should go for it. Ashley certainly seems to be willing." She pauses. "Such a shame when people can't work things out. Alyssa is a sweetheart, beautiful too, and their wedding was exquisite."

She flips her hair and walks away, leaving me confused. Was Brynn trying to give me advice? Or was she trying to get under my skin by talking about Owen's ex-wife? I'm hesitant to trust anything that comes out of her mouth because I know how manipulative she can be, but maybe being married to my brother is finally starting to change her.

At least now I know I can't have any more sunrise conversations on the balcony.

Unfortunately, I know Brynn's right about Ashley. The way she's been hanging around and the comments she made to me about Owen being single, she's already making her move. This being the case, I need to make a decision about whether I'm going to let it happen or step in and do something about it.

This could be the chance I've been waiting for since we picked flowers (weeds) together for our mothers—I think we were eight at the time. Anyway, that's when I was old enough to realize I liked him. This is probably much too long to carry a torch for someone.

All of a sudden I feel anxious. My post-waterfall relaxation has begun to fade at the thought of me and Owen as more than just family friends. As romantic as it would be for something to happen between us, I'm reminded there are other people here on this vacation, and privacy would definitely be out the window as I've already learned, based on Brynn's sneaky balcony behavior.

Hah. And here I am getting way ahead of myself, assuming there's even a chance something could happen between Owen and me. A walk on the beach and a few flirty comments doesn't mean there's any kind of a future or even a present with him. For all I know he could be looking for someone to hang out with on this trip and any kind of romance could be the farthest thing from his mind.

Anyway, I refuse to let Brynn bother me. I jump off the couch and head to my room to shower. I'm definitely not going to be late for dinner tonight.

Chapter Thirteen

*T*here's something about hotel robes and slippers that make me feel so fancy.

I take a long hot shower after our hike and day at the falls. I'm about to sit down and do some reading when there's a knock at my door. It could be any of my family members, but secretly I'm hoping it's Owen. A girl can dream, right? Unfortunately, when I open the door, I find Jackson on the other side.

"Hi." I try to hide my robe-clad body behind the door.

"Hey, did I wake you?"

"No, I was just going to read for a while." *In other words, I'm not in the mood for visitors.*

A smile spreads across his face. There were countless times during our relationship when I wanted to sit and read while he wanted to go running or hiking or hang gliding. This is what I mean by him getting bored with me eventually.

"Oh, well, can we talk for a few minutes?"

I don't know how to answer this question. Judging by the serious tone in his voice, I have a feeling this could be an awkward conversation. I've reached my limit of these types of conversations for one day, but maybe it's better to get it over with so we can move on.

I glance down at my robe and sigh. Obviously I'm comfortable enough around Jackson to only be wearing a robe.

"Uh, sure. Come in." I open the door wide enough for him to step in and close the door behind him.

"Do you want to sit out on the balcony?" he asks.

I think about Brynn listening to my conversations and shake my head. "It's kind of warm outside right now, not to mention the balcony walls have ears. Let's just talk in here."

He gives me a curious look but doesn't ask what I mean.

I sit down on the edge of the couch and pull the belt of my robe tighter.

He sits in the chair across from me and rests his forearms on his legs.

For some reason he looks nervous, which makes me feel nervous. It's crazy that you can spend so much time with a person and then feel like you have nothing to say.

"I wanted to talk to you about Tara."

Ah, I think I know where this is going. Now I know why he looks uncomfortable. "Okay."

"I'm sure you know we've been hanging out since we got here and before anything …" he pauses and takes a deep breath. "I want to make sure you're okay with us hanging out," he says quickly.

I push my hair behind my ears while I try to think about how to respond to the idea of him and my cousin hooking up.

"I know we're not together anymore," he continues, "but, I'm here with your family, and I want to be respectful of your feelings."

For a split second I feel a twinge of jealousy, which I have no right to feel. I'm sure it's normal to experience this feeling even though I'm the one who made the decision for us not to be together. The truth is Tara would be a much better match for him, despite what my sister thinks. Tara's life is exciting. Jackson wouldn't ever have to worry about her staying home and reading. Her career allows her unique opportunities, and I know Jackson would love to tag along with her every chance he could.

I fold my arms. "Jackson, you're free to spend time with anyone you want. You don't need my permission."

He clasps his hands together but doesn't say anything for a few seconds. "I had fun at Waimea today. It was nice hanging out with you, like it used to be—especially when you were teasing me about doing research."

I smile. "You know I had to do it. And I was only joking. That's one of the things that makes you who you are."

We both grow quiet again. I knew coming here and being with my family would be interesting, but Jackson being here in my hotel room is still surreal.

"I miss this," he says not looking up from his hands. "I told you I'm okay with being friends, and I am. But honestly, there's still a part of me that wishes things could be different."

Here we go. I knew this was coming as soon as I saw him at the airport. It was hard enough to end our relationship, and now I feel like I'm reliving that day all over again. "Jackson—"

"I know," he interrupts. "And I promised you things wouldn't be weird between us, especially while we're here. I'm not trying to make things hard. I felt like I needed to be honest with you."

"That's not what I was going to say," I tell him. "I understand why you're feeling this way. You being here with my family feels natural."

He nods in agreement. "So natural."

"When we broke up, I told you I didn't want to hold you back. You deserve to be with someone who's all in, someone who's open to going on exciting adventures with you."

He opens his mouth to protest. "I told you that didn't matter to me. I need someone who balances me, not someone who's the same as me."

This takes me back to the conversation we had when our relationship ended.

"I know you did," I reply. "I—"

I'm interrupted by a knock at the door.

"Hold on," I say, getting up from the couch. I hope it's Maya, because I'm going to drag her into the middle of this conversation, by her hair.

When I open the door, I stand frozen in my slippers.

Owen is standing there with a covered tray. He looks down at my robe and smiles, causing a jolt to shoot through my body. Oh hell, I don't know what's happening right now.

"Hi, am I catching you at a bad time?"

I glance over my shoulder. *This can't be happening.* Jackson, the robe …*Damn.*

"No, I was—"

"Hey, man," Jackson says joining me at the door.

Crap. Why did I answer the door—the first time?

Owen looks at Jackson and presses his lips together. I can only imagine what he's thinking, and me being in my robe doesn't help the way this looks.

"I'm sorry," he says.

"It's totally fine. We're just talking," I tell him. Hopefully, neither man detects any desperation in my voice.

He hands me a tray. "My mom asked me to bring this to you."

I lift the cover to see a plate of fresh pineapple and berries with a side of honey and a book. I smile. "She's the sweetest. This is the book she was telling me about."

He nods. "Yep, she ordered a plate of fruit for herself and said she was ready to curl up with a book for the afternoon. She mentioned something about a conversation you had with your mother earlier."

I wish I were curled up with a book right now. Instead I'm standing here in my robe with my ex-boyfriend and my childhood crush. *How did I end up here?* "She's the best."

"Anyway, I'll let you get back to your ... conversation. See you guys tonight."

He takes off down the hall before I can say anything, and there's a part of me that wants to drop the tray and run after him. Instead, I rest it on one hand and close the door behind me.

I can't help but wonder why Alaina didn't bring me the tray and the book herself. Is there a reason Owen was playing delivery boy? Not that I'm complaining, not at all. I just wish he hadn't shown up now. *Ugh,* I've got to get Jackson out of my room before anyone else gets the wrong impression.

"You okay?" Jackson asks, eyeing me curiously.

I nod absently. "Yeah, I'm just tired."

I'm not tired—more confused than anything.

"Oh, okay. I'll let you get to your reading," he says, walking past me to leave.

He opens the door and pauses. "It wasn't my intention to make things awkward again, especially because it seems like we're in a good place. I just didn't want to do anything without being completely honest with you. Will you at least think about what I said?"

I'm barely listening to him. *What does he want me to think about?* "Okay."

"See you later," he says.

I close the door behind him and put the tray down on the table. I sit on the edge of the bed and replay the last ten minutes. I don't know what to think about Jackson and Tara. On one hand, it's weird thinking about them being together. And what if their relationship did progress? Would family events be even more awkward than they already are? I did tell Jackson he should find someone who would enjoy life the way he wants to, and I meant it, but at the time I never considered it would be with a member of my family.

I take a strawberry off the plate Owen brought me and pick up the book. This is the novel Alaina said she couldn't put down. This is exactly what I need right now. Sometimes it's just easier to get sucked into the pages of a book in order to escape from real life.

After enjoying a few chapters, I take my time getting ready for the luau.

I add some loose beach waves to my hair and finally decide to wear my new strapless floral-print jumpsuit.

Confession—the only reason I got this outfit is because it makes my chest look bigger. That should put a stop my mom's comments about me not being able to fill out that stupid coconut bra for the dreaded family picture. Maybe I'll just wear it over this jumpsuit? We're all going to look ridiculous anyway, so why not?

I check my reflection in the mirror, and I'm actually quite pleased. The more I think about it, the more I don't want to spend my entire vacation confused about men. I'm in one of the most desired travel destinations in the world, and I can't let anyone else keep me from enjoying it.

When I arrive in the lobby, I see Peepaw and Evelyn sitting together on one of the couches. I stand back for a few minutes and watch their interaction. Peepaw has his arm around her, and she's whispering in his ear. He has the biggest smile on his face, and she looks like she's glowing. It's very sweet to watch them together.

"What are you looking at?" a voice whispers, sending a familiar chill through my body.

Why does he keep doing this to me?

I turn around to see Owen looking superhero-level hot in a V-neck white T-shirt and Hawaiian shorts. I suck in a breath and quickly gather my thoughts. "I was watching my grandfather and his girlfriend together."

He looks over my shoulder in their direction. "Your grandfather is the man," he says. "I hope I can be like him when I grow up."

I smile. "He's definitely one of the best."

Owen runs his hand through his hair the same way he did when he was standing at my hotel room door earlier, and the same way he used to when we were teenagers.

I quickly look away so I don't do something dumb like drool or reach up and touch his hair myself. I used to imagine running my fingers through it and ... *Stop it, Cora!*

"Speaking of great, you look beautiful tonight," he says, flashing me a warm smile.

I feel heat fill my cheeks. "Thank you. I think there was something about that waterfall. I've felt so refreshed since we left there today."

He leans up against the chair. "I know what you mean. I crashed after I came back from your room. It was the best nap I've ever had."

Now is my chance to explain why Jackson was there and I was in my robe.

"About that ... I wanted to explain because I know how it looked when you stopped by, and with Jackson being there—"

He shrugs. "Hey, you don't need to give me an explanation. It's none of my business."

I put my hand on his chest and then quickly pull it away. "I want to, because I don't want anyone to get the wrong idea in case it gets out. The reason he came to my room was to talk to me about him and Tara."

He raises his eyebrows. "Really? Your ex-boyfriend and your cousin, huh?"

I grit my teeth. "Yeah."

"How do you feel about that?"

I'm trying to decide how to answer his question when Peepaw calls us over. He has perfect timing. I need to thank him later.

I give my grandfather a kiss on the cheek and sit down on the couch across from him and Evelyn.

Owen sits down beside me. I immediately breathe in the divine scent of his cologne, which makes me feel like I'm walking through the men's fragrance department of Nordstrom. He's sitting close enough to me that the sides of our legs are touching.

I'm so busy thinking about his close proximity I don't realize Evelyn is saying something.

"I'm sorry, what did you say?" I ask, when I stop feeling dizzy by the fact that Owen's hand is on his leg, which is touching mine. Not that I'm complaining, not one single bit.

Evelyn and Owen start talking at the same time about the perfect weather we've had since we arrived.

I glance at my grandfather, who looks amused. Sometimes I wonder if he can read other peoples' minds, especially mine. I remember my grandmother telling me Peepaw was very observant and he enjoyed sitting back and watching how people interacted with others.

"You look very pretty tonight, young lady. Don't you agree?" he asks pointing to Owen.

Okay, this is only slightly humiliating.

"She does. In fact, I just told her the same thing," Owen says, nudging me with his elbow.

"Thank you," I reply. "So, what did you two do this afternoon? Are you enjoying your vacation so far?"

Peepaw looks at Evelyn and gives her a wink.

Owen and I give each other a side-glance, and he covers his mouth with his hand to hide his smile. As much as I love how much of a tease my grandfather is, I'd rather not listen to him joke about the intimate details of his relationship.

Evelyn playfully pats him on the arm. "Oh, Louie."

Louie? I still can't get used to that. Even my grandmother didn't call him by that nickname, or at least I don't think so.

"We rented one of those pool cabanas and played cards," she continues. "He let me beat him at gin rummy three times. It was lovely to have some alone time together."

She smiles and points back and forth between Owen and me. "How about you? I hope you two have had some alone time. There are certainly a lot of us here."

Oh, crap. She thinks Owen and I are together. I bite my lip as I try to think of an answer.

"We went with the whole group to the Waimea Valley and waterfall today," Owen chimes in. "It's a beautiful place."

She nods knowingly. "Oh yes, well, you just make sure you spend some quality time with each other, too. It's such a romantic place."

Why did I sit here again? I remind myself she's an old woman and she just made an assumption since Owen and I are sitting together. I mean, she can't even seem to remember my name no matter how many times I correct her.

"I think that's a great idea," Owen says.

I glance at him, and he stares back at me. Only this time it feels different, like he's trying to tell me something. Regardless, it's not the time nor the place to have this conversation.

"Hey, everyone," Ashley says loudly. As usual she has to make a grand entrance.

I drag my gaze away from Owen toward her and see she's wearing a skintight, low-cut white dress that hugs her perfectly. I watch as she conveniently leans over in front of us to give both Evelyn and Peepaw kisses on their cheeks.

I stand up, and Owen follows my lead.

"Hi, cousin, you look so pretty," she kisses me on both cheeks and then turns toward Owen.

"Hey, you." She slowly leans into him and kisses him gently on his cheek, causing my blood to boil. "Are you ready for a *fun* night?"

I'm not sure if she's referring to the luau or something else.

I awkwardly push my hair behind my ear and look away. Thankfully, the remainder of our group arrives within the next few minutes.

I remind myself that I don't want to think about anything complicated right now, so I put what Owen said to Evelyn out of my mind. I'm here to have fun, and that's what I'm going to do.

Chapter Fourteen

'*ve always wanted to attend an authentic luau, and it's
everything I expect, just like I've seen in movies. They
actually roast the pig in the ground for several hours. The pit is called
an *imu* according to Jackson, who, as expected, did his research on
traditional luaus.

The dinner begins, and of course the Fletchers don't disappoint and
provide plenty of entertainment before the stage show even starts. At
least this time I have a better seat, between Alaina and my sister. Well,
maybe not my sister. Every time I think I'm going to forgive her for
bringing Jackson, something else happens. Like him showing up in my
hotel room and Owen assuming the worst.

It's like a comedy of errors as the evening goes on. As soon as we're all
seated, Tara asks the server if there's a detailed list of the caloric intake
on the menu. He politely tells her no and doesn't seem to be offended
by her rant about being more health conscious. She also loudly makes
gagging sounds at the mention of the pig being roasted. Perhaps she'll
take after her mother and order her dinner from the bar? Although a

dinner consisting only of alcoholic beverages isn't a healthy option either.

As if our poor server doesn't have enough to deal with from my cousin, my uncle nicknames him Big Kahuna and laughs every time he says it. There are a few moments when I think Big Kahuna, er, our server, may take him down with one throat punch or poison his food with some weird island herbs.

All this being said, so far nothing compares to Ashley flashing the crowd when she goes to sit down on the ground. Her wardrobe choice wasn't practical for this type of event.

Anyway, despite the cringe-worthy moments, the drinks are flowing, and everyone seems to be enjoying themselves.

"Thanks for the book," I say to Alaina after things calm down. "I started it this afternoon. It was exactly what I needed."

I kind of want to tell her about Jackson coming to my room, but now isn't the time. Especially with all the extra ears around the table who like to listen to my conversations.

She gives me a warm smile. "Oh, good. I was going to call your room to make sure you were there, but then Owen offered to take it to you." She looks across the table to where he's engaged in a conversation with my brother. "I'm so glad he came on this trip. It's been a difficult time for him."

I nod. "I was sorry to hear about him and Alyssa."

She hangs her head. "It was such a shock to us. But he claims it was the right decision, so we have to love and support him." She pauses as she continues to watch him. "I just hope he didn't make a mistake."

Hmm ... this sounds familiar. I guess all mothers have these concerns for their children.

I take a sip of my water as I listen to her. I'm definitely interested in hearing about Owen. "So, you had no idea there were issues going on between him and Alyssa?" I ask softly.

"I try not to pry into his personal life too much," she whispers. "Since then, he's thrown himself into his work, which I know is paying off because the firm is having a lot of success. At the same time, we keep telling him to slow down and deal with his divorce, even though he swears he's fine about it. I even offered to go down and stay with him in San Diego for a while. Of course, he didn't like the idea."

I listen intently as she talks. This gives me a lot to think about and reminds me that no matter the amount of flirting between Owen and me, he's still recovering from his marriage ending. I'm sure this will have lasting effects on him, despite his being okay with it.

Our conversation is interrupted by the lights dimming. Suddenly the sound of soft drumbeats fills the air, followed by the sound of a horn.

"They call that blowing the *pu*," I hear Jackson say. "It signals the start of the traditional ceremony."

Listening to Jackson explain details of a traditional luau reminds me of being with him. As I said, sometimes his research got on my nerves.

"This is so exciting," Maya squeals.

Suddenly the performers take the stage, and I become completely engrossed in the show. They perform traditional dances from different islands—Hawaii, Tahiti, Samoa, and Tonga. It is so fascinating. I always thought it was just hula dancing.

I overhear Tara telling everyone that she learned a few dances from a dear friend who grew up in the islands. She describes everyone in her industry as a dear friend, but there has to be drama in the professional dance world, right?

After some very exhilarating authentic dances, a few of the performers come to our table and ask us to join them on the stage. Tara, Ashley, and Brynn are the first to volunteer, and they drag Jackson, my brother, and Owen with them.

"Will you look at them?" Maya asks in disgust. "They always have to be front and center. I'm not going to let them steal this show, too. Let's do this, Hunter." She grabs her husband's hand and practically drags him toward the stage.

I stay safely at the table with the *grown-ups*. I guess I'm technically a grown-up too, but I'm the only one sitting down who's under the age of thirty, so there's that.

As I watch the performers teach the volunteers some traditional dance steps, I can't help but notice the way my cousins dance around Jackson and Owen, and admittedly it bothers me a little. Fortunately, I'm quickly distracted when Alaina makes a comment which sends my aunt into a tailspin.

"Wow, that girl is certainly comfortable in her own skin," Alaina exclaims. "I can't believe the way she's throwing herself at my son in front of all these people."

As soon as I hear those words come out of her mouth, I look to see my aunt's reaction. DeeDee is very protective of her daughters.

"Throwing herself at him?" Aunt DeeDee snaps. "How dare you?"

Aunt DeeDee somehow manages to channel her inner Scarlett O'Hara when she gets upset. She puts on her best offended Southern belle accent. I expect her to clutch her chest and yell *I declare* at any moment.

"They're just dancing, and it doesn't look like your perfect, precious son has a problem with it."

Alaina raises her eyebrows. "Calm down, DeeDee. I didn't mean to offend you," she says softly.

My aunt rolls her eyes. "Now come on, Alaina. Why don't we just put the cards on the table. We don't like each other."

Oh, crap.

I look around the table to gauge everyone's expressions. My parents, Evelyn, and Ken look shocked at DeeDee's admission, my grandfather looks amused, and Uncle Sterling takes another sip of his cocktail. There's a part of me that wants to get up and leave, but mostly I want to stay and watch the fireworks. This is more enjoyable than shaking my hips on stage anyway.

"That's ridiculous," Alaina says. "At least on my part. Why don't you throw back another drink?"

"Lainey," Ken says under his breath.

"It most certainly is not ridiculous," my aunt yells as she jumps out of her chair. Her face has turned bright red, and for a second I think she may jump across the table and attack Alaina.

The people at the next table are now watching and pointing.

"Anyway, why are you even here? This is a *family* event. Warner and Leann are good people to invite you, but you should've declined instead of infringing on our family time. You don't belong here."

"DeeDee," my uncle interrupts. *Too little too late.*

"No, Sterling," she says holding up her hand. "I won't tolerate that stuck up bitch insulting my daughter. She's a phony and an opportunist. She's been waiting for years to push me to my limits, and well, it's finally happened. I'm madder than a wet hen right now."

And there it is.

Alaina's mouth drops open before she rises to her feet. All of a sudden they are screaming at each other across the table. What the hell is happening?

My aunt pauses long enough to drain her glass. "Leann, Warner, I'm sorry to disappoint you, but I'm going back to the hotel for the night. I think I'm getting a migraine. Let's go, Sterling, now."

My uncle does as he's told and waves to everyone as he follows my aunt toward the entrance.

I glance at Alaina, whose face has turned bright red. She's obviously upset.

"I'm terribly sorry," she apologizes. "I shouldn't have engaged and made such a scene."

She sits down and then bursts into tears.

"Ah, don't concern yourself," Peepaw says with a laugh. "That daughter-in-law can be a real pistol. My son has always had his hands full with her. Anyway, you provided some good entertainment for the evening. Hell, this was better than the fire dancers."

Evelyn pats his hand to get him to be quiet.

Hah! Good luck with that.

Alaina rises to her feet and rushes over to my mother and hugs her. They begin whispering to each other, but unfortunately I can't hear a word they're saying.

A few seconds later, Owen returns to the table, interrupting the lingering tension still following the spontaneous outbursts. The others are still on the stage, including Jackson who looks like he's really enjoying himself as Tara and Ashley dance on either side of him. They are no longer doing traditional Polynesian dancing, and it's getting sexier by the second. Somehow we've gone from Pacific Island dancing to a club scene. I notice a few people pointing and whispering.

"Someone remind me never to get on a stage again," Owen says, dragging my attention away from the show my cousins were putting on. "I don't think anyone wants to see me move my hips like that."

Hmm ... that's not true.

He scans the table and then looks at his mother. "Mom, are you okay? What happened?"

"Just a misunderstanding," my mom says, patting Alaina on the arm.

Owen gives me a confused look.

Alaina walks toward him. She kisses him on the cheek. "Honey, we're heading back for the evening, but you stay and enjoy yourself."

My parents, Owen's parents, and Peepaw and Evelyn all get up from the table, leaving Owen and me by ourselves.

He takes a sip of water. "Okay, you have to tell me what just happened. Did I say something to scare everyone off?"

I give him the sordid details about the argument between his mother and my aunt.

"Are you kidding? I can't believe I missed that. Your aunt must've really pushed my mother's buttons because she's usually very calm, even in confrontations."

I shrug. "I think she snapped after being called a phony and an opportunist. It was pretty ugly, and technically it's your fault."

He laughs. "I guess so. My mom can be really overprotective sometimes."

This reminds me of what she said about him not dealing with everything going on and overworking himself. "Yeah, she mentioned she's been worried about you."

He shakes his head. "Let me guess. She was referring to my divorce."

Before I can answer his question, Brynn and Shawn return to the table. "That was so much fun," Brynn says excitedly. "Cora, why didn't you come up there?"

I grit my teeth.

"Oh, never mind. I know why you didn't come on stage," she says giving me a smug look.

I swear, every time I think Brynn has become a better person, she proves me wrong by showing her true colors.

"I have no idea what you're referring to," I say flatly.

She laughs. "Sure you do. Wasn't it our sophomore year when we were doing the event with the Kappa Lambda Nus?"

I scowl.

"What happened?" Shawn asks eagerly.

I give him a dirty look. Seriously though, you would think my brother wouldn't want to dredge up cringe-worthy moments from my past, but no such luck.

Of course Brynn jumps at the chance to share one of my many embarrassing moments, despite the fact that it has nothing to do with me not going on the stage tonight.

She happily tells the story of me announcing and welcoming our new pledges with the back of my skirt tucked into my underwear.

"Poor Cora," she says sympathetically. "We tried to get her attention and warn her not to turn around."

I frown. "Yeah, you tried so hard to tell me. Thankfully, Fran practically rushed the stage to help me." I pause and look at my brother. "You remember Fran, right, Shawn?"

I see Brynn's jaw tighten, and all of a sudden Shawn doesn't seem as eager to hear the rest of the story. Good, serves him right.

"So, where did everyone go?" he asks, finally noticing our table is empty.

Owen tells him the *grown-ups* all returned to the hotel. He also leaves out the details of his mother and the fight.

The luau show is officially coming to a close, and everyone else returns to the table. It's obvious this party is over, and I'm ready to head back to the hotel myself. I think I've had enough excitement for one night.

"So, who's ready to go to The Volcano?" Brynn asks. "Cora, should we tuck you into bed before we head out? We could read you a bedtime story and bring you a glass of warm milk."

Wow, Brynn is certainly in rare form tonight. I'm sure my mentioning

Fran to Shawn didn't help the situation. Hah! At least I know how to get under her skin.

"No, she's coming with us," Maya insists. "Come on, sis. Have some fun for once."

I sigh. As much as I'm ready to crawl into bed with my book, I don't want to give Brynn any more satisfaction tonight. "I'm in. Let's go."

Chapter Fifteen

_____

he view from The Volcano is unreal. It's a big open-air rooftop area encompassing the entire twenty-seventh floor of the neighboring hotel. It's filled with gorgeous tropical flowers, palm trees, a small "volcano," and a waterfall leading into a pond. There are several couches and chairs alongside the glass walls overlooking the ocean. The lighting is dim and cozy, making it feel warm and inviting. There's a band playing in the corner, which adds the perfect touch to the ambiance.

I'm sitting on a loveseat watching the waves when my sister sits down next to me. She has a bright blue drink in her hand, and she holds it out to me.

"You have to try this—it's called a Blue Lagoon. I don't know what's in it, but it's so dreamy."

I shake my head because I've had enough drinks for the night. I'm still nursing the same glass of wine I ordered when we arrived.

"Why didn't you didn't tell me Jackson went to your room today?"

I shrug my shoulders. "When was I supposed to tell you, at dinner when all hell was breaking loose?"

She shrugs. "Well?"

I hold my hands up. "Well, what?"

She points at Jackson who's sitting at the bar with Tara. "He told Hunter that he asked you about Tara. What exactly did he ask you? Please tell me you discouraged him from letting anything happen."

I nod. "He did ask me about her, and I told him he didn't need my permission to hang out with another woman."

She groans. "I figured you said that. Seriously though, it has to bother you a little, seeing him with someone else, especially a family member, and Tara—of all people. It doesn't get any worse. Yuck."

I look over at Jackson and Tara with their heads together. Okay, so maybe it bugs a little. I'm sure if it didn't there'd be something wrong with me.

My attention is drawn away from Jackson to the bar where Owen is talking to Shawn, Brynn, and Ashley.

"Cora."

"What?"

She gives me a strange look. "Are you okay?"

I snort. "Good question."

Hunter joins us, which gets me off the hook from spilling my guts about Owen showing up when Jackson was in my room. Thankfully, Hunter drags my sister to the dance floor.

The crazy thing is, I've never been someone who let relationship drama affect me. Unfortunately, no matter how hard I try, I feel like all of this is distracting me from enjoying my vacation.

I take a deep breath and another sip of my wine. I'm done for the night. It's time for me to head back to my room. Thankfully, tomorrow is a free day because I'm in desperate need of time to clear my head.

I sneak out of The Volcano without letting anyone see me and slowly make my way back to my hotel room. On the way, I walk out onto the sand and find a place to sit for a few minutes. What was it Fran told me to do? Something about immersing myself into the island or cultures? I feel like I did at the falls. Maybe now I should do something here on the beach—meditate, yoga, burst into a song from *Moana*. That would surely clear my auras, right? Maybe I should take her advice. I could go to the spa or maybe try the sunrise yoga on the beach my cousins were raving about. I cringe at the thought, but I promised myself I'd make the most of this trip no matter what, and that means doing hard things.

I open my eyes when I hear my alarm going off. An alarm on vacation, damn, this is just wrong. Yesterday morning I got up early because I couldn't sleep, but today I was enjoying my rest until the alarm sang its hideous song. It's one thing to wake up early for breakfast, but for exercise, wow, I must really be stressed out.

I drag myself out of bed and peek out the curtains. It's still dark outside. This sunrise yoga better be worth it.

I check my phone to find a text from Fran. She's sent me a picture of Kiwi, which makes me smile. This is exactly what I need to start my day.

I send her a quick reply to thank her and mention I'm heading to sunrise yoga. She'll be so proud of me for participating in the island activities.

I make my way down to the lawn where the yoga instructor is setting up for the practice. I pick a mat in the back row and sit with my legs crossed. I've done maybe two or three yoga classes in my life but never one overlooking the ocean. I admit this is kind of cool. Maybe this won't be so bad after all. And I can take a nap poolside if I need to later.

"Good morning."

I'd know that voice anywhere. I turn to see Owen standing next to me. He looks like he's half-asleep.

"Hi."

He sits down on the mat next to mine and rubs his eyes.

I suddenly wish I'd paid more attention to how I looked when I left my room this morning. I try to casually fix my ponytail, and I check to make sure my clothes aren't inside out or that my underwear isn't on over my pants. I know it sounds crazy, but I've been known to do some wild things when I'm half-asleep.

"I think it might be a crime to wake up this early on vacation," I say. "And two days in a row is just tragic."

He snorts. "I think you're right. What made you get up?"

I look out at the water. I definitely don't want to tell him I'm stressed out because of men. "I thought it might be good for me to take some time to myself and de-stress. My roommate told me I needed to relax or reflect, so I figured I'd give it a shot. What about you?" I ask.

He yawns widely. "I like yoga, and I've never done a sunrise class, so when Tara and Ashley were talking about it yesterday, I figured I'd give it a shot." He pauses. "Alyssa did yoga all the time, and she's the one who got me into it."

I nod at the mention of his former wife. I wonder if Alaina was right and he's going through the motions following his marriage breaking up.

"Have you talked to your mom at all?" I ask, changing the subject. "I was wondering how she was doing after what happened last night."

He shakes his head. "They were already asleep when I got in. But I'm sure she's fine. My mom gets over things pretty quickly."

Two more people join the class and choose mats in the front row.

"I'm glad to hear that. My aunt can be really harsh. I hope it doesn't keep your mom from enjoying this vacation. DeeDee was out of line because your parents are family—all of you are."

He smiles. "I appreciate it. Most of my childhood memories include the Fletchers."

I make a face. "Oh, I don't know if that's a good thing or a bad thing."

He laughs. "It's a good thing."

"Well, you know I have to ask," I say. I point and flex my toes to warm up my legs. I think this is part of yoga practice—it seems like it would be.

"I was thinking about the time you and your mom brought dinner and cupcakes over for us. I think my mom had had surgery or something, I can't remember exactly, but it was some kind of medical procedure."

I start to blush because I remember that night very clearly. It was the one time I felt like Owen and I had a *moment*. It was right before he left for college, and he was watching a horror movie in their loft when we arrived. My mom made me go upstairs to take him a cupcake, and of course I didn't object.

I remember very vividly sitting down on the couch next to him. Before I knew it, I became enthralled in the movie. When a terrifying scene came on the screen, Owen and I grabbed onto each other. We were both so scared we held on to the other for the duration of the movie. After it ended, neither of us said anything about it, and I filed it safely away in my memories.

"I think that was one of the last horror movies I ever watched," he says, interrupting my thoughts. "I had nightmares for days."

"Me, too."

"I don't even remember the name of it. Do you?" he asks.

"Aloha kakahiaka," the instructor says, interrupting our conversation.

Both Owen and I sit up straight and listen as she welcomes us and gives instructions. She begins the class with lots of breathing and focus exercises.

I close my eyes and try to focus on the sound of the ocean. It takes all of my inner strength to concentrate on why I got out of bed at five thirty and not on my trip down memory lane with Owen. I'm here to relax and clear my mind. It doesn't help that the boy I adored throughout my childhood is stretching right beside me.

"Clear your mind of everything else as you breathe in and out. Focus on what is right here, right now, on this beach."

No problem there.

"Focus on what you can control in this place."

I let out a deep breath. I don't know if I'm in control right now. One thing is for sure, I'm still one hundred percent attracted to Owen. The years away from him haven't changed that. And even though I know I made the right decision to break up with Jackson, it's uncomfortable seeing him with Tara.

"Let yourself relax, connect with the earth below you, and come up into downward-facing dog."

I follow her instructions as I try to bring my mind back to the present. I quickly glance next to me at Owen, who's in perfect downward-facing dog position. He has really nice arms, and legs, and everything.

Come on, Cora.

All of a sudden I start to feel self-conscious while my butt is up in the air. I casually turn my face to the side to double-check if I put deodorant on, considering I was half-asleep when I left my room.

Thankfully, I did.

Somehow I make it through the rest of the class, and before I know it, I'm lying on my back in a position called *savasana*. The instructor is no longer speaking, and the only sound is from the waves crashing against the beach. I don't know how long I'm lying still, but when I open my eyes everyone else has already rolled up their yoga mats.

I quickly jump up and start to roll up my mat.

"Take your time, my dear," the instructor says. "There is no rush. *Savasana* is very important to your practice. I like to think of it as the reward you give yourself, and I believe it makes the practice complete."

Hmmm … I wish Fran were here so she could decipher what this instructor is saying. They could speak *yoga* and *zen* to each other. Maybe I should ask the instructor if my aura looks compromised today.

"Thank you so much for this class. It was very helpful," I say.

She bows her head to me. "This was your practice. Thank yourself for being here."

I pretend to know what she's talking about, but I'm not sure what I'm supposed to do. Maybe I'm supposed to stand in front of a mirror and say *Thank you for waking up before dawn to do yoga, Cora* or maybe give myself a hug?

"Did you fall asleep?" Owen asks when she walks away.

I frown. "No, why?"

He shrugs. "You were so still. I don't blame you. It was very relaxing."

"I don't think I fell asleep, but I didn't hear anyone get up ... so maybe."

We put our mats on the cart and begin to walk back toward the hotel.

"What are your plans for the day?" he asks.

I smile. "I'm hoping to find a quiet spot near the pool so I can read all day. You?"

"The plan is to go golfing with the men." He lets out a deep sigh. "I think I'd rather be chilling at the pool."

Ah, yes. I remember my mother mentioning that at dinner last night. She said the men would be gone for the day, so it would be girls only at the pool. My aunt started talking about margaritas and lifeguards. I don't know what she was saying because I tuned her out when she started drunk dancing and slapping her butt. Of course that was before all hell broke loose. More reason for me to find a quiet corner if possible, especially now because of the situation between Aunt DeeDee and Alaina.

As soon as Owen and I approach the elevator, the door opens, and Jackson steps out. He narrows his eyes at Owen.

"Morning. What are you guys up to?"

Owen tells him how we both ended up at the sunrise yoga class.

Jackson looks annoyed, and I can only assume he's bothered by us being together. Not to mention Owen did show up at my room yesterday while he was there. I'm sure his imagination is running wild.

"Cora, you got up for yoga?"

I nod. I'm not offended by the surprise in his voice because normally this wouldn't happen.

"Did Ash and Tara make it? We all hung out at The Volcano pretty late."

"Nope, just us," Owen says.

Jackson doesn't say anything.

"So, you golfing today?" Owen asks, clearly trying to change the subject.

"Yeah, I'll be there. I need get my run in first. Later."

He takes off without another word. Owen looks at me and raises his eyebrows, and we step into the elevator together.

"So, he was obviously pissed off."

I shrug. "Nah. I mean, I don't know why he would be."

Owen smirks. "Because he wants you back. I'm sure when he saw us together, he thought ..." He pauses. "Anyway, doesn't he know how long we've been friends?"

I rock back and forth on my heels. "Yes, he knows, and he shouldn't care who I hang out with since he's trying to hook up with my cousin."

Owen shakes his head. "Yeah, I hate to break it to you, but they're just using each other to pass the time."

I don't disagree with him.

"You're probably right," I say. "And Ashley isn't much better. She's notorious for whirlwind romances and engagements, so you better watch your back."

The elevator door opens, and we step out onto our floor.

"Oh, I already know about it. She told me all about breaking off her engagement, and she was asking me about my divorce."

"Yeah, she was asking me about you."

We arrive in front of my room.

"Really?" he asks with a gleam in his eye. "And what did you say?"

I shift from one foot to another. "She asked what you were like, and I told her we hadn't seen each other in a long time." I stop. "Anyway, you came back to the table, and she stepped in and asked her own questions."

He bites his lip, which is so incredibly hot.

"I better let you go. My dad doesn't like to be late for tee time. Have a good time golfing."

He smiles. "Thanks, and you have fun avoiding your family today."

I scowl. "I didn't say I was doing that."

He throws his head back and laughs. "You didn't have to."

I try not to laugh, but I'm unsuccessful. "Fine. See you later."

I slide my key into the slot to open my door.

"Hey, Cora."

I turn around quicker than I'd like.

"Maybe we can hang out again later and catch up some more. You know, in case anyone else has questions about me, you'll know what to say."

Be cool, Cora. Be cool.

"Um, sure. Sounds fun."

I did it.

He tells me he'll be in touch and takes off down the hall.

I'm very careful to close the door behind me before I scream into a pillow and jump on the bed.

Chapter Sixteen

_____

I call Fran as soon as I calm down to give her an update and to check up on my sweet Kiwi. She, of course, gives me a lecture about how to proceed with Owen.

"First of all, I'm so proud of you for getting out of bed for yoga," she says. "And as far as Owen goes, you need to let things progress naturally. Don't try to fight the chemistry between you. If the universe wants you together, it will happen."

I take a sip of water. "Fran, the man is newly divorced. Even his mother says he hasn't dealt with it properly." I remind her about this important detail because it's playing over and over in the back of my mind already.

"Mother's don't always know what's best. You know that better than anyone."

That's for sure.

"Didn't he tell you the reason he got divorced was because it wasn't right? Maybe he's ready to move on. He definitely wants to spend time with you." She pauses. "Cora, isn't this like your dream come true? The universe wants you to enjoy it."

The universe again, huh? Or it could be I'm the only normal person here, so I'm the best option to spend time with. I don't want to read too much into it. Not to mention the Jackson thing is still going on.

"What do you think about Jackson hanging out with Tara? It's weird, right?"

"Oh, no you don't. I get it's weird to see him with your cousin, but that's a closed door—keep it that way."

This is why she should be here with me. I'm alone on the island and could use my friend to help me navigate through this.

"That reminds me, I mentioned you to Shawn, and I think Brynn wanted to kill me. It was hysterical."

Fran doesn't think it's as funny as I do. "You girls love to push each other's buttons."

I stretch out on my bed and rest the phone on my neck. "Too bad. She's been trying to get under my skin since we got here. I can't even have a private conversation on my balcony."

"Stay away from her. She's a toxic person who needs to put someone down to make herself feel better."

I groan. "I wish my brother could see that. He worships the ground she walks on, and it's nauseating."

I fill her in on the other craziness that's happening. When I get off the phone, I take a quick shower and grab my pool bag. But first, breakfast.

～

When I arrive in the restaurant, I find my mother and Alaina sitting together. It looks like they're having an intense conversation.

"Good morning," I say cheerfully. I give them both kisses on their cheeks, but neither of them looks like she's in a good mood.

"Is everything okay?" I ask. "Did something else happen with Aunt DeeDee?"

My mother lets out a very dramatic sigh, which in Leann Fletcher terms means everything is definitely not okay.

I hang my bag on the back of the chair and sit down. "What's going on?"

My mother takes a long sip of her mimosa. "Cora Ann, please tell Alaina they absolutely cannot leave early."

I gasp. And admittedly my first thought is about *who* she's referring to. Does she mean just Alaina and Ken? Or Owen, too? As much as I love Alaina, I'm hoping she won't take Owen with her if she goes.

"Of course you can't leave!" I exclaim. "I hope this isn't because of what Aunt DeeDee said last night. She was just being overly dramatic, and I hope you know we don't agree with all the terrible things she said."

Alaina begins talking about how they shouldn't have come and it should've been a family-only celebration.

"You are family," I insist.

My mother nods in agreement. "Yes, and you know I'm closer to you than I've ever been to DeeDee. She's my sister-in-law, and I love her, but it's not the same."

Alaina reaches across the table and puts her hands on both my and my mother's hands. "I think it'd be best if you spend the remainder of your vacation with just family, and I mean the Fletchers," Alaina says. "The three of us already talked about it before the men left to play golf."

Hearing this makes my heart sink. So, she was talking about Owen as well.

My mother begins to dab the corners of her eyes while Alaina pats her on the arm. She looks at her watch and jumps up from the table.

"I have to get to the spa. I'm sorry to rush out, but I'll meet you at the pool in an hour. Please don't do anything yet—at least let me talk to Warner. Cora Ann, please talk some sense into her."

She squeezes my hand before leaving.

Once she's out of sight, I plead with Alaina to stay, "You can't leave me alone with these people. Other than Peepaw, the rest of them are too much to handle by myself. And Peepaw is so enamored with Evelyn, I'm not sure I'll be able to spend time with him anyway."

She gives me a sympathetic smile. "Last night was awful," she says sadly. "I knew DeeDee could be volatile, but she brought out the worst in me. Our being here together makes things uncomfortable for everyone else, and it's not fair to any of you."

I groan. Typical Alaina, she's always concerned about those around her. "I know this sounds terrible, but I'd rather they leave," I whisper.

She shakes her head. "You and I both know that's not going to happen."

Of course not. My aunt and uncle are taking full advantage of this free vacation.

"What do Ken and Owen think?"

Especially Owen.

She sighs. "At first Ken didn't agree with me, but the more we talked about it, he understood. He's willing to leave if I really want to do. And Owen, well, he flat out told me he wasn't leaving."

This makes my heartbeat speed up.

"We talked about this being a family-only trip, and he brought up Jackson being here, too."

Huh, well this is interesting.

"He's exactly right—you were all invited because you're important to my parents, including Jackson. Please don't let what Aunt DeeDee said force you to leave. This is their anniversary, not hers. We want you guys here, more than you know."

Alaina takes off her glasses and rubs her eyes. "I'll think about it, but if we stay, we will be doing our own thing, other than the anniversary party of course."

I guess that's understandable.

"So, no family picture?" I ask raising my eyebrows.

She puts her hands in prayer position and presses her lips together. "Well, if there's one good thing to come out of this ..." she says with a wink.

I let out a laugh and beg her to help me come up with an excuse to get out of it, too.

"I pleaded with Leann to consider something else, but she has her heart set on everyone wearing the traditional attire," she says, grimacing.

"You know how she is once she's set her mind on something."

"I do. Anyway, if we stay, we'll have to skip the picture. We really shouldn't be in it anyway."

My stomach growls loudly.

"Oh dear, go get yourself some breakfast. I'll get a refill on my coffee."

I finally get up and make my way to the buffet. The early morning yoga practice definitely made me work up an appetite.

Alaina sits with me while I eat, and we change the subject away from them leaving.

We're about to leave the restaurant when we run into my aunt and Ashley.

"Oh, you're still here," my aunt says rudely.

Ashley is busily typing something on her phone, obviously trying to avoid the drama.

"Aunt DeeDee, please stop. This tension is really upsetting Mom," I tell her. "Can you two get along a few more days for my parents' sake?"

Alaina is the first to agree. "DeeDee, I do want to apologize for yelling last night. My behavior was uncalled for."

She sighs dramatically. "Fine. We will be civil for Leann and Warner," she says and walks away from us and into the restaurant. Of course she didn't apologize. I pat Alaina on the shoulder as we walk toward the elevator. This is really frustrating, and I'm afraid any progress I made in convincing her to stay was for nothing.

Okay, so Owen was right about me trying to avoid my family all day. I'm successful with finding a secluded corner by the pool where I'm able to read. The best part of the day is the complementary poolside foot massage. What a wonderfully unexpected treat.

Everything is perfect until my sister finds me.

I had a feeling the peace and quiet was too good to last.

"We need to talk," she says in a loud whisper.

I sigh. "Maya, come on. I'm really enjoying the relaxation. No more drama."

She ignores me and sits down on the edge of my chair, giving me a nudge to move over. "I just came from the spa, and Brynn was there."

I stare blankly at her. "So?"

"Is there something going on with you and Owen?"

My stomach sinks. I knew it—Brynn will never change. She couldn't resist blabbing about what she heard.

"What are you talking about?"

Maya tells me Brynn accidentally let something slip about my balcony conversation.

I remind her who she's dealing with. "You know Brynn loves to create unnecessary drama, especially when it comes to me."

My sister gives me a skeptical look. Even if she doesn't believe me, she knows I'm right about Brynn.

"I hope so, because that's weird," she says making a face. "Owen is like our brother."

I completely understand what she's saying because with Maya being the youngest, Owen was like a big brother to her. It always felt different to me, maybe because I had Shawn. There is more of an age gap between Shawn and Maya.

"Owen and I have known each other our whole lives. Why does Brynn always have to stir the pot?"

She shrugs. "I don't know, but she seemed pretty confident something was going on with you two."

"I don't know, but we've got bigger issues. Alaina and Ken are thinking about leaving."

Thankfully, I'm able to change the subject by telling her about my conversation with Alaina.

She folds her arms. "Personally, I wouldn't mind if Aunt DeeDee left and took Tara with her."

I know the whole Jackson and Tara thing is still bothering her, but I steer clear of that conversation. I definitely don't want to discuss Owen or Jackson with my sister.

"I'm sure Mom will convince them to stay. She'll turn on the tears and work her magic."

She's right.

"I'm going to get a drink. You want anything?" she asks.

Peace and quiet?

"I'm good, thanks."

She finally leaves, and I return to the pages of my book. I'd much rather read about the drama than live it.

Chapter Seventeen

*A*ll is quiet until the late afternoon when once again things begin to unravel. I'm relaxing in my room when we find out the latest news.

On a positive note, Maya gets her wish when Tara informs everyone that she was called up to compete for a spot on some new dance show, so she's planning to take the next flight back to LA.

"She's out of here," Maya says excitedly. "Now we can all hang out together without her crawling all over Jackson. That had to be uncomfortable for you, at least a little bit."

I don't deny it was a bit awkward.

"Good, so will you hang out with us, please?"

I reluctantly agree so I can get off the phone, but I remind her yet again that Jackson and I are friends and nothing more. She assures me she understands, but I can almost see the wheels turning in her head as she plans on throwing one more Hail Mary at matchmaking.

I'm getting out of the shower when I'm summoned to my parents' room.

As soon as I arrive, my mom hands me a box containing the outfits for the family picture, which has been moved up to today before Tara flies out.

I don't know whether to be relieved we're getting it over with or upset I don't have more time to get out of it.

"I need you to help me deliver these right now," Mom says, pointing to the large box.

I peek inside where I see individual plastic bags marked with our names. *Ugh*, why do I have to be the delivery girl? Why can't her loyal assistant Brynn deliver these hideous things?

"Why isn't Brynn helping today? I thought she was by your side every step of the planning process?"

I do sound kind of catty, but it's a valid question.

"Brynn has already helped me so much, and I didn't want to interrupt her time with Shawn."

Figures. I guess she assumes I don't have anything to do since I'm traveling solo. Or maybe this is my punishment for not giving into her demands and reconciling with Jackson.

"I was thinking, it's probably good we're moving the picture up, in case Ken and Alaina decide to leave, too," she says, as she rushes around her room looking for something.

I guess she isn't aware that Alaina was relieved at the possibility of missing this nightmare photo session.

"Hey, Mom, maybe you should let Alaina and Ken off the hook from the picture. Things are already awkward enough with Aunt DeeDee." The least I can do is try to save Alaina and Ken from having to endure the picture with the rest of us.

My mother gives me a horrified look and reminds me of the one promise everyone made was to be a part of the family photo. She looks completely frazzled, so rather than upset her any more than she already is, I do as she asks and head out to deliver these costumes.

Now would be a good time to break out the Xanax. I've done a great job of surviving this vacation without it, although this family photo is enough to push anyone over the edge.

My first stop is to my cousins' rooms, and as expected, they are excited about the coconut bras and skirts. I'm not the least bit shocked by this, and I don't doubt they'll look great wearing them. According to Ashley, this isn't her first time wearing this kind of attire. I don't even ask for more information because frankly, I don't care.

The next stop is my aunt and uncle's room.

"Thank you, sweetie," Aunt DeeDee says. "I hope Miss Priss Alaina isn't going to be a part of our family picture."

I pretend to not know anything about the subject and tell her I was only given the important task of delivering outfits for my mother.

"Now you sit and have a chat with me," she says. I do as she asks. I could use a break from the task at hand anyway. I consider asking her for a drink, but I probably shouldn't encourage it.

"You have no idea how difficult it has been all these years to bite my tongue."

I can imagine. Aunt DeeDee isn't the silent type.

"I've always felt like the Webbers were more important to your parents than we were," she says, hanging her head. "Let me tell you something I don't want you to ever forget. Blood is thicker than water, Cora Ann. Friends come and go often."

She dramatically dabs the corners of her eyes with a tissue in between taking sips of her cocktail, naturally.

"I'm sorry you feel that way, but you shouldn't," I say, trying to sound sympathetic. "My parents love you very much."

She closes her eyes and takes a few breaths.

"I'm sorry to rush out. I better get the rest of these delivered before my mother loses her mind."

She gives me an understanding nod, and I'm finally able to escape.

I go to Maya's room next. She opens the door, and I hand her the outfits.

"Somehow I got stuck being the bearer of bad news. Mom says she didn't want to interrupt Brynn and Shawn."

She takes the bags and shakes her head. "At least we're getting this over with so it's not hanging over our heads. Another positive about Tara leaving early."

"I was thinking the same thing. Want to help me drop off the last few?"

She shakes her head. "Hunter and I were going to take a quick nap."

Of course they were.

I knock on Jackson's door, but he doesn't answer, so I leave his outfit with Maya. I still can't believe he's going to be in our family picture. The good news is I don't plan on displaying the photo in my house, ever. As far as I'm concerned, it'll never see the light of day, until my mother sends out her Christmas cards.

I need to talk to her. Maybe Alaina can help me convince her not to use the picture. I'm not confident about it, but it's worth a shot.

Brynn answers her door with her makeup and hair already done. She's another one who isn't upset about the coconut bra, which doesn't surprise me. I still believe she has something to do with choosing the horrendous outfits.

"Oh, good," she says, taking the outfits from me. "You know, this picture is really important to Leann. Everyone should stop complaining about the outfit and be supportive."

And by everyone, she means me. I know Brynn well enough to know she's going to remind us that she's been the dutiful daughter-in-law, helping my mother make plans since day one.

I politely excuse myself and make my way toward Peepaw's door.

I'm not emotionally prepared for what I see when he opens it. Let's just say seeing my grandfather in leopard-print boxer shorts and his girlfriend in a matching leopard-print silk robe is enough to scar anyone for life.

"Thank you for dropping this off, Cara," Evelyn says. "You're such a devoted daughter."

I don't even bother correcting her. Instead I apologize for the interruption and make a quick exit.

My last two stops are to Owen and his parents. I decide to knock on Owen's door first, hoping he can help me convince his parents to stay longer.

When he opens his door, he's in a pair of gray joggers and nothing else. This is a much welcome sight following the visit to Peepaw and Evelyn's room. I drag my eyes away from his abs and back to his face.

"Well, this is a nice surprise," he says, a smile spreading across his face.

I take a quick glance at his chiseled abs.

Yes, it is.

My pulse begins to pick up like it always does when I'm in his presence.

"Hi, I, um ... My mom has me delivering these ridiculous outfits for the family picture. I'm sure you heard she's moved it up to today."

He leans against the doorframe and reluctantly takes the bag out of my hand.

"Yeah, I just found out about this. I didn't think I was included since I was late to the party."

I laugh. "Oh well, you know how Leann is. She probably ordered your outfit in case you ended up coming. I have your parents' outfits, too ... although when I saw your mom this morning, she was still upset about everything that happened last night."

Keep your eyes up, Cora. Focus on his gorgeous face, not his amazing body.

"She is." He pauses. "You want to come in?"

That's a silly question.

I walk past him into his room, putting the now empty box on the floor. He turns off the music coming from his phone.

"I was doing some sit-ups and push-ups."

Of course he was, because sunrise yoga and all-day golfing isn't enough physical activity for this man.

I shove my hands into the back pockets of my denim shorts.

"I'm sorry to interrupt you and with such bad news."

He laughs as he pulls a shirt on over his head.

Truthfully, I don't know whether to be relieved or disappointed that he put a shirt on. Probably a little of both.

"I guess Mom told you she wants to leave," he says, opening a water bottle and offering it to me.

I take it from him and take a sip before telling him about the conversation I had with his mother this morning and how I tried to reason with her. "I told her she's as much a part of our family as anyone else. Families aren't always biological. Your parents need to stay. All of you do."

He sits down on the edge of the bed. "Oh, I'm not leaving," he says. "Your parents were so generous to include me on this vacation. I'm not going to hurt their feelings by taking off because your aunt had a tantrum."

I smile. "Even if it means you have to wear this outfit for a picture?"

He reaches for the bag. "Let's see what this thing looks like. I haven't even seen a picture of it yet."

I cover my mouth in an effort to keep from laughing.

He eyes me curiously. "What? Why are you laughing? I heard it was some kind of Hawaiian outfit. So, what is it? A Hawaiian shirt, and maybe a skirt? I'm secure enough in my manhood to wear a skirt for a few minutes."

Before I have a chance to break the bad news to him, he opens the bag and pulls out a green Speedo and floral-print loincloth.

I cover my face. *Why am I here?*

He bursts out laughing. "Very funny. Is Shawn behind this?"

I shake my head. "I wish I could tell you this was a joke, but unfortunately this is for real."

He holds up the loincloth. "So, all the men are wearing this thing?"

I cringe. "Yep."

He pauses before holding it against himself. "All the men, including your dad, my dad, and your grandfather?"

I sit down next to him on the edge of the bed. "If it makes you feel any better, we girls have to wear plastic grass skirts and coconut bras."

He rubs his forehead. "And by girls, you mean …"

"All of us, including our mothers and Aunt DeeDee."

We're both quiet for a few seconds. Then he starts laughing, and his laugh becomes contagious. Before I know it, we're both laughing hysterically.

"Thanks, I really needed to laugh," I tell him through my tears.

When we finally stop, he playfully bumps into me with his arm. "Do you still want to hang out later?" he asks, leaning into me. Once again his breath tickles me on my neck.

When I turn to look at him, our faces are only a few inches apart, which causes a stir within me. "Yes, I would like that," I say softly.

He's about to say something else when a loud knock makes me jump up from the bed.

Why are we always getting interrupted?

"Honey, are you decent?" Alaina calls.

He rolls his eyes and gets up to open the connecting door.

When his mother walks in, she gives me a confused look. "Oh, hi, honey."

I quickly grab their costumes and hand them to her. "Here are your outfits for the picture. My mother gave me the dreaded task of delivering them," I tell her.

At least I have a valid reason for being in her son's hotel room.

"Mom, you didn't tell me I had to wear a Speedo," Owen interjects.

She puts her hand to her mouth. "Leann told me the Speedo would be covered."

"Yeah, it's covered by a tiny piece of fabric." He tosses the loincloth to his mother who catches it midair.

She examines it. "Oh dear, your father is going to have a fit."

"Your coconut bra is in the bag," I tell her, forcing a smile. "And since you have to be in the picture anyway, you have no reason to leave early."

I look at Owen who's watching me. "Mom, I told you I'm not leaving," he says adamantly.

My heart is beating so quickly I worry it's loud enough for them to hear. I can't wait until later when I get to spend more time with Owen, alone.

"Okay. I promised Leann I would do this for her," Alaina says, talking a deep breath. "We'll see how this evening goes before we make a decision."

I already know how this evening is going to go. We're all going to show up half-naked for this train wreck, and we're taking a photo to document it. I remind myself I came on this trip knowing this was going to happen. Of course, I had no idea Owen or Jackson would be here when I agreed to it.

"I guess I should break the news to Ken," she says, eyeing the bag.

Owen laughs. "Let me know how that goes."

Alaina finally heads back to her room with their outfits, leaving Owen and me alone again.

"Do you think they'll stay?"

He shrugs. "I think so, but you never know with them. Regardless, I meant what I said. I'm not leaving."

I clear my throat. "I'm glad."

Owen takes a step toward me when his phone starts buzzing. He reaches for it and smiles when he looks at the screen. "It's from your mother. Looks like it's go time. In exactly one hour, we have to meet on the beach dressed and ready for the picture."

I roll my eyes at my mother's group text. "That's my cue to get ready." I walk toward the door, picking up the box from the floor.

"I guess I'll see you in an hour," he says.

I sigh. He'll definitely see a lot of me—of all of us. "Yep."

I'm approaching the door when I feel his hand on my arm. When I turn around, he's right behind me, and without a word he takes my face in his hands and gently kisses me.

I drop the box and put my arms around his waist, pulling him in to me. I'm in complete disbelief that Owen Webber is kissing me right now. I can't count the number of times I imagined this moment, dreamed about it, and wrote about it in my journal. The entries about Owen were long and detailed.

He moves his hands through my hair then clasps them around my lower back. Our kiss continues, speeding up and then slowing down.

We're interrupted by another knock on the door.

"You still decent?" Alaina calls.

He lets out a low growl.

"I need to go anyway," I whisper.

He hesitates but doesn't let go of me. "Okay. I'll see you soon."

He kisses me one more time before opening the door for me.

I grab the box and practically float back to my room. If I'm dreaming right now, I don't want to wake up, ever.

Chapter Eighteen

*W*hen I return to my room, I fall down on my bed and run my fingers over my lips. They are still tingling from Owen's mouth touching them. I close my eyes as I replay the last few minutes. I can still feel his hands on my face, his arms around me, and his body up against mine.

I know I need to get ready, but my heart is pounding so fast right now.

I reach for my phone and send Fran a text letting her know we need to talk tonight. When I finally pull myself together, I look at the plastic bag containing my outfit for the picture. The sooner I put the thing on, the sooner I can take it off.

I stand in front of the full-length mirror, trying to adjust everything. I lift, separate, bend, snap—basically anything I can do to make sure things stay where they are supposed to. Although the outfit doesn't look terrible on me, I definitely don't fill out the top as well as the other girls will.

I put on a light pink blouse and knot it right in the center, the coconuts are peeking out at the top. This addition actually doesn't look too bad, and my plan is to wait until the very last second to take the blouse off for the picture.

I curl my hair and put more makeup on than I usually do, anything to draw attention to my face and away from everything below my neck.

As I add gloss to my lips, I can't help but think back to being in Owen's room. I shake my head to shift my focus back to the task at hand. I slide my feet into my sandals and do one more check in the mirror.

Let's get this nightmare over with.

There are many things I wish I could unsee, but seeing my Peepaw and Evelyn proudly walk down the beach in their Hawaiian outfits is probably at the top of the list. And I thought seeing them in their matching leopard lingerie was bad enough.

They are walking hand in hand and don't seem bothered by the outfits one bit.

My mother rushes to give them hugs. I'm sure she's thrilled they've embraced her idea. Clearly, it doesn't even phase her that everyone is almost naked. As much as I adore my grandfather, that's a lot of bare skin.

Honestly, the men have it much worse than us women. I bet Owen is now wishing he didn't come, especially because he had no time to mentally prepare himself for wearing the loincloth.

My cousins and Brynn are proudly wearing their coconut bras, and as expected they look amazing in them. Hunter and Jackson are taking pictures of each other flexing and posing. And don't get me wrong, Jackson looks good in his outfit too, not that I didn't expect him to.

"So, this is different," Jackson says, coming up beside me. "I don't think I've ever experienced anything like this."

I laugh. "I'm assuming you're referring to taking a family portrait in matching Hawaiian outfits."

"Yep," he says. "It's kind of fun, though."

Fun? No wonder my mother loves him so much.

"How did you get away with wearing a shirt?" he asks.

I peek around him at my mother, who's now mimicking a hula dance. I let out a long sigh. "I'm not getting away with it. I told her I was wearing this until the moment we take the picture, and then I'm planning to put it right back on as soon as the photo shoot is over. These things don't fit everyone the same."

He shrugs. "I think you look great, if not better than the other girls."

I smile. "Thanks, Jackson. You always know exactly what to say to make me feel good."

"We're heerrrree."

We all turn to see Aunt DeeDee spinning around in her hot pink skirt. Let's just say the coconuts don't do anything for her.

"*Ugh,*" Jackson says under his breath.

"I heard that," I say over my shoulder.

My mother and DeeDee are talking to the photographer who's setting up a tripod and some big white umbrella lights.

Other people on the beach are staring at us. Not that I blame them—we look completely ridiculous. I don't doubt our faces (and bodies) will be splashed all over social media if they aren't already.

A few seconds later I see Owen. He's walking behind his parents. Both Owen and his father are wearing swimsuits and open button-down shirts.

"That's a shame," Ashley whispers. "I was looking forward to seeing Owen in a Speedo."

I don't say anything. *Although I'm a bit curious myself.*

My mind immediately returns to being in his room earlier, feeling his lips on mine, being in his arms—this memory makes my heart race. Maybe if I focus on that, I won't think about what's happening right now.

My parents walk over to greet them, and I see my mother pull Alaina and Ken into a big hug. My dad puts his hand on Owen's shoulder and leans in to say something to him. They both start laughing.

The rest of us walk over to them and stand around as my father starts talking.

"Thank you all for being here. I would like to reiterate that Leann selected these outfits. I went along with it because the couch hurts my back."

Everyone laughs.

I zone out as he continues, and I catch Owen's eye. He looks at me and smiles. Oh, how I wish we were somewhere else right now.

"I know some tempers flared last night," my dad continues. I glance at Alaina who looks down. "I think we all had a long day, but I hope we can all put our differences aside for a little while longer and have a nice evening."

When he's done, I immediately notice my aunt and uncle walking away from the circle. Aunt DeeDee is going on and on about family and how my uncle should say something to his brother. She's not making any effort to speak quietly.

Owen makes his way over to me. "Hey."

"Hi."

We're standing a few feet away from each other, but my stomach is still full of butterflies.

"Cute shirt," he teases.

I look him up and down.

"Cute swimsuit," I reply.

He laughs. "After you left, I tried on that thing your mother chose. There was no way in hell I was walking through the hotel wearing only that," he says. "I'll drop my pants when it's time."

All of a sudden it's getting really warm, and I don't think being on the beach has anything to do with it.

"My cousin will be happy about that. She was very disappointed when she didn't see you in your Speedo."

He moves a little closer to me. "This thing is so uncomfortable. Every time I move, it rides up."

I try not to giggle. "The good news is you never have to wear it again."

I watch as he runs his hand through his hair. I feel like I've gone back in time every time he does this.

"I'm looking forward to hanging out later," he says under his breath.

Before I can respond, my brother comes over and starts teasing him about not being able to hang because he's wearing a swimsuit.

While I'm standing back and listening to them, I notice Jackson giving me a funny look. It's the same expression he had when he saw Owen and me together after sunrise yoga.

My mother calls everyone over as the photographer is ready for us. Those of us with extra clothing remove it, namely me, Owen, and his parents.

"I would prefer my family to be on the opposite side of the picture from the Webbers," Aunt DeeDee announces.

Alaina rolls her eyes but doesn't say anything.

"Who do you want to stand next to?" Brynn whispers to me. "Since you're obviously very popular here. I think both Jackson and Owen would like to stand with you."

I give her a dirty look.

"I would prefer to be on the left," Tara says. "My left side is better."

The photographer begins posing and moving people around. My grandfather and Evelyn are placed in the middle. I stand back and watch as everyone takes their places. Maya grabs my arm and drags me over to where Jackson is standing with Hunter.

"Maya."

"What? Is it a problem that I want my sister next to me in the family picture?"

I raise my eyebrows and shake my head. We all know she cares nothing about being next to me. This all about Jackson and me being in the picture together.

The photographer pushes me toward Jackson and then turns my shoulders so I'm standing right in front of him. I know my mother is behind this, but I don't object. Right now, all I care about is getting this over with.

I look over at Owen, who's awkwardly standing between his parents. He has his hands folded in front of his loincloth. Ashley was right though—he does look really good in his outfit.

Once everyone is in position, the camera flashes start. The photographer takes several pictures of all of us then some of just the women, the men, and individual families. There's also a few with just the Fletchers, to which Aunt DeeDee makes a few comments about this being the way it should be. And she goes on to say how rude it is for certain people to push their way in to a family reunion.

I have to give credit to Alaina who doesn't respond and truly is the better person in this situation. She plasters a smile on her face and endures taking pictures being half-naked and wearing a coconut bra. She's the perfect example of a true friend.

After what feels like hours of posing and smiling ... and adjusting, the family fun photo session is finally over.

I quickly put on my shirt and pull it closed. I'm so happy this is over with I could cry. I'm about to say my good-byes when my mother informs me she wants to have dinner with our immediate family, meaning my parents, siblings, and me. I'm about to decline, but she hurries off to talk to Alaina who's already covered up and ready to leave.

My aunt and uncle and cousins are now doing their own photo session.

Owen walks over to me, looking much more comfortable now that he's covered up.

"I was just informed I'm having dinner with my family," I tell him.

"No problem," he says. "Shoot me a message when you're done."

"I will."

He flashes me a smile. "Now if you'll excuse me, I've got to get this thing off. The chaffing has begun."

I grit my teeth. "Ouch."

He grimaces. "Ouch is right."

He turns to walk away but stops. "I'm looking forward to tonight."

Heat rushes into my cheeks. "Me, too."

I try to hide my giggle as he waddles away.

Now that I'm mostly covered, I wander over to where Peepaw is still sitting. I feel like I've hardly spent any time with him since we've been here. Although, I'm pretty confident Evelyn has been keeping him busy. As I approach, I overhear their conversation.

"When do you want to tell them our news?" Evelyn asks.

News? Ohhhhh...

"How about at the party? The perfect time to make a big announcement."

I back up so they don't suspect I heard anything. I think I can guess what their announcement is, and I'm really happy for Peepaw.

Everyone is now making their way back to the hotel, which means I can change out of this outfit, never to wear it again.

It's been quite a day, and even though the past hour has been mostly unbearable, if my mother hadn't asked me to deliver the outfits, Owen and I wouldn't have shared that unbelievable kiss.

Thankfully, the picture is over, and I can't wait to see what tonight will bring.

Chapter Nineteen

*W*hen I return to my room, I have two missed calls from Fran. I remove the coconut bra and toss it across the room. I call her back and tell her about the magical kiss Owen and I shared.

She gives me some important *best friend* advice, and that's not to freak out.

I sigh. "I'm trying, but you know how long I've dreamed about this. I still can't believe he's here."

She reminds me that we only have a few more days before returning to our lives and I need to let the magic of the islands guide me. I'm not sure what she means, but it sounds cool. I ask her to give Kiwi a hug for me and hang up to get ready for my evening.

I happily put on some regular clothes: a black strapless dress and a pair of gold sandals. I twist my hair up into a bun on top of my head and add some fun jewelry. I'm putting on the last few touches when there's a knock at my door. I excitedly rush toward it, hoping it's Owen.

But once again I'm met with Jackson on the other side.

I try to hide my disappointment. "Hi, I'm just leaving for dinner."

He smiles. "Me, too. I figured we could head downstairs together."

I open and close my mouth. I should've known this immediate family dinner would include him. I don't bother to protest and grab my handbag and key card.

"That was an interesting family shoot. Your family is very entertaining," he says as we ride down to the lobby.

I shake my head. "It was awful. I'm so glad it's over. That picture has been looming over me like a dark cloud."

We arrive in the lobby to find my parents having a discussion.

"I don't care, Warner. He's your brother. Why can't you talk to him? We have three more days here, and I want them to be enjoyable. I'm sorry, but the world doesn't revolve around DeeDee."

She stops talking when she sees me and Jackson. She gives us both hugs.

"Cora Ann, you look so pretty tonight."

"Thanks, Mom."

She squeezes my hand and pulls me away from Jackson. "You need to tell me how things are going. Are you enjoying yourself?"

I put my hands on her shoulders. "I'm having a very good time."

She looks over at Jackson. "And?"

I plaster a smile on my face. "If you're asking about Jackson, you already know the answer."

She frowns, but thankfully everyone else arrives, so she doesn't have time to lecture me.

We all make our way to Mahalo's, the hotel's upscale beachside restaurant. When my father starts talking about their golf game from earlier in the day, Shawn brings up Owen.

"Owen Webber is a phenomenon. That guy hasn't changed a bit. How is he so good at every sport he plays, even golf? It's infuriating."

"Owen's been through a lot," my mother says, taking a sip of her wine. "His divorce was hard on everyone in the family."

"What exactly happened?" Maya asks. "They were married for like five minutes."

My mother tells us Owen called his parents after he was only married a few months and told them he was moving out.

"He claimed he made a mistake," she says with a shrug, "and they rushed into the wedding without thinking things through."

Owen told me the same thing, but I don't speak up.

"That wedding cost a fortune," Maya exclaims. "You would think he would've realized it wasn't right before they dropped all that cash."

"Alyssa was really heartbroken," Brynn chimes in.

We all stare at her. I certainly didn't expect her to say that.

"How do you know that, babe?" Shawn asks.

Brynn tells us she and Alyssa started messaging each other about Alyssa's wedding planner because Brynn was in charge of the events for her best friend's wedding.

"Based on what Alaina said, it sounded like Owen was in the driver's seat," my mother says. "So tragic. I thought they made a beautiful couple."

She's not exaggerating. I remember when I saw their engagement photos that were taken at the La Jolla cliffs. They looked like they could've been clipped from a magazine.

Brynn takes a sip of her wine.

"Yes, Alyssa told me they were having some problems and talked about counseling. But he was the first one to suggest the divorce. It wasn't long after they got married."

I'm hanging on every word they're saying about Owen's divorce, and then I notice Jackson watching me. I'm pretty sure he senses something's there with me and Owen. *Is it that obvious?*

Or maybe Brynn mentioned something to him about my balcony phone confession to Fran. I wouldn't put it past her, especially after she already let it slip to Maya.

"Anyway, it's still sad for all of them," my mother says. "I know Alaina is hoping they find their way back to each other."

No!

I take a sip of my water, and the conversation shifts to the blowup between my aunt and Alaina. I hear my phone buzzing from my bag, and when I look at the screen, I find a message from Owen.

> How's dinner? Want to meet up at the end of the beach near the rocks?

I look up from my phone, and thankfully everyone else is intently listening to my parents talk.

That sounds perfect.

"We had no idea they felt that way about Ken and Alaina," my dad says. "It's really stupid because they have their own friends they do things with. Apparently, years of dislike finally boiled over when the Webbers were invited on this trip."

I'm trying not to watch the clock, but I can't help it. I've waited most of my life to spend time alone with Owen, and it's finally happening. I guess a few more hours won't matter at this point.

After dinner, everyone orders coffee, and they serve a delicious pineapple upside-down cake.

Shawn and Brynn are the first to leave, followed by Maya, Hunter, and Jackson, who announce they're heading to the Hula Hula.

"You want to come with us?" Jackson asks me.

I can't help but notice the eagerness in my mother's face.

"I think I'm going to stay with my parents for a bit."

Surely my mother would prefer me to spend time with her over a man.

"Okay. You want to meet up with us later then?"

I shrug. "I'm not sure. It's been a long day."

His face falls, but he doesn't push the issue.

"Poor guy," my mother says as soon as he's gone.

"Leann, give it a rest," Dad exclaims.

I give him a grateful smile.

"I will not, Warner," she scolds. "Don't you remember when I broke up with you? You were pretty devastated until my friend Cheryl convinced me to give you another chance. Look how that turned out. What would've happened if someone discouraged me?"

Not this story again ... although this time I can hear my father's side.

"Did it really happen that way?" I ask him.

He sips his coffee. "For the most part, but I wasn't *devastated*. More shocked than anything. It was totally out of the blue."

"And I'm sure Jackson felt the same when Cora Ann broke up with him," my mom interrupts. "She did the same thing to him that I did to you."

I let out a frustrated sigh.

"Mom, please listen to me. I don't understand why I need to keep repeating myself, but here goes ... Jackson is kind and a good person, and I know you would love for him to be an official part of the family, but—"

"He is a good person," she interjects.

I ignore her and continue talking. "But something is missing. Yes, he's fun and attractive, but there's no spark."

Not like the spark I feel around Owen.

"Spark is important," my father interjects.

My mother glares at him, and he shrugs.

"Please stop trying to force this. It's really making me uncomfortable," I plead. "Our hotel rooms being next to each other and then the family picture today—it's too much, Mom."

She clears her throat. "I want you to be with someone who will take care of you. There are some terrible men out there. My friend's daughter just went through quite an ordeal." She lets out one of her usual dramatic sighs. "As your mother, it's my job to worry and want the best for you."

Owen immediately pops into my head.

"I appreciate that you want what's best for me, Mom. I promise I'm not going to settle like—" I stop myself before saying my brother's name.

"Anyway, I'm going to head up." I stand up from my chair. "I love you both."

I give them each a kiss on the cheek and hurry back to my room to freshen up. I didn't give my mother a chance to say anything else, but I actually think she was more upset with my father for not backing her up. I think he's as tired of hearing about Jackson as I am.

When I get back to my room, I quickly brush my teeth and touch up my makeup. I'm both excited and terrified to be alone with Owen for the first time since our kiss in his hotel room. I don't know what to expect, but I've never been more ready for anything in my life.

Chapter Twenty

---

*W*hen I was in college, there was a cliff in the mountains overlooking the whole city where couples would go to hook up. The spot where I'm meeting Owen reminds me of that place, only with the ocean crashing against the rocks. It looks like the setting you would see in a movie, and it's so romantic I may never want to leave. Lydia was right about this place.

As I make my way along the shore, I rehearse several different scenarios in my mind. I'm not sure what to expect or how I should act. I guess the best way is to let things happen naturally like Fran said.

Thankfully, I don't run into any of my family members on my way. That's another question I have—I'm not sure if we're keeping this meeting a secret or what. As far as I know, the only people who noticed our interaction are Jackson and Brynn. Everyone else has been preoccupied with my aunt's outburst and fight with Alaina.

When I arrive, Owen is already there, sitting on a blanket, looking out at the ocean.

I take a few deep breaths to try to calm my nerves.

"Hey."

He turns around and rises to his feet. He immediately pulls me into a hug, so I wrap my arms around him and hug him back. The top of my head nestles perfectly into his neck, and I feel him rest his chin on the top of my head.

When we finally separate, he takes my hand. I sit down next to him, and he asks me about dinner with my family.

"Oh, you know, we talked about the vacation and of course my aunt and her behavior." I conveniently leave out that his personal life was part of our discussion. "How was your evening?"

He shrugs. "It was okay. My mom is still bugged about the situation with your aunt."

I shake my head. "Aunt DeeDee is way out of line. I knew she was feisty, but she's really being nasty. My parents said they had no idea she was so threatened by their friendship with your parents."

He groans. "They are still thinking about switching their flights. I spent most of dinner trying to convince them to stay, especially for the anniversary party. I asked them why they're going to let DeeDee get to them. She obviously loves to stir things up."

I nod. "Yes, she does. Thanks for trying, though. My mom will be heartbroken if they leave early."

We're both quiet for a few seconds.

"What about you? Are you still staying?"

He runs his fingers across my hand. "I told you I wasn't leaving. I ..." He stops and clears his throat. "Cora, I don't know how to explain this"—he points back and forth between us—"the only thing I can tell you is when you walked in late to dinner, I felt something the second I saw you. So many memories came flooding back to me at once, and all I could think about during meal was that I wanted to talk to you."

I know the feeling.

"I feel so comfortable with you." He pauses and scratches his head. "I guess it's because we've known each other for so long."

"Only since we were babies," I remind him.

He laughs. "That's true." He stretches out on the blanket and rests his chin on his hand. "Do you think this is weird? I mean, our families have been close for such a long time, and I know you've always thought of me as another annoying brother ..."

Well, that answers one of my questions. Obviously he never knew I was in love with him for the majority of my childhood.

"Say something," he begs. "And please tell me I'm not making a complete ass of myself right now."

I stretch out on the blanket and face him. "I have so many thoughts going through my mind right now," I tell him. "I'm trying to come up with the right words."

I look into his familiar hazel eyes, and the memories flood back to me. How I wished he would've returned my feelings. And then I remember how sad I felt when I heard he was getting married. I want to tell him everything, but I don't know where to start.

He reaches over and pushes my hair behind my ear.

"I was dreading coming on this trip," I say. "But that changed after our walk out here the first night."

I lie on my back and stare up at the stars.

All of a sudden Fran's words play through my mind. I need to embrace this moment because in a few days we're going back to our real lives. We're lying on the beach in Hawaii under the stars, and it's now or never. I'm not even sure what I'm so afraid of. I turn my head to look at Owen, who's also looking up at the sky.

I slide a little closer to him, and our faces are now inches apart. "This is so surreal," I tell him. "You have no idea how long I've thought about this."

He gives me a curious look. "What are you talking about?"

I cover my face with my hands and let out a low scream. I need to just tell him. When I uncover my face, he's leaning up, looking at me. "Here's the deal, you probably suspected this, but I had the biggest crush on you when we were younger, and it lasted for years."

And I don't think I ever got over it.

His mouth curls up into a smile. "Are you serious? When?"

"Come on. You really didn't know?"

He lies back down and rubs his forehead. "So, you're telling me I had a chance with you all along."

Um, yes.

I bite my lower lip and let out a loud sigh. "Oh, what the hell. Yeah, you had a chance."

All of a sudden I get a wave of courage from out of nowhere and tell him everything. I bring up the celebrations our families spent together —the Fourth of July, Thanksgiving, Memorial Day—the list goes on. I tell him about spending hours selecting my outfits and getting ready hoping he'd notice me. And then about how I would freeze when he was around, so I'd sit back and watch him play sports with Shawn while I pretended to be reading.

"Cora, we played together all the time when we were little, and then as we got older you barely talked to me," he exclaims. "I figured you thought of me as another annoying brother you were forced to hang around with."

I shake my head. "I never thought of you as a brother. I was so nervous around you, especially as we got older. You became this hot baseball playing superstar, and I was … well, me."

He reaches over and gently caresses my cheek. "You don't give yourself enough credit. You're sensitive and patient. After what your mother and sister did to you on this trip—most people would explode, but you've taken it in stride. And you're beautiful. I always thought you were pretty, but now …"

I can feel heat fill my cheeks. Thankfully, the moon casts enough lighting for us to see each other but it still hides my blushing.

"And since we're confessing things, I wanted to make a move when you were at my house the night before I went to school. When we were watching the movie and you were in my arms. I thought about that night for weeks afterward. I came close to calling you more times than I can count, but I didn't because I figured you would think I was crazy. The truth is I was always attracted to you."

His confession leaves me feeling exhilarated. Now I know I didn't imagine or fabricate the connection between us that night. I actually convinced myself I was making it all up in my head because I wanted it to happen so badly.

At the same time, I feel sad and full of regret. What if I hadn't been so scared and told him how I felt all those years ago? Maybe things would've turned out differently. What if we could've had all this time together?

"Are you okay?" he asks, pulling me out of my thoughts.

"Yes. I was thinking about what would've happened if I'd told you how I felt."

He grows quiet. "I should've said something that night." He pauses. "Damn, I wish I could go back in time."

I know the feeling.

I reach up and run my hand through his hair. "Sorry. I've been wanting to do that for as long as I can remember."

He scrunches his nose. "What? Play with my hair?"

I giggle. "Yes, you always ran your hand through it before you put on your baseball cap. I thought it was sexy."

Seriously, Cora? Talk about putting everything out there. I don't know who I am right now.

He puts his hand on my waist.

"Since we're discussing this now, I think the way you chew on your lip while you're reading is sexy."

Oh, my gosh, I totally do that. "How did you know?"

He runs his finger across my lip before leaning in and kissing me. He pulls me on top of him, and I don't put up a fight. His hands are in my hair, on my back ... my waist. My eighteen-year-old self is insanely happy right now, as her wish is finally coming true. I push all my doubts, questions, and concerns out of my mind and allow myself to be in this moment. It's long overdue, and nothing else matters right now.

Chapter Twenty-One

One of the reasons I read so much is to escape into the pages of a story and immerse myself into someone else's life. Life is challenging enough, and I believe everyone needs a break from time to time. I love a good story full of drama and romance. And right at this moment, I feel like I'm living out a scene from a book.

In this story, the heroine reconnects with someone from her past, and it's everything she dreamed it would be. I know it seems cliché, but it's happening right now, and I'm loving it. With every touch and every kiss Owen gives me, I feel myself becoming even more drawn to him, if that's possible.

"We probably should stop," he whispers as he plays with my hair. "This is a public beach."

"Mmmm ... you're probably right."

We lie side by side on the blanket, and he lets out a deep breath as I rest my head against his shoulder.

"There's so much I want to talk to you about," he says. "Where do you live? I want to hear about your job, your friends—I want to know what you've been doing for the last eleven years. My mom has given me updates on your whole family but not many specific details."

I answer his questions while trying to ignore his arms around me. I admit I keep expecting to wake up at any moment.

"What about you?" I ask. "I know you played college baseball, and you played in the minor leagues, right?"

He nods. "For a very short amount of time, until I hurt my shoulder. That was the end of my career."

I remember hearing about this from my mother. When she'd bring up Owen, I'd have mixed feelings. It was like I wanted to know everything about him, but it was also too painful. After all, he was the one who got away. I'm trying to avoid the topic of his marriage, but I shouldn't. It's a part of his life.

"And of course, I know you were married."

He clears his throat. "I want you to know everything, but talking about my marriage might be a downer. I'm sorry."

I tell him not to apologize and take the opportunity to address his mother's concerns. I've already shown all my cards, so there's no point in hiding anything now.

"You said you made the right decision getting divorced, but it had to be difficult."

"It was extremely difficult," he admits. "We made a commitment we thought would last a lifetime, and I felt like I failed at that commitment."

I tell him about what his mother said about being worried because he was throwing himself into work.

He groans. "She's right about me becoming a workaholic, but that's only because business has really taken off for our firm, like I told you. I admit in the beginning I threw myself into my job because I was struggling, and it was the perfect distraction. I wanted to be busy, so I worked at least fifteen hours a day. I ate at the office, and some nights I slept there, too. Even though deep down I knew Alyssa and I weren't right for each other, I didn't know how to deal with it. And I still don't have a social life. I've been on one date since Alyssa and I split up, and that was another mistake. I let my co-worker set me up because he was relentless about it. Never again."

This makes me think about Jackson.

"Same for me. I let Maya set me up with Jackson against my better judgement," I say. "I knew better, but I wasn't meeting anyone on my own, so I took a chance. I didn't think about how complicated it would be for everyone else if things didn't work out for us. Seriously, he's my brother-in-law's best friend, and as you can see, it's a disaster."

Even through the almost darkness I see him frown.

"What?"

"It's obvious they're really pushing you to get back together with Jackson."

"Tell me about it. My mom thinks because she broke up with my father and they reconciled, the same should happen for me." I rub my temples. "She says she wants me to be with someone who's good, and Jackson is a good guy. Just not the guy for me."

I stop talking and replay everything I'm saying in my mind. When is it too much information, and when should I shut my mouth?

"Anyway, we were talking about you," I say, changing the subject. I would say I'm sorry things didn't work out with his marriage, but that's a lie. I never met Alyssa, so I don't know what type of person she is, but the idea of him being with someone else makes me sick to my stomach. This reminds me of Brynn bringing up Alyssa.

"Did you know Alyssa and Brynn started messaging each other after your wedding?" I ask.

"Alyssa mentioned Brynn reaching out to her, but I didn't realize they stayed in touch."

"She told us tonight at dinner. She also said Alyssa was really upset by the divorce. I'm assuming it wasn't a mutual decision?" I cringe at my boldness. I have no filter tonight. "Sorry. I hope I'm not overstepping."

"You're not overstepping at all. I want you to feel like you can talk to me about anything." Owen assures me he's fine with being open about all the details of his life, including his marriage ending.

I still can't get over how comfortable I feel talking to him. For as long as I can remember, I was so nervous that it was easier to ignore him. My fear and insecurity caused me to lose precious time. And with only a few more days here, I'm not letting that happen again. I'm taking advantage of the time we have and making the most of it.

"To answer your question, I'm the one who suggested the divorce because things were not going well. As soon as the excitement of the engagement and wedding was over, real life set in, and it became more apparent we weren't compatible. I was ready to be more settled, while she clearly wasn't."

I know exactly what he means because that's how I felt with Jackson. Even though he said he wanted to settle down, I knew he wasn't ready.

We both grow quiet, and he wraps his arms around me even tighter.

As I lie in his arms, listening to the ocean, I begin to wonder what happens next. I know I'm getting way ahead of myself, but I can't help it. Is this just something to add excitement to a family vacation, or could there be more for us?

"What time is it?" I ask.

He pulls out his phone to look at the screen. "It's almost one."

I groan. "My mother scheduled an early morning dance lesson for us girls tomorrow."

"What are you doing after the lesson?"

I shrug. "Another free day. I was planning to visit Pearl Harbor." I'm about to invite him to come, but he beats me to it.

"I was wondering if you'd spend the day with me," he asks.

I look at him and smile. "Yes. I'd like that."

Owen leans in, gives me another kiss, and then stands up and pulls me to my feet. I help him fold up the blanket, and then we walk back to the hotel, hand in hand.

We arrive at my room first. Owen hasn't let go of my hand since we left the beach. We look at each other and smile. It's obvious neither one of us wants to leave the other one.

"Since we're all about honesty tonight, I really, really want to come in, even though you haven't invited me yet," he says with a wink.

I giggle quietly. "I really, really want you to come in."

He sighs. "You need to get up for your dance lesson, and I'm planning on doing sunrise yoga again. We should probably rest up for our day tomorrow."

I frown, but I know he's right. I know we should take things slow, but considering we haven't seen each other in years, how much slower can we go?

"Good night, Cora," he says, kissing me on the cheek and then lingering right in front of my lips before giving me one more gentle kiss. "I need to get out of here before I change my mind," he whispers before taking off down the hall.

I enter my room and drop down onto the bed. Tonight happened, I wasn't dreaming, and I didn't imagine any of it.

I slowly change into my pajamas and pull on the fluffy hotel robe. I go out on the balcony, sit down, and look out over the ocean. I need to get some sleep, but after tonight I have no idea how.

I'm spending the day with Owen tomorrow, just the two of us. No matter what happens, I owe my parents big-time. This vacation has been life changing. I'll never have to wonder *what if* when it comes to Owen Webber, even if this vacation fling ends when we board those planes back to our lives.

I pull the robe tightly around me and hug my knees to my chest.

But what if this doesn't end when we go home? Is it possible for us to continue what we started here? We live over two hundred miles away from each other—he has his life, and I have mine.

I don't check the time I finally crawl into bed, but I know I'll have sweet dreams.

Chapter Twenty-Two

*W*hy did I sign up for this? Who wants to have a dance lesson at eight a.m.? Why couldn't she have scheduled it for ten? I put my sunglasses on and sit down on the lawn.

"Where is everyone else?" my mom whines. "It's already after eight. What's so difficult about arriving places on time?"

I almost say something to her about rescheduling the lesson for a later time, but it's too early to get into an argument with her. And since I'm already here, I'd rather get it over with.

I notice Evelyn is standing under a tree, cooling herself with a paper fan. It's a good thing she seems so laid back to be able to put up with all of this nonsense.

Brynn is talking to the dance instructor and has already begun what looks like her own private lesson. Not to mention, she's wearing her bright yellow grass skirt from the family picture. I'm surprised she's not wearing the coconut bra, but as usual she knows exactly what to do to make herself look like the best daughter-in-law in the world.

Maya sits on the ground next to me. "You look tired."

I yawn. "Yeah, I couldn't sleep."

She eyes me curiously, and for a second I wonder if she knows something about last night.

Owen and I aren't hiding it ... at least I don't think we're hiding it. We didn't exactly discuss what we're going to tell everyone, or if we need to. Maybe we'll show up at the anniversary party together and let everyone figure it out for themselves. Hmm ... that's not a bad idea.

"Well, the good news is Mom said Tara already flew back to LA. Good riddance to her."

I wonder how Jackson's handling Tara's early departure. Just a few days ago he was asking my permission to hang out with her.

My mother puts her hands on her hips. "I only had a few small requests of everyone on this trip. Is it really too much to ask for all my girls to be here for an hour hula lesson?"

"I'm sorry I'm late. I completely overslept," Alaina calls as she rushes toward us.

I think it's safe to say my aunt and Ashley are not coming, because of Alaina.

"I'm just glad you're here," my mother says, throwing her arms around her. Who knew this hula lesson meant so much to her?

She tells the instructor we're ready to start. And so begins our Polynesian dance lesson with Brynn as the star of the show, at least in her mind.

"Oh, this dancing is so spicy," Evelyn exclaims excitedly. She starts wiggling her body in an awkward manner. "Can you teach us to do the lambada next?"

Ugh. Is she serious?

The instructor gives her a half-smile.

"I think lambada is a South American style of dance," Brynn says knowingly. "We had a dance instructor come and teach many different styles for one of our sorority charity functions. Remember, Cora?"

I nod. "I remember."

How could I forget? It wasn't my favorite activity because I don't love being front and center. And we had to perform the dance on stage after only two lessons. At least I can thank my mother for putting me in dance classes when I was young because the steps came easy to me.

"That was a lot of fun," Brynn says, as she sways her hips to the music. "But I love this. Leann, this was such a great idea."

I glance at Maya who rolls her eyes.

"I would love to learn the lambada," Evelyn says. "Did you know they call it the forbidden dance? And do you know why they call it that?"

I have a feeling she's about to tell us.

"It's because it's a sexy, dirty dance," she says as she does a little shimmy with her shoulders.

I can't help but laugh because even though it's gross to think of her and Peepaw in that way, she has an authentic zest for life that's contagious.

"Evelyn, you have to give us your secrets," Brynn exclaims.

Um, no, she doesn't.

"I hope Shawn and I still have the kind of fire you and Peepaw have in our later years."

I tune out their conversation. It's bad enough to think about the intimate details of Peepaw's personal life but adding in Shawn and Brynn's crosses the line for me.

"I see the fire in all of your relationships," Evelyn says. "And you have excellent role models, thanks to your parents. We're all here because of their love and devotion to one another for forty years."

My mother smiles proudly.

The instructor interrupts our conversation to give us the next instructions.

"And you too, Cara. I see the fire with you and your handsome young man."

What?

"Cara?" Brynn pauses as she looks at me. "Oh, you mean Cora."

I grit my teeth and look at my mom, who's beaming at Evelyn's suggestion.

"I told you, Cora Ann. Other people can see the connection you and Jackson have. Now you have to be willing to open your heart."

I don't respond as I wait for the other shoe to drop. I'm pretty confident Evelyn isn't talking about Jackson.

Thankfully, the instructor steps in and brings our focus back to learning the steps.

After what feels like hours, our hula lesson is finally over.

"What are you doing today?" Maya asks, wiping her forehead with a towel.

I take a long sip of my water. "I'm heading out to explore the island."

This isn't a lie. I am planning on exploring the island, except I'm going with Owen.

"Oh, where are you going?" Brynn asks, joining our conversation.

Ha, like I would tell her. "I'm not exactly sure. I still have to map out my itinerary."

She tells me she and Shawn have a couples' massage booked, and then they plan on leaving the resort for the day also. She takes this opportunity to ask the dance instructor for some recommendations of local spots to visit.

I use this moment to escape before I get any more questions or before Evelyn tells everyone that *Cara's* romantic connection is actually with Owen, not Jackson.

I grab some coffee and a bagel on my way back to my room. When I return, there's a text message from Owen waiting for me.

MEET AT 10:30? CAN'T WAIT TO SEE YOU.

I quickly jump into the shower and get ready for my day. I try to take my time, but I find myself rushing. The sooner I see Owen, the better. I finally decide on a white eyelet sleeveless shirt, a pair of denim shorts, and cute white sneakers. I have no idea what we're doing, so I throw on a hat and grab my sunglasses.

When I arrive in the lobby, all is quiet, and none of the Fletcher party is around. I see Owen sitting in an oversized chair, looking at his phone. As I expect, he looks totally hot in a light blue V-neck shirt and gray shorts.

He stands up as I approach him and kisses me on the cheek. I guess we aren't trying to hide anything after all. Okay, good to know.

"You ready?"

I've been ready for years.

I smile and nod.

When we exit the lobby, there's a sleek black car waiting. Owen leads me toward it and opens the door.

I stand back and look at the car. "This is for us?"

He laughs. "It sure is. How did you think we were going to get around?"

I hadn't thought about it—maybe a taxi or an Uber? I certainly didn't expect to be picked up in some fancy car, but I don't mind. I grin as I climb into the back seat.

He slides in next to me and immediately takes my hand in his.

As much as I would love for him to kiss me, I really love how tender he's being with his subtle gestures. Kisses on the cheek, gentle touches, and handholding. He could be all over me, but he's being very respectful.

He asks me about the hula lesson, and I give him to the sordid details of Evelyn and her desire to learn how to lambada.

He laughs. "Is the lambada even a thing anymore?"

"I don't know. But the woman is eighty-five years old, so for her it must be a big deal. Maybe it's one of those bucket list items?"

I also tell him Brynn asked about my plans for today. I figure it's a good segue into how everyone finds out we've been spending time together.

"What did you tell her?"

I shrug. "I said I was exploring the island, but I didn't say who I was going with. I didn't know what to say."

He gives me a thoughtful look. "Are you thinking we should keep this a secret?" he asks.

"Are you?"

He shakes his head. "No. I don't think we owe anyone an explanation. We're adults. If people see us together, fine."

Hmmm ... I like this.

I look out the window as we drive along the freeway. "Where are we going?"

"You said you wanted to see the island, so let's do it. I hope you don't mind that I went ahead and made some plans."

He hasn't let go of my hand since we left the hotel, which is totally fine with me.

"I don't mind at all. This is amazing."

I ask him about his parents, and he tells me they're still on the fence about leaving early because they're afraid if they stay it'll ruin the anniversary party. At this point they should just stay anyway since the party is tomorrow night.

He changes the subject and asks me about my life back home.

"I live with my best friend, Fran, and my high maintenance cat." I swipe through my photos and show him pictures of Kiwi.

"Has my mom seen these pictures? She'll be obsessed."

I shake my head. "Not yet, but I told her all about Kiwi."

"She reminds me of Buttons."

I open my eyes widely. "I totally forgot about Buttons."

Buttons was an abandoned cat Alaina had found when we were young. Unfortunately, the cat was very sick and didn't live long after Alaina found her. It was so sad.

"Kiwi is a good cat, very smart. Although she can be a pain in the ass, I think she knows when I need to work because she sits on my laptop. It's her way of telling me she wants attention. She's affectionate too, unlike most cats. Well, except she didn't like—" I stop talking before I mention Jackson.

Owen raises his eyebrows. "She didn't like Jackson?"

I shake my head. "Not at all. She's never had that kind of a reaction to any of my friends, so who knows?"

"Maybe she could sense things wouldn't work out between you two, so she didn't want to get too close," he says. "I've heard some crazy stories about pets and their owners. Pets saving their owners, sensing when something isn't right. I totally believe it."

I've heard about that, too. Although I don't see Kiwi saving me from anything except maybe overworking myself. She certainly knows how to keep me from opening my laptop.

"Do you have any pets?"

He shakes his head. "Unfortunately not. Alyssa never wanted a pet because of the hair, and she thought they were messy. And I've been working so much since we split up, getting a pet has been the last thing on my mind. But I'd love to get one. My place is lonely."

This makes me think about Owen going home alone and what's going to happen after this. It's much too soon to bring this up, and as amazing as the last twenty-four hours have been, I haven't seen Owen in years.

The car comes to a stop, and I look out the window and gasp.

"What are we doing here?"

He smiles and opens the door. "I told you we were seeing the island." He takes my hand and pulls me out of the car.

"We're going on a helicopter?" I shout excitedly.

He tells me he asked Kalaina the concierge about the best way to see the island, and she recommended this tour.

"Oh, my goodness, I've never been in a helicopter," I say nervously.

"It's an amazing experience everyone should try at least once."

I bite my lip. I admit I'm a little nervous, but at least it's not parasailing or bungee jumping.

"I'm actually afraid of heights," he says as we walk toward the building. "But I tried a helicopter tour in the Caribbean, and it was very smooth."

I'm not afraid of heights, but I am afraid of falling—so there's that. My nerves are overshadowed by how amazing Owen is for planning this on such short notice. I'm in a daze as the pilot goes over the rules and safety measures.

When he leads us out to the runway, a feeling of excitement takes over me. I'm about to fly over Oahu in a helicopter.

After we get strapped in, I triple-check my seat belt, and we put on the noise-blocking headphones.

Owen reaches over and squeezes my hand, and a few minutes later we're airborne.

I can't decide what is more amazing—this view or feeling Owen's grasp tightly around my hand. No matter what happens, I'll never forget this for as long as I live.

Chapter Twenty-Three

There are no words for this experience. I look out the window as we fly over Waikiki, Diamond Head, and Pearl Harbor. Owen holds my hand firmly in his, and we listen to the pilot tells us about the island. He goes into detail about the historical events leading up to the bombing of Pearl Harbor, and I feel emotional thinking about Peepaw, who's a veteran.

I still can't wrap my head around the fact that less than a week ago I was mapping out a plan to see these landmarks on my own, and here I am with Owen Webber, of all people. This is completely mind-blowing and for me a dream come true.

"What do you think?" Owen asks into the microphone.

I look back and forth between him and out the window. "I think this is the best day ever."

He laughs. "Agreed."

Our journey continues as we sail through the air above the green mountains and crystal blue waters. I may not know what's going to happen between us after this, but I don't know how anything could top this day.

When we're safely back on the ground, the pilot takes some photos of us so we can document our excursion. I can't wait to send a picture to Fran.

"This was, without a doubt, the best way to see all of the island," I tell him as we walk toward the awaiting car. "Thank you for today."

"It's not over yet."

"What do you mean? We're not going back to the hotel?" I ask.

Owen leans his head to the side. "Do you want to go back?"

I shake my head as I climb into the back seat.

He slides in next to me and puts his arm around my shoulders.

"I thought after the helicopter tour we were done for the day."

He shakes his head. "No way. I said we'd spend the day together, and we still have a lot of the island to explore on the ground."

I'm completely speechless right now. I would think seeing everything from the sky would be sufficient. I guess Owen has a different idea.

Our next stop is lunch at an amazing sushi place on Waikiki Beach. We talk about all the places we saw while we were in the air, and of course I express how cool it was to fly over Pearl Harbor.

"Good thing we're headed there next," Owen says.

I clap my hands excitedly as we make our way back to the car. I feel like a kid going to a toy store. Without thinking, I begin to talk about a recent book I read about Pearl Harbor, and then I stop abruptly. "I'm sorry. I'm sure you don't want to hear about the books I've been reading. It's not exactly super exciting."

He laughs. "Why wouldn't I want to hear about them? There's nothing wrong with your love of books."

"I know," I say. "The truth is I'm incredibly boring. I like to read, and I love my cat. The most interesting thing about me is my job—the one aspect of my life that gets action."

Did I really just say that out loud?

He grins. "I appreciate your honesty."

Oh well, I need to be honest with him. This is who I am, and there were many times I felt like I couldn't be myself when I was with Jackson. Not because he made me feel that way, either, but because of the pressure I put on myself. I know how much he enjoyed trying new places and things, and I wanted to be supportive. Don't get me wrong, I didn't always mind. It was fun to do new and spontaneous things once in a while.

"I'll be honest with you, too," he says. "I'm probably more boring than you think *you* are. All I do is work, go to the gym, and order takeout food. I have no pet, no social life, and I watch TV when it's baseball season. And when it's not baseball season, I'm wishing it was baseball season."

I laugh.

"Okay, maybe we should just agree that our lives are equally boring."

He moves his face closer to mine until our lips are barely touching. "Fine. I agree."

Our lips touch, making the memory of last night flood back to me. This is the first time he's kissed me all day.

"Confession—I was wondering when you were going kiss me," I whisper in between his kisses.

He briefly pauses. "Confession—I've wanted to kiss you all day, but I didn't want you to think I did all of this only because I'm unbelievably attracted to you. Or because I find you incredibly sexy."

I put my hands on my cheeks to hide my blushing.

He opens his mouth widely. "You're blushing."

I playfully push him away. "Shut up."

He pulls me even closer to him. "I can make Cora Ann Fletcher blush. Who knew?"

I scowl. "Very funny."

After a bit more playful teasing and a few more kisses, we pull into the parking lot at the Pearl Harbor National Memorial Park. As we walk hand in hand, I can't help but feel emotional. This is one of those places I've always wanted to visit, and now I'm getting to experience it with Owen.

We walk through the monument, listening to the events of that fateful day in history. We hop on a boat and sail around the harbor. Owen has his arms around my waist, and I lean my head against his chest. This is without a doubt the best date of my life.

My thoughts are interrupted when I hear my phone buzzing from my pocket. I'm greeted with a message from my mother.

> DINNER 7PM. GOING TO CELEBRATE YOUR GRANDFATHER'S BIRTHDAY TONIGHT SINCE WE'RE ALL TOGETHER.

This message is a reminder that this day and my alone time with Owen won't last forever. I have to return and face my family tonight, and in a few days we all go home.

"You okay?" Owen asks.

I nod and show him the message from my mother. He kisses me on the forehead.

"We have a few more quick stops to make, and then I'll have you back in plenty of time."

I don't want to go back.

Although, I do want to celebrate Peepaw's birthday. And there's still the announcement I overheard him and Evelyn talking about.

After we finish our tours we head back to the car, and I drop my phone back into my bag. I'd rather not have any more distractions. I will see my family soon enough, but for now I want to soak up the remainder of the day Owen has planned for me.

I can't believe how much thought Owen put into our outing today, considering I was with him until late last night and we left the hotel this morning at ten thirty. When I ask him how he organized it so fast, he tells me he contacted Kalaina first thing this morning, and she helped put it together in no time. Talk about fantastic customer service. I assumed she just recommended the helicopter tour.

Our last few stops are the real-life Dole Planation, where I pick up Lydia's chocolate-covered pineapple. And she was right about it being absolutely delicious.

Our last stop is the coolest little surf town called Haleiwa on the North Shore of the island. I feel like the ultimate tourist as I snap pictures. I want to document every bit and remind myself that this day happened. Owen and I take lots of selfies, and we ask a fellow tourist to take a picture of us standing on the beach together. The photo turns out perfect, and Owen asks me to send it to him.

Both Owen and I are quiet as we journey back to the hotel. I'm resting my head on his shoulder as he leans his head on mine.

"I don't know how to thank you for today," I say, interrupting the very comfortable silence.

"Thank you for joining me," he says as he kisses the top of my head.

As we travel, I'm trying to push out the impending questions about what happens a few days from now. After so many years without him in my life, I had long ago come to terms with it.

Now I don't know—this vacation has changed everything for me. And I don't know how I'm going to go back to a life without him being a part of it.

Chapter Twenty-Four

*a*fter Owen drops me off at my room, leaving me with a kiss that sends shivers through my body, I finally return Fran's texts and phone calls.

"Cora Fletcher, you have a lot of explaining to do," she scolds. "And before you ask, the cat and I are doing just fine."

I start by telling her about last night and then give her the play-by-play of today's events. I finally realize I've been talking non-stop and she hasn't said a word. I look at my phone to make sure we didn't get disconnected. "Fran, you still there?"

"I'm still here. I'm just processing everything you've told me."

I totally understand what she means. I'm still trying to process it myself. I can't believe I almost didn't come on this vacation then basically came kicking and screaming, and now in just a few days so much has happened.

"How are you feeling about everything?" she asks.

Fran is so good at this stuff. She's such a good listener, and she gives the best advice.

"I'm ... actually I'm not sure how I am. My mind is spinning right now." I tell her about how much I loved spending the day with Owen, but it also makes me sad knowing this won't last.

"And how do you know it won't last? Did you two talk about it?"

I gasp. "No, of course not. I didn't want to ruin a perfect day by asking what happens next. For all I know, this is nothing more than a vacation fling. We're both here, we're single, we have a history, and this place is super romantic. It's the perfect scenario."

"That's understandable." She stops talking, which means she's probably reading my aura, if she can do that over the phone. "You know the subject of what happens next has to come up at some point."

"I know, and I'm okay with discussing it *when* it comes up."

I look at the time. "Fran, I have to get ready for dinner. I don't need my mother fussing at me for being late."

"And you don't want to be late seeing Owen," she teases.

I laugh. "That, too."

I ask her to give Kiwi a hug for me, and we get off the phone. I know she's right about Owen and me having *that* conversation, but at the same time I'm nervous to talk about what comes next and fear this could be it for us.

I try to concentrate on getting ready for dinner while daydreaming about the most perfect date ever. No wonder Alyssa took their breakup so hard, especially if today is a regular example of the kind of man Owen is when in a relationship.

Then again, I'm not so naïve to the fact that Owen was trying to impress me today. And he totally succeeded.

When I arrive in the restaurant fifteen minutes early, I find Peepaw sitting by himself. Wow. This is the first time since we arrived that I've seen him without Evelyn glued to his side. Don't get me wrong, I like her a lot, but it would be nice to spend a few minutes alone with my grandfather.

"Hi, Peepaw." I lean down and give him a kiss on the cheek.

"Hello, dear girl. How are you tonight?"

I don't wait a second longer to tell him about my experience visiting the Pearl Harbor memorial, conveniently leaving out the view from the sky, of course. I know it's not a big deal to share that part of the story with him, but I'm not ready to get into it yet. It will be common knowledge soon enough.

"It's quite a place. Very peaceful," he says with a serious tone in his voice. "I'm glad you took the time out to see it."

"Me, too. I just finished reading a book about it, and it was on the top of my list of places to visit."

He gives me a thoughtful smile. "You remind me so much of your grandmother. She had a true love for learning just like you."

This isn't the first time I've heard him say this, but I still love to hear it. Especially since I feel like such an outcast in my family sometimes. Hearing that I remind him of my grandmother makes me happy, like I fit in somewhere.

"I know, and I'm very proud of that."

"You should be. She was incredible," he says softly. "She was kind, patient, and selfless. Those are necessary qualities you need to put up with this wild bunch."

No kidding.

"She was beautiful too," he adds. "You have her eyes."

This is also true. I look like my dad, who looks like his mother.

I notice a sad expression come across my grandfather's face. I imagine it's still hard to talk about her, even several years after her death.

"Where's Evelyn?"

Shifting the focus onto something happy might help to lighten the mood.

"She's getting her hair done." He looks at his watch. "She should be down very soon."

I put my hand on his arm. "She's a nice lady, and it's obvious she adores you."

He sits up straight and proud, "Can you blame her? I'm a pretty good catch."

I laugh. "I don't blame her one bit. You're definitely one of the best."

I knew changing the subject would bring a smile back to his face. As wonderful as it is to spend time with him alone, I know Evelyn means a lot to him.

"I'm glad she makes you so happy," I tell him. "You deserve it more than anyone."

He shakes his head. "Well, mostly everyone. What about you?"

I lean my head to the side. "What about me?"

"Are you happy?" he asks, giving me a curious look.

Am I happy?

What a question. I think, like most people, I go through the motions of life, and I'm generally a happy and content person. If he's referring to right this second, I'm over the moon after the day I had.

This makes me wonder if I could I be happy with Owen. I haven't been around him in many years, and I don't know his day-to-day habits. But I know the way he makes me feel. And I love that I can be myself around him, quirks and all.

"Right at this moment, I'm very happy because I'm here talking to you."

He gives me a skeptical look. "I'm pretty swell, but I have a feeling I'm not the reason for your current mood. Are you going to tell me what's made you light up like a Christmas tree … or should I say *who?*"

"Hello, Cara."

I turn around to see Evelyn has finally joined us, and I stand up to greet her. I don't even bother correcting her at this point. She's in her eighties, and she's convinced my name is Cara, so *Cara* it is.

"Hi, Evelyn. You look very nice," I say, giving her a hug. "I love your hair."

"Yes, you do look lovely," Peepaw chimes in.

Evelyn sits down next to him, and he kisses her hand.

"You look very pretty too, Cara," she says. "I recognize a woman in love when I see one."

I freeze. *In love?* What's she saying? I laugh nervously. "I'm not sure what you're talking about."

She raises her eyebrows. "Sure you are."

Damn, this woman is good. I'm not saying I'm in love, but I definitely have strong feelings for Owen. I find it interesting that Evelyn barely knows me and can't even remember my name, but she senses the connection Owen and I have.

"Speaking of love. What about you two?" I ask, purposely trying to change the subject. "How long before you take your relationship to the next level?"

I hint around, hoping to find out more about the top-secret announcement I overheard them discussing.

"You never know what can happen," Peepaw says. "I like to keep some mystery alive, and right now we're enjoying each other's company."

Evelyn looks at him adoringly.

"How exciting," I gush. "I can't wait to see what's next for you."

He winks at me. "Likewise."

We continue to chat while we wait for the rest of the group to arrive. Slowly but surely everyone, including Ken and Alaina, joins us for dinner. I guess this means they aren't leaving, which makes me happy. Not only for my mom's sake, but because I like having them here.

When Owen arrives, he doesn't hesitate for a second and takes the seat next to me, then casually puts his arm on the back of my chair.

"Hi," he says with a huge grin on his face.

I say hi and pray my face isn't beet red. I place my hands on my cheeks.

"Don't worry. You're not blushing," he whispers. "But, what do you think would happen if I kissed you right now?"

Okay, so now I'm blushing. "Sounds good to me," I whisper back.

He gives me a mischievous smile.

A few seconds later Ashley makes a grand entrance. She's wearing a halter top with a long maxi skirt. Her very toned stomach is showing, and as usual she looks like a fitness model. She sits down on the other side of Owen and slides her chair a little closer to his.

"Hey, you," she says, nudging him with her elbow.

I give the girl credit. She goes after what she wants.

Jackson is the last to arrive, and he doesn't look happy. Maybe the novelty of the Fletcher family fun has worn off? I'm sure the combination of my rejection and Tara leaving early has put a damper on his vacation. He grabs a menu but not before glaring at Owen, who still has his arm on the back of my chair.

Admittedly, I feel bad for Jackson. I never wanted to add more pain to this situation. Unfortunately, his joining us on this trip and my not changing my mind about our relationship probably opened an old wound. Even if he's okay with being friends, rejection never feels good.

"Hello, everyone," my father says. All of a sudden, silence falls over the table. "Leann and I are so happy you're all still here with us. I know things have been tense, but tomorrow night is our big anniversary party, and we wanted to share some exciting news about the evening we have in store for you."

More exciting news? I wonder if this has anything to do with Peepaw and Evelyn's announcement. I'm not sure I can take much more. So far I've made it through the family fun without taking a Xanax, but I have it ready in case something major blows up.

"Tomorrow night, right before the anniversary party, Leann and I will be renewing our wedding vows at sunset."

Cheers and excitement erupt from everyone at the table.

I watch as my mom reaches over and takes his hand in hers. She has tears in her eyes, and she places her hand on his face.

It's a very sweet gesture, and I can understand why she's been working so hard to get Jackson and me back together. She wants me to experience the exact joy she's feeling right now. There's a part of me that feels guilty about giving her such a hard time. Watching my parents together does give me hope for my future. I want to find love, and the same kind of love my grandparents had for all those years. I deserve that as much as anyone, and I wish the same for Jackson.

"It would mean so much to us if you could all make an effort for the remainder of this vacation. We brought you all here because you all mean so much to us."

I notice Aunt DeeDee look down at her plate. Maybe she feels guilty about the way she's acted, or maybe she doesn't. She's definitely quieter tonight than she has been, or she might just be sober. It's only seven o'clock though, plenty of drinking hours ahead of her.

"We're hoping tomorrow evening will be a night to remember for all of us," my mother adds.

I give Owen a side-glance, and he looks at me and winks.

Thankfully, everyone has their party manners on for the rest of the evening.

The interesting thing is Owen has made several not so subtle gestures showing his interest in me, but no one has noticed. Well, except Jackson, who at one point drains his glass while Owen and I have our heads together. He's showing me a cat video on his phone, so most people would never pick up on us being anything more than friends.

And maybe we're just good friends who have kissed a few times? Even though we've admitted our feelings for one another, I still don't know how to label our situation. The fact is, we have separate lives waiting for us back home, and a lot to talk about.

Just when I'm feeling comfortable with Owen's arm not leaving the back of my chair, Brynn has to be the one to sabotage my enjoyment. What else is new?

"Cora, what did you do today?" she asks.

I notice the other conversations die down while waiting for my answer. Oh well, it's now or never.

I clear my throat. "Owen and I went out and explored the island. I was just telling Peepaw about our visit to the Pearl Harbor monument."

"We're going there tomorrow," Alaina chimes in. "Ken's father went to Japan during the war."

Miraculously my explanation sparks a conversation about history among everyone at the table. I look at Brynn and shrug my shoulders while she looks away.

Hah! Like I didn't figure out what she was trying to do by calling me out in front of the whole table. She thinks she's so crafty, but I know how she operates.

"Not one of them batted an eyelash when you said we hung out today," Owen says under his breath.

I pick up my water glass and take a sip. "That shows you how truly uninterested they are in my life," I whisper from behind my glass. "Well, except for Maya and my mom, of course. Sometimes I wonder if they only want Jackson to be a member of the family because they adore him. It might have nothing to do with me. Maybe they should just adopt him, although I don't think my dad cares either way."

He's right though—not one person questioned Owen and me hanging out today. That proves how shocked they'd be if something romantic happened between us.

"Well, Jackson is definitely bothered by us hanging out," he adds. "He just walked out."

I look over, and Jackson's no longer at the table.

"Oh, no. Did he say something before he left? I wasn't paying attention."

Suddenly I feel incredibly sorry for Jackson. I don't want to hurt his feelings any more than I already have, but what can I do? I'm not going to stop my life because he can't move on. He didn't have to come here.

"Cara, what other places did you visit today?" Evelyn asks, leaning over to me.

"Cora," Owen corrects her.

She laughs and shakes her head. Seriously though, does she think we're kidding?

"I'm glad you two were able to spend some time together," she says softly. "There's something special about this place. It draws people together."

I glance around the table, but everyone else is immersed in their own conversations.

"It has been magical," I agree.

She reaches over and pats my hand. "Now you hold on to him. He's a good one."

Huh ... I can't figure this woman out. At one moment she seems ditsy and forgetful (hence my constantly incorrect name), but then she says meaningful things that make sense.

"We'll see," I say nervously. Would it be appropriate to tell her about my concerns? It's probably not the place, but I don't know if she'll remember having this conversation after tonight. "The future is very uncertain."

Evelyn gives me a wistful look. "Yes, but sometimes we have everything we need right in front of us. Take some advice from someone who's a little older than you—don't waste a single moment, or life just might pass you by."

I'm about to say something else, when my mother asks Evelyn a question.

Ashley is now talking to Owen about her vegan meal plan. I can't help but notice the way she leans her chin on her hand while she's talking to him. If she gets any closer to him, she'll be in his lap.

Surprisingly Jackson returns a few minutes later with another drink in his hand. I can tell by his mannerisms that he's pretty buzzed.

I quickly grab my phone out of my bag and text Maya.

> I THINK JACKSON IS GETTING DRUNK. CAN HUNTER GET HIM TO
> SLOW DOWN?

She looks at her phone and then at Jackson, who's now telling Shawn a story about a time when he and his friends chased a coyote through the foothills. I've never heard this story, but it wouldn't shock me if it was true.

I watch as Maya whispers in Hunter's ear. He shrugs his shoulders like it isn't a big deal. Not that I'm surprised by is reaction, Hunter is so oblivious to things around him if it doesn't have to do with himself. He's by far one of the most narcissistic people I've ever met.

Oh well, I probably should stay out of it anyway, because what Jackson does isn't my business.

We're finishing dinner when my mother speaks up. "Attention, ladies. I'm calling an emergency meeting in my room immediately after dinner."

No! I was really looking forward to spending the evening with Owen.

At the same time, Ken announces that the men are taking my dad out for his 40th anniversary bachelor party. Hmmm ... I had no idea that existed. I'm afraid to think about it.

Owen looks at me, and we both frown.

"I guess this means I won't see you tonight?" he says under his breath.

Ugh. He's right though. I would bet money that my mother has every intention of keeping us girls busy for the remainder of the night.

"What's this emergency meeting about?" Ashley asks.

My mom rubs her hands together like she has some big elaborate plan. Oh hell, I don't even want to know.

"Well, it's not actually a meeting," she says. "It's more like an anniversary bachelorette party. If the men can celebrate, so can we. We're having a ladies' night out."

I should've known. I can see it now—my mother wearing a bright pink feather boa, doing shots, and prancing around like it's her last night of single life.

"Let's do this, Warner," Jackson yells, startling me. He walks over to my dad and picks him up in a bear hug.

I give Maya a knowing look. I told her he was getting drunk.

Owen leans over and whispers in my ear, "I don't want to go to a fortieth anniversary bachelor party."

I laugh. "I'll switch with you. I'd much rather hang with my father tonight."

"I wish I could see you later."

Why are my parents doing this?

"Owen, come on, bro," Shawn calls, interrupting our moment.

Seriously, sometimes I hate my brother.

Owen tells me good-bye after the guys call him again. They start chanting my father's name as they leave the restaurant.

This isn't how I expected my evening to go, but I need to roll with it. Unfortunately, my time to spend with Owen is quickly dwindling.

Chapter Twenty-Five

We're back at The Volcano, and as I feared, my mom is acting more and more like a bachelorette as the night goes on. She's drinking colorful beverages, and somehow she's found a pink feather boa. I don't know where she got that thing. Alaina and Aunt DeeDee are both buzzed and taking turns glaring at the other. I fear another altercation could occur before the night is over.

I can't believe I'm spending my night babysitting these women instead of hanging out with Owen.

"You and Shawn should come out to Lake Tahoe with us," I overhear Aunt DeeDee say to Brynn. "We'd have a good ol' time."

Brynn takes a sip of her drink. "Yes! I love Tahoe."

I'm glad Brynn is keeping her busy. The more we keep her and Alaina apart the better.

I glance at Alaina, who's sitting at a table by herself. She's swaying her head to the music and sipping on the same drink my mother has.

"You doing okay?" I ask.

She pats the seat next to her. "I'm having a great time," she says slowly. "I don't do these ladies' nights very often."

All of a sudden I see Brynn run over to the DJ. She whispers something in his ear, and he nods his head. A few seconds later Snoop Dogg's voice comes over the speaker, and the DJ calls my mother and her friends out onto the dance floor. Alaina and DeeDee get up from their seats, and I watch as the three of them try to drop it like it's hot, and surprisingly they're doing a pretty good job.

Evelyn seems to be having a great time, too. I think we were all shocked when she smacked our server on the butt and called him a hunk. I'm hoping we don't end up at some male revue after this. I may never recover from watching these women stuff dollar bills into Speedos.

"Are you getting sleepy, Cora?" Brynn asks, swaying to the music. "It is a little late for you, right?"

I take another sip of my wine and plaster a fake smile on my face. "I feel pretty good tonight, but thanks for checking on me. It's so nice to know you care so much."

She smirks and leans closer to me. "I know what's going on with you."

I lean even closer to her. "I don't care what you *think* you know."

Brynn's expression changes. Maybe I surprised her when I didn't freak out about what she thinks she knows. And maybe she does know about Owen and me. At this point I honestly don't care what she says or what my family finds out.

Owen and I agreed we aren't keeping our, um, *friendship* a secret. We sat together at dinner, and although we weren't all over each other like my brother and Brynn are during meals, we were appropriately affectionate. It's not my fault my family is oblivious to me except when it's convenient for them.

"Does that mean you're ready to tell everyone?" Brynn asks snidely.

"Tell everyone what?" Ashley asks, putting her martini down on the table.

A mischievous grin spreads across Brynn's face. She lives to torture me, but I'm not going to give her the satisfaction of taunting me.

"Brynn was just asking about where Owen and I went today."

Ashley narrows her eyes. "Where did you go?"

Damn. If looks could kill, I'd be in trouble right now.

"I told you at dinner," I say with a shrug. "We explored the island."

I give them a quick rundown of all the places we saw, on land of course.

"Cora, are you interested in Owen?" Ashley asks. "I thought you were all like siblings."

Brynn folds her arms tightly against her chest. "I was asking Cora the same question."

"Yoo-hooo. I need all my girls out here on the dance floor," my mom yells.

Ashley, Brynn, and I turn to look at her.

She's clearly surpassed her alcohol tolerance for the day (or year). She's swaying her arms in the air, and she's barefoot. I think it's time to take her back to our hotel.

I walk away from Brynn and Ashley and their inquisition, and I grab Maya, who's laughing at something Evelyn is saying.

"Maya, we need to get Mom back her room. She's completely smashed."

Just as Maya looks over my shoulder, the inevitable happens, and my mother vomits all over the floor. Well, this is a first for us, having to put our mother to bed after a night of partying. At least she can now say she had an authentic anniversary bachelorette party.

After apologizing to the manager, Maya and I manage to get our mother downstairs and outside before she vomits again. The others are close behind.

"Sweet Leann has always been such a lightweight," Aunt DeeDee says. It's so nice of her to be supportive of the woman who paid for her vacation.

"I have the best girls," my mother slurs, touching our faces. I try to hold my breath and not gag over the stench of fresh vomit.

Somehow we make it all the way up the elevator without my mother getting sick again, and we get her cleaned up and into bed. She's snoring as soon as her head hits the pillow.

My father hasn't returned from his bachelor party yet, which makes me wonder what the men are up to.

"Hopefully she's okay tomorrow," Maya whispers. "You know how upset she'll be if the party and ceremony don't go perfectly."

I nod as I shut the hotel room door quietly behind me. We walk down the hall toward our rooms.

"Can you believe this vacation is almost over?" she asks.

Ugh. I don't want to be reminded.

I frown. "I know."

She eyes me curiously.

"Well, look at you. You're actually having a good time. I guess it's a good thing I made such a big deal about you being here."

I giggle. "Don't you mean it's a good thing you gave me a guilt trip about not being here for our parents?"

She shrugs nonchalantly. "Whatever. You're here, aren't you? You owe me."

My little sister is very proud of herself right now. And she's right, her guilt trip is one of the reasons I finally decided to come. Now I'd hate to think what would've happened if I hadn't.

"Fine, I owe you, Maya. Thank you for making me realize I was meant to be here."

She puts her arm around me. "Does this mean you're over the Jackson thing and you forgive me?"

I purse my lips. The truth is, I'm not upset about it anymore. Although not ideal, I know their intentions were good. "Yes, I forgive you."

She squeezes my shoulders.

"On one condition," I add.

"What?"

"You accept that Jackson and I won't be getting back together, and no more sneaky plans behind my back. Not Thanksgiving or Christmas, my birthday, or a random Sunday night. No more."

"Okay."

I go on to tell her how much I appreciate that she wants me to find love, and I understand how easy it would be for Jackson to officially be a member of our family.

"I know," she agrees. "It makes me sad, but I understand."

"Thank you."

She's quiet for a few seconds. "Cora, you're going to find someone who completely sweeps you off your feet. I know it."

What if I've already found this person?

"Hopefully you find someone like Hunter. I only want the best for my big sister."

I force a smile. I'm not going to tell I don't want a man like Hunter. Some things are better left unsaid.

We come to Maya's room first and give each other a hug before she goes inside. As I walk to my room, I think about the sister bonding moment Maya and I just shared. That's why we're here, right? Aren't family reunions supposed to be for moments like this, to build stronger relationships with your loved ones?

Although, the thought of Brynn and me bonding makes me cringe.

I remind myself that not all family relationships are perfect, and it's important to at least tolerate each other. I probably should be the better person when it comes to Brynn, and not let her snarky comments bother me. Besides, what's the worst thing she can do? I don't care if she tells everyone about Owen and me. At this point it doesn't matter. Like I told Peepaw earlier tonight, I'm really happy. For now anyway.

I had every intention of getting up and doing one last sunrise yoga practice this morning, but I completely slept through it. I didn't sleep well and was restless for most of the night. I kept waking up, thinking about Owen and going home tomorrow. I want to know if we're going to continue this after we leave Hawaii. If this is it for us, I'll try to deal with it. I hate not knowing.

I received a text from Owen telling me the men got back in the early morning hours from their bachelor party fishing excursion. It sounds like the perfect party for my father, fishing in the middle of the night with a bunch of men. What a way to celebrate his last night of being married for thirty-nine years. *That sounds so weird.* And I'm sure he didn't get wasted and vomit everywhere like my mother did. She wanted a big celebration, but I doubt that's what she had in mind.

Even though I don't make it to yoga, I force myself to get out of bed and throw on some joggers and a T-shirt. It's my last full day here on the island, my plan is to find a great spot on the beach and relax (hopefully with Owen).

Naturally, breakfast comes first.

I make my way downstairs and find Ashley sitting at a table with half of a grapefruit and her laptop. I hesitate at the entrance for a few seconds. But, I'd rather deal with Ashley than Brynn.

"Morning."

She looks up from the screen. "Oh, good morning, Cora."

I grab a cup of coffee and sit down at the table with her.

"How's Aunt Leann today? I imagine she's feeling pretty bad."

I stir my coffee. "I haven't talked to her yet today, but I agree with you. I can guarantee she's going to wake up feeling miserable."

We both grow quiet. I'm not sure what to say.

"What are you doing?" I ask, pointing to her computer.

"Checking emails. It's back to the grind tomorrow."

I hang my head at the reminder. "Unfortunately." I take a sip of my coffee, and we're both quiet as she taps away on her keyboard.

"I'm okay with leaving. I have two trips coming up, and I'm having my apartment redecorated," she says not looking up from the screen.

At least she knows what's next.

"Have you seen anyone else this morning?" I ask. "It seems really quiet, so I can only assume everyone else is sleeping off their bachelor and bachelorette parties."

She finishes typing and closes her laptop. "I haven't seen anyone down here, but I did see something very interesting this morning when I returned from yoga."

My curiosity is piqued, and when it comes to this family, it could be anything.

"Ooohhh, tell me."

She cradles her coffee in her hands. "After I finished with yoga, I ran up to my room to get my laptop. When I came out of the room, I saw an absolutely gorgeous woman at Owen's door. I hung back for a few seconds, and then I saw her go inside. Unfortunately, I was too far away to hear what they were saying."

I feel a twinge of jealousy shoot through my body.

"I don't know who she was, but *she was stunning*," she says adamantly.

I don't reply as I try to process what she's telling me. Okay, so a woman went into Owen's room. I'm sure there's a good reason. Housekeeping? Concierge? A co-worker?

"Maybe the woman you saw works here at the hotel?" I ask. It definitely could be the concierge. Owen was able to book and plan a full day of excursions in a matter of hours. That has to be it. Maybe he's planning something else? Wishful thinking, but I don't want to assume the worst.

Ashley shakes her head. "No way. The woman I saw was on vacation. She was wearing a very short backless dress and a wide-brimmed hat. Oh, and her shoes were to die for."

I'm trying not to overthink this. There has to be a good explanation.

"Anyway, I guess that's my answer about Owen and me having some fun together," Ashley says with a laugh. "Not like it's some huge loss. I was just looking for someone to keep me company while I was here. Obviously he had other plans."

I take another sip of my coffee. I'm so confused right now.

Before I can ask any more questions, Ashley packs up her laptop.

"I'm going to hit the spa one last time. You want to come?"

I shake my head. "Thanks, but I should probably check on my mom," I reply.

She blows me a kiss good-bye and leaves me alone with my thoughts.

I take my phone out of my bag and stare at it. I want to send Owen a message, but what do I say?

I heard you have a woman in your room. Does she know we spent the whole day together yesterday?

Gah. The last thing I want to do is appear possessive and stalker-ish. It's best for me not to say anything because he doesn't owe me any explanation. If he chooses to tell me about this woman later, that's up to him. We had a lot of fun yesterday, and we're obviously attracted to one another, but at the end of the day, he has his life in San Diego, and I have my life.

I put my phone back in my bag without sending him a message. I'll be home soon enough, and this vacation and my time with Owen will be a distant memory.

I wish I believed this.

I decide to drown my confusion in a big plate of waffles.

No matter what happens today, I know I made the right decision to come on this trip. I needed to be here with my family, good or bad. It's time for to me to move on from past issues and embrace the fact I'm a Fletcher, differences and all.

Chapter Twenty-Six

"Thank you, Cora Ann," my mother says placing a cold towel on her forehead.

After my very interesting and informative conversation with Ashley, I go to my parents' room to check on my mother after her big night. Sure enough, I find her lying in the bed, drinking a cup of coffee.

It's official, my mother is hungover.

"What was I thinking last night?" she whines. "I'm not in my twenties anymore. To think I could drink that much was a terrible mistake, and now I'm paying for it."

I sit on the edge of the bed next to her. "Mom, how much did you have to drink?"

She shakes her head. "Only a few glasses of wine at dinner. Then the bartender at the Volcano place was making drinks for us. They were so fruity and delicious, I had a few of those. I guess I didn't realize how they would affect me. I can assure you I won't be doing this again."

I look over at the beautiful white dress hanging on the closet door. "Your dress is stunning, Mom."

She nods from under her washcloth. "I had to get it taken in two times after I did the keto diet thing."

My mother has always been health conscious, so when she decided to eat keto, I wasn't surprised. She even forced my dad to change his diet. He said he wouldn't complain as long as he could have bacon and coffee. And he made it obvious that he embraced his new fit lifestyle— he proved that when we did his airport exercise class.

"Cora Ann, are you okay?" my mom asks worriedly. "You seem distracted this morning. You're not getting sick, are you? I can't afford for you to get me sick on our last day of vacation, and we have to fly tomorrow."

She covers her mouth with her hand while I shake my head. "Mom, I'm fine."

She takes the washcloth off her head. "I hope so." She rubs her temples. "Anyway, I'm glad you're here because I've been thinking I owe you a huge apology, honey."

I really don't want to get into this. I'm tired of this same conversation. "Mom, you don't—"

She holds up her hand. "No, please hear me out."

I let out a sigh while she continues. As expected she gives me the same story about why she invited Jackson and how she wants me to be happy. How many times do I have to hear this? Perhaps the guilt of trying to force Jackson and me together has officially taken over.

"I know things can be complicated with this family," she continues. "But I want you to know we all love you very much."

I swallow the lump in my throat. "Thanks, I appreciate you saying that. Sometimes it's hard to find my place."

She sits up with a huge groan. "You don't have to *find* your place; you have a place. You're my Cora Ann."

Just then my father comes into the room with a shopping bag in his hand. My mother lies back down and replaces the washcloth on her forehead.

"Hey, Dad."

"Good morning. How's my favorite girl today?"

I stand up from the bed and give him a hug. "Mom's doing okay."

He chuckles. "I'm glad to hear, but I was talking about you this time." He begins to unload his bag of items that should help cure my mother's hangover. Bananas, Gatorade, pickles...

"Now, let's get you back in tip-top shape," he exclaims. "We have a big night ahead of us."

"Don't remind me, Warner," Mom wails. "Those damn fruity drinks. I'm convinced they lace those things with something so you keep drinking them. I really should press charges."

I glance at my father and try to hide my smile.

We spend the next few minutes googling the fastest way to get rid of hangovers. There are more remedies than I ever imagined. Unfortunately, there isn't enough time for her to sleep it off. I hang out in my parents' room for a while, and before long my mom begins to act like her old self. By the time I'm ready to leave, she's out of bed and threatening to go back to The Volcano to give the bartenders a piece of her mind.

The truth is I don't want to leave my parents' room. I feel safe with them, and it's a good distraction from Owen and the mystery woman.

When I finally return to my room, I check my phone. A wave of disappointment comes over me because there's still no word from Owen. After much contemplation, I send him a casual text, asking him how he slept and what his plans are for the day. I also mention I'm heading out to the beach on the chance he'll decide he wants to join me. I hold my finger over the send button for a few seconds and read through the text two more times. I decide to hurry up and send it before I change my mind. Then I call Fran.

"How do you know Ashley's not lying?" Fran asks calmly.

I kick off my flip-flops and stretch out on my bed. "She's not lying. Why would she fabricate a story about seeing someone go to his room?" I ask, rubbing my forehead. "She gave a very detailed description of the woman, down to her shoes. I know she wasn't making it up."

"So, maybe she exaggerated," Fran says. "It's possible she wanted to discourage you because she saw the strong connection you two have."

I groan. "I guess it's possible. Brynn was trying to start drama at the bachelorette party last night. Ashley asked me if I was interested in Owen, but our conversation was interrupted when Mom puked all over the place."

Hmm ... this makes me wonder. Could Brynn be involved in this somehow? Wow, I'm really reaching now.

"Cora, why don't you ask him?"

Is she serious? Because I would sound like a stalker. I don't want him to think I'm watching him. That's extreme, even for me.

"Fran, I'm not going to blurt out that Ashley saw a woman go into his room. It's none of my business who he's hanging out with anyway."

"It is your business," she exclaims. "He went above and beyond to wine and dine you yesterday. There's a very good explanation. I feel it in my gut."

She continues her exposition. "Remember, not everything is how it appears," she says knowingly. "I don't believe the universe would bring you back together after all this time for it to be meaningless."

I sigh loudly. "I don't know what to think. But again, he doesn't have to explain anything to me. We had a great time together yesterday, and we're going home tomorrow."

I'm interrupted by the sound of a text coming in.

> I'M SORRY I HAVEN'T BEEN IN TOUCH TODAY. TAKING CARE OF SOMETHING THAT CAME UP UNEXPECTEDLY. LOOKING FORWARD TO SEEING YOU LATER.

A feeling of relief washes over me as I read the text to Fran.

"There you go. He responded and apologized for not being in touch," she says, sounding proud of herself. "I knew there was a reason, so don't get discouraged. Take some cleansing breaths and find a quiet corner to meditate."

She's right—well, about everything except the meditating. I can't let this ruin my last day here, and he mentioned seeing me later, which makes me feel better.

"Okay, I'm going to the beach. I will let you know what happens later."

"Good for you," she says. "Enjoy your day and try not to worry."

I thank her for listening and end the call.

I read Owen's message one more time before responding.

ME, TOO. HOPE EVERYTHING IS OKAY.

I grab my beach bag and head out for my last relaxing day in paradise.

I'm going to miss this.

I lie back on my lounge chair and watch the waves hit the shore. I've been trying to read all morning, but I'm really distracted. And yes, because of Owen.

We had such a great day yesterday and I can't for the life of me understand what's going on with him today. He said something came up that he had to take care of. Maybe it has to do with his job? I can't even count how many times Alaina has mentioned she's been worried about him overworking himself. It's probably something as simple as that.

At the same time, I'm starting to doubt my decision to be so honest with him about my feelings. Maybe spending all day with him yesterday wasn't the best idea. I knew going into it we'd be going home, but I was happy to be with him, so in that moment I didn't care.

The sad part is I was looking forward to spending more time with him today because I knew this was it. Then again, the more I think about it, not seeing him today will probably make leaving easier.

I go back to my book and try to find the place I left off, but no such luck. I sigh loudly as I put the book down and stare out at the ocean. Out of the corner of my eye, I see Jackson walking toward me.

Damn. I don't know if I can handle any more stress today.

"Hi, is anyone sitting here?" he asks, pointing to the chair next to me.

I shake my head. "It's all yours."

He sits down and scans the beach. Neither of us says anything for a few seconds.

"How's your day been so far?" I ask finally.

As I feared, our interaction feels awkward and forced.

"It's been great. Hunter and I hiked Mount Ka'ala this morning."

I don't know what he's talking about, so I ask him.

"It's a very rigorous seven-mile climb. It was challenging but fun. I needed it today."

I ask him more questions and listen intently because I'd rather talk about hiking than him and me or Owen and me.

"How about you? I'm surprised you aren't with Owen today."

Aha, I knew it was a matter of time before he brought Owen up. I press my lips together while I think about how to respond. "Actually, I had plans to do exactly this on my last day, relax and read on the beach."

This is totally true because Owen and I didn't make set plans. Even though I was hoping to spend the day with him, of course I don't tell Jackson that.

He smiles. "Sounds perfect. It is your favorite thing to do."

I nod.

"Cora, I owe you an apology, actually several apologies."

Wow, between my mother, Maya, and now Jackson, I've been getting a lot of apologies in the last twenty-four hours.

He looks down as he twists his fingers around each other.

"Jackson, it's okay."

He holds up his hand. "Please let me say this. Cora, I shouldn't have come on this trip. I knew why I was invited, and although part of me that was hopeful we could figure *us* out, I've known it was over for a while now. I think I got caught up in the mood and the excitement of being here with you."

I reach over and put my hand on his arm. "I completely understand. This island is magical, and it's hard not to want to share it with someone else."

My brain immediately rushes back to the helicopter ride with Owen yesterday. The knot in the pit of my stomach is growing as I think about him and another woman in his room.

"About that ... what's really going on with you and Owen?" He stops. "Sorry, you don't have to tell me. I'm just curious."

I chew on my lip. It should probably feel weird to talk to Jackson about another man, but for some reason it doesn't.

"Owen and I have known each other our whole lives. We were both heading out to see the island yesterday, so we went together." I push my sunglasses up on my nose.

Jackson leans his head to the side. "Huh, well if you want my opinion, there's more between you and him than a childhood friendship. I can tell by the way he looks at you."

Now this is definitely not a conversation I imagined myself having with Jackson.

"We're comfortable around each other. Sometimes it's easy when you have a history." I pause and bite my lip. "Don't get me wrong. I enjoy spending time with him, but we live over two hundred miles from each other. I don't see us getting together very often after this."

Jackson shakes his head. "Interesting."

"What?"

"That's a lot of excuses. You must have intense feelings for him, or you wouldn't be trying so hard to justify it."

I open my mouth to disagree but stop myself. Honestly, what's the point because he's right. "It doesn't matter what I feel. Like I said, we have our own careers, homes, and live in different cities. Feelings or not, it just won't work."

Jackson reaches over and takes my hand in his. "Cora, you deserve to be happy more than any person I know. Last night I watched the two of you interact, and although it bothered me, I could see how happy you were with him."

I squeeze his hand. "I'm sorry, Jackson. I know this must be difficult for you. You deserve to be happy, too. That's why I keep saying you should be with someone who wants to experience all the excitement life has to offer."

In other words, I don't want to talk about Owen anymore.

Thankfully, he takes the hint and goes to the bar to get us some drinks.

While he's gone, his words replay in my mind. I didn't think I was imagining the connection Owen and I had, and it really seemed like he felt the same. I check my phone, and there's a message from him. My stomach does a flip.

> ARE YOU STILL AT THE BEACH? CAN WE MEET UP BEFORE THE PARTY? I HAVE TO TELL YOU SOMETHING.

Okay, Cora, calm down.

I'm not going to drop everything and run to him, even though I'm anxious to hear what he has to tell me.

I look back at the bar where Jackson is still getting us drinks.

After giving it some thought, I reply to his message.

> STILL AT THE BEACH. WANT TO COME DOWN? OR I CAN MEET UP IN AN HOUR.

I put my phone down and wait for his reply.

Jackson returns and hands me a club soda. "I heard Leann got smashed at the bachelorette party. I wish I could've seen her in that state."

I laugh. "You didn't miss much, although I don't think we'll be welcome at The Volcano ever again. Mom says she wants to press charges against them for serving her delicious drinks."

"At least you didn't go on a midnight fishing trip," he says. "It was a bad idea because I was already pretty buzzed. Throw in the motion of the boat, and the smell of fish—"

He stops talking and pretends to gag. "I fell asleep on the boat and barely remember most of it."

He's right though—it doesn't sound as interesting as our night at The Volcano.

I ask him about Tara, and as expected he figured out very quickly just how chaotic her life is when she left in such a hurry.

"She was cool but too high maintenance." He pauses. "Although we did talk about going sky diving together."

Apparently, this is something they both always wanted to try. And this is a perfect example of why Jackson and I aren't compatible. There's no way in hell I would ever jump out of a plane.

We end up sitting on the beach and talking for a while before he heads out to go kayaking. I pack up my stuff and make my way back to the hotel. On my way I send Owen a text.

HEADING BACK TO MY ROOM NOW.

I'm in my room for about two minutes when my phone buzzes. I'm disappointed that it's a message from Maya.

MOM HAS OFFICIALLY LOST HER MIND. SHE WANTS US TO BE BRIDESMAIDS AT THE CEREMONY.

What the hell? Do you have bridesmaids when you renew your vows? Then again, I didn't think you were supposed to have bachelor and bachelorette parties either, but what do I know? I type a quick response.

ARE YOU KIDDING?

My phone buzzes a few seconds later.

NOPE. COME TO MOM'S ROOM ASAP. HURRY. SHE'S IN EMERGENCY MODE.

I sigh. Another emergency according to my mother. I get two more text messages from Maya in the ten minutes it takes me to change.

On my way to my mother's hotel room, I send Owen a follow up text.

CHANGE OF PLANS, HAVE TO HELP MOM GET READY FOR THE CEREMONY. HOPEFULLY IT WON'T TAKE TOO LONG.

My phone buzzes with another text from Maya.

I sigh. I should've known this wouldn't be a relaxing vacation day. The Fletcher family reunion isn't over yet, and I'm sure it's going to finish off with a bang.

Chapter Twenty-Seven

*T*he good news is my mother's hangover is completely gone, but the bad news is she's in full-blown bridezilla, or anniversary-zilla, mode. I don't know if that's a thing, but it is now.

Maya was right, she's in rare form. As soon as I arrive at her room, she asks me what I'm wearing to the ceremony and party. She seems happy when I tell her about my pale pink halter dress.

"I'm wearing a pink dress, too," Maya says.

"Pink is good. Now we're just waiting on Brynn," Mom says, breathing a sigh of relief.

I scowl. Oh, joy. I should've known Brynn would be a bridesmaid, too.

"Mom, what about Alaina?" I ask. "She's your best friend."

My mother continues to dig through her suitcase and pulls out three different pairs of shoes.

"Alaina wanted to be a part of the ceremony but decided she didn't want any more backlash from DeeDee." She holds up the shoes against her dress. "Which shoes look the best?"

A few minutes later Brynn shows up, and as expected she begins offering suggestions as soon as she walks through the door.

Mom motions for us to quiet down when she gets on the phone with Kalaina the concierge. She's talking really fast about setup and flowers.

"How's your day been, Cora?" Brynn asks sweetly. She loves to put on this fake act in front of my mother.

"It's been fine," I reply as I organize the mess my mother is making.

"Okay, girls, let's go out to the beach to check the setup," Mom says as soon as she gets off the phone. She takes a long sip of her coffee. Personally, I think she's had enough for the day, but I keep my opinion to myself.

Brynn claps excitedly and links arms with my mother. Maya and I groan and follow behind.

As soon as we get to the elevator, the door opens and Owen steps out.

I suck in a breath.

"Hello, ladies," Owen says, giving me a weak smile.

"Hi, sweetie," Mom says. "We can't chat right now. We're on a mission."

Brynn throws a side glance at me.

"A mission? Very exciting," Owen says, raising an eyebrow. He's been around long enough to know you don't mess with Leann Fletcher when she's on a mission.

My mom, Brynn, and Maya step into the elevator.

Now is my chance to talk to him for a few seconds. "Mom, I'm going to run to my room and use the restroom really quick. I'll be right behind you."

She holds up her hand to protest. "Cora Ann, you can use the bathroom downstairs. This is urgent," she scolds as she holds the elevator door open for me.

Brynn smirks. I know she's loving every second of this.

Rather than make a scene, I step into the elevator.

"I'll see you all soon," Owen says, shifting his gaze to me.

My heart is absolutely racing.

The door closes, and we journey down to the lobby. My mother is talking a mile a minute about flowers and how to do her hair. Honestly, you would think this was her actual wedding day.

I don't hear a word she's saying because I'm still thinking about Owen and how much I want to talk to him. I'm going straight to his room as soon as I'm free from my mother turned bridezilla.

When we arrive on the beach, there are a few white chairs being set up. The ocean is the perfect backdrop for a romantic ceremony. When and *if* I ever get married, I would love to come back here because this is magnificent.

My mother and Brynn are now talking to the event coordinator, leaving me and Maya to look through the flowers.

"Mom is taking this to a whole other level," I say, touching the petal of an orchid.

"Are you surprised?" Maya exclaims. "When doesn't she go overboard?"

She has a point.

"Well, you're her favorite. Why don't you try to talk her down?"

She opens her eyes wide. "Are you insane? I know better. Besides, I think Brynn's taking my place as Mom's new favorite."

I glance at Mom and Brynn giving instructions. I think Maya's right.

"What's up with you?" Maya asks. "You seem kind of out of it."

I shrug my shoulders. "I think I'm sad about leaving."

One corner of her mouth turns up. "Ahh ... and to think you almost didn't come. It's a good thing I'm such a good sister and talked you into it."

Didn't I just hear this last night? She's never going to let me live it down. We will be old ladies, and she'll be reminding me about this vacation.

"You encouraged me to come, but I would've anyway. Mom probably would've disowned me if I hadn't."

"Cora, Maya," Mom calls.

We hurry over to where she and Brynn are standing. She begins rambling about the position of the sun and which direction she should be standing so she doesn't have shadows on her face for the pictures. After making some adjustments, she's finally satisfied with the setup, and I make my escape.

I rush through the hotel and pound on the elevator button. I'm heading straight for Owen's room because I can't wait any longer to find out what's going on.

～

When I arrive at our floor, I walk to Owen's room and stop. I take a deep breath and knock loudly. I silently pray he's alone inside the room.

A few seconds later he comes to the door.

"Hey. I'm glad you're here. Come in."

He closes the door behind me, and before I can say anything, he wraps his arms around me.

All of a sudden all my doubts and worries vanish. I want to ask him about what happened earlier today, but I'm too busy breathing him in. Being in his arms feels so right, like this is where I'm supposed to be.

"I'm so sorry," he says into my hair. "I really wanted to spend today with you, but this morning was chaotic. Something happened I wasn't expecting."

Something or *someone*?

We both let go of our embrace, and he leads me over to the couch.

"Is everything all right?" I ask worriedly. "You said in your text you had to tell me something."

He lowers his head and nods. "I had a visitor this morning, and it threw my whole day into a tailspin."

I'm assuming that visitor is who Ashley was referring to. My heart is pounding against the wall of my chest.

I clear my throat. "Owen, I should tell you that Ashley mentioned something to me about seeing a woman here this morning. It's totally not my business, but—" I stop before I say something I shouldn't.

He narrows his eyes. "Did she really?"

I shrug. "I mean, it's totally fine because—you can see whomever you want." *Ugh*, I sound so stupid right now as I fumble over my words.

He clinches his jaw. "Alyssa's here."

Wait. *Alyssa?*

"Alyssa—as in your ex-wife?"

He tightens his lips and nods. "Apparently, she saw some photos online of me and my parents here and felt the need to fly all this way."

I'm so confused, but I listen as he continues talking. *Alyssa?* Wow. I wasn't expecting this.

"She showed up at my room this morning when I was on my way to yoga."

This explains why Ashley said the woman she saw was gorgeous. I've seen plenty of pictures of Alyssa, and she is flawless. But I still don't understand why she came all this way. Something about this seems odd to me.

"So she flew to Hawaii to talk to you?"

He runs his hand through his hair. "She says she's been thinking about everything that happened with our marriage, and she wants to know if we can try again. She thought being here in such a romantic destination might help rekindle what we lost." He pauses and rubs his forehead. "Honestly, this came out of the blue. I haven't seen or heard from her in months."

Until now in Hawaii.

My mind is swirling as I try to make sense of this. And suddenly a thought pops into my head. Is it possible?

"Brynn," I say out loud.

Owen gives me a confused look, and then his mouth drops open.

"You really think Brynn would contact her?" he asks.

I shrug. "I'm not sure. She knows about, um, us spending the day together. I don't know if she would actually call her, but I can guarantee she posted the photos."

He stares off into space, and I notice his jaw tighten.

"Alyssa said she saw the photos of me and my parents being here with your family, and it made her think about how much she misses all of us. She had a great relationship with my parents. She also claims she's been wanting to reach out to me for a while, and she finally got up the nerve."

Yeah, I'd say she definitely got up the nerve, considering she flew across the Pacific Ocean to tell him how she felt. Although, Owen is pretty spectacular, so I can't imagine what it would be like to lose him.

And I don't want to.

"So where is she now?"

He shakes his head. "I'm not exactly sure. She said she wanted to see my parents."

I nervously clear my throat. I want to ask him how their conversation ended and more importantly if they're going to give their marriage another try.

"Huh, well this is definitely a surprise. Did you invite her to my parents' anniversary party?"

He frowns. "No, why would I?"

I look out the window to avoid making eye contact with him.

"Hold on. Cora, I hope you don't think we're getting back together."

I bite my lip. "I didn't know …"

He reaches over and takes my hands in his.

"Alyssa and I are over. I told you that. We have been for a long time, even before our divorce."

I feel a wave of relief wash over me … although I still have questions. Mainly, what's going to happen when we leave here tomorrow? I need to be honest with him.

"I'm glad," I say, my voice only slightly above a whisper.

"Are you?" he asks, giving me a worried look.

I nod. "I'm still sad though, because we're leaving tomorrow and going back to our own lives."

He pushes my hair behind my ear. "I was up half the night thinking, and I was hoping we could talk about it today. Then that didn't happen …"

So, he has thought about it, too. At least I know I'm not the only one who's had this on my mind.

We're interrupted by both our phones going off at the same time. I have a pretty good idea as to who's texting.

Owen gets up to check his phone. "Your mother just sent a detailed itinerary for tonight."

I sigh. "I probably should get ready. She called an emergency meeting, and apparently I'm a bridesmaid in this vow renewal ceremony I knew nothing about."

I don't move from my spot on the couch, and Owen sits back down next to me.

He slides an arm around my shoulder. "I really want to continue this conversation," he says as he runs his fingers through my hair. This sends shivers down my spine.

"So do I."

He lifts my chin with his finger. "Cora, I'm not ready for this to end just because we're leaving Hawaii."

My heart begins to race as he presses his lips against mine. He caresses my face with his finger, and I melt under his touch.

There's no way this can end here. I haven't been able to get Owen out of my system for most of my life, and that was before this vacation. Losing him now would be devastating.

I don't know what's going to happen tomorrow, but we still have tonight, and I'm going to make the most of it.

Chapter Twenty-Eight

When I arrive at my mother's room, she's in the bathroom, and Brynn's sitting on the bed. She's wearing a salmon-colored gown with iridescent beading; her hair is in loose curls flowing down her back.

"Cora, you look beautiful," she says with a warm smile. "That color suits you."

I fold my arms and plaster a smile on my face. "You look nice too, Brynn."

She stands up and runs her fingers through her hair.

"This is such an exciting night for your parents," she squeals. "I feel so honored they want to share this milestone with all of us."

I pick up my mother's bouquet and breathe in the glorious floral scent.

"So, I talked to Owen earlier."

She raises her eyebrows. "Oh, how did it go?"

"He's had quite an interesting day," I exclaim, gently placing the bouquet down. "Would you believe Alyssa came all the way here to talk to him?"

She frowns. "What do you mean?"

"Alyssa—you know, his ex-wife—came to Hawaii to talk to him. I guess she saw some pictures posted online. She decided she missed him so much that she wanted to fly out here and tell him she wants to give their marriage another chance."

I smile at her sweetly, but she doesn't smile back. She actually looks kind of upset.

"Is something wrong, Brynn?" I ask innocently.

She opens her mouth to say something when my mother comes out of the bathroom in tears.

"I—I—can't zip it up. It won't zip up. How can this be happening? I'm going to have a panic attack." She begins to fan herself with her hands.

Both Brynn and I rush to help her.

"Calm down, Mom."

"Breathe in slowly," Brynn demands.

"Let me try zipping it up for you."

My mother flops dramatically onto the bed. "I don't know what I was thinking," she wails. "I lost weight to fit into this dress, but I've been eating and drinking since I arrived here, and now it's too snug."

Brynn gets her a glass of water.

"I should've thought this through better," she says, taking a sip of the water. "We could've done the ceremony at the beginning of the week and then eaten and drank and been merry for the remainder of the vacation. What was I thinking?"

She's still having a tantrum when Maya arrives, so we fill her in on the dress being too tight.

"Mom, look at me. You need to relax," Maya says calmly. "Stand up and let me try to zip it up for you."

Of course she stands up when Maya asks her to. Her *baby* girl has the ultimate power of persuasion.

Maya begins to try the zipper.

"What about wearing the dress with body-shaping undergarments?" Brynn suggests.

That's a good idea.

"I didn't bring any with me. I was so proud I wouldn't need them," Mom wails.

Although I understand why she's upset, she's being extremely overdramatic.

"I'm sure someone has a pair you can borrow," Brynn says, looking at me.

I glare at her. It figures she'd suggest I'd be the one to have the undergarments that hold everything in.

"No, Brynn, I don't have any," I snap.

"I was referring to Alaina or DeeDee," she adds.

Sure you were.

I offer to hunt down the body shapers before my mother officially has a panic attack or worse.

I decide to ask Alaina first because I'd prefer to avoid my aunt if possible. When Alaina answers the door, she invites me into her room, and I finally come face-to-face with Owen's ex-wife, Alyssa. She's as beautiful in person as in the pictures I've seen. She's tall with shoulder-length blonde hair and has the longest legs I've ever seen. I feel completely inadequate standing next to her, even though I'm all dressed up.

Alaina puts her arm around my shoulder and introduces me.

"It's nice to finally meet you," Alyssa says. Her voice is very sultry and soothing. "I've heard so much about you, I feel like we know each other."

I'm not sure if she's heard about me from Alaina, Owen, or Brynn.

"You, too. What brings you to Hawaii?"

She and Alaina exchange a glance.

"I had to resolve a few matters."

The mood shifts in the room, and I can tell by Alyssa's expression that she's disappointed with the way things turned out. It takes every ounce of inner strength to hold in my excitement.

"You look gorgeous, Cora. All ready for the big night?" Alaina asks, obviously trying to change the subject.

Crap. Meeting Alyssa totally made me forget why I came here.

"Oh, I almost forgot. Do you have any body shapers? Mom's in major crisis mode."

I explain my mother's dress issue, and Alaina shakes her head.

"She told me it was snug after the alterations. She must be panicking right now."

I snort. "You have no idea."

Alaina digs into her suitcase and produces the coveted garment.

"Alaina, you're a lifesaver. The *Best Friend in the World* award goes to you."

I say a quick good-bye and hurry back to my mother's room. The whole time I'm thinking about what made Alyssa decide to come here. Did Brynn tell her about Owen and me? Would my sister-in-law really stoop so low and try to sabotage my chances with Owen?

As soon as I return, Mom goes to the bathroom, and we wait in silence.

When she comes out, we all hold our breath as Maya tests the zipper on her dress. Slowly but surely it zips up to the top, and we all cheer excitedly.

It's a tight fit, but thankfully she brought a different cocktail dress for the anniversary party (just in case). It's a good thing she doesn't have to sit down during the ceremony or pictures, because I'm not sure how long this dress is going to make it. We will all be holding our breath through the ceremony, Mom especially.

Brynn basks in the success of her brilliant idea, and I wish I had thought of it first because this will go down as a permanent moment in the Fletcher family history. I already know Brynn will tell everyone she meets that she saved her mother-in-law from having a nervous breakdown right before renewing her wedding vows.

Maya, Brynn, and I all adjust our own dresses and touch up our hair and makeup. Finally, we're ready to head down to the beach. Another dramatic crisis averted, and as usual, never a dull moment with the Fletcher clan.

Having the ceremony at sunset was a genius idea. Stunning florals line the path leading out to where the ceremony will take place. In the background the sky is a brilliant mix of pinks, blues, and yellows. Brynn, Maya, and I walk in front of my mom as we make our way across the sand to where my father is standing with Shawn and Hunter.

As we approach the chairs, Owen and I lock eyes. A big smile spreads across his face and causes my heart to beat even faster. I can't wait for this big production to be over so I can finally spend time with him for the remaining hours we have left.

The three of us stand on the opposite side of the men, and we all watch as my mother moves slowly across the sand. My father walks up the path to meet her, and then they approach us together.

The service begins with the minister delivering a captivating speech about eternal love. He talks about finding your soul mate and working together to make a solid union. My parents then read their own set of vows they wrote. I only cringe slightly when my mother recounts breaking up with my father before realizing he was the one for her all along. It's obvious I'll be reminded about this story until the end of time, or until I finally settle down, whichever occurs first. They talk about Shawn, Maya, and me and drop hints about being excited for grandchildren. Thankfully the pressure is on my brother and sister for that one.

I casually look at the guests a few times. My emotions are all over the place right now, so my heart beats extra fast each time Owen and I exchange glances.

Although almost everyone has tears in their eyes, Evelyn and my aunt and uncle are all crying hysterically. Even Jackson dabs the corner of his eye. The ceremony is heartfelt and romantic, and the sun begins to disappear on the horizon as it's ending.

My parents exchange a long kiss, and everyone cheers loudly. Following the cheers, the photographer makes us pose for several pictures. I'm hoping these pictures will go on Mom's Christmas cards instead of the infamous coconut bras and loincloths picture.

My parents announce that it's party time and begin to make their way toward the hotel. I hang back as Shawn and Brynn and Maya and Hunter are close behind them, with everyone else following. Except Owen.

"The ceremony was very touching," he says once the others are gone. "I've never seen anyone renew their vows."

"Me neither. It was very sweet."

He moves a little closer to me and puts his hands on my waist. "You look absolutely gorgeous tonight."

I wrap my hands around his neck and pull his face toward mine. I don't bother moving slowly at this point. It's the last night, and I promised myself I would make the most of the time I have left with him.

Our lips touch again, and I wish there was someone around to capture a picture of this moment. There's a faint bit of light left in the sky, and there's a soft breeze with the ocean behind us.

I know I need to get to the party before my mother freaks out again. Luckily, my time as a dutiful bridesmaid is coming to an end and I can enjoy the rest of my evening.

"You ready to go inside and face them?" he asks, taking my hand firmly in his.

I hold up our hands. "You mean crash the party like this?"

A wicked smile spreads across his face. "I think it's time to have some fun. Don't you?"

I pull him toward the hotel. "Definitely. Let's do it."

Chapter Twenty-Nine

*O*wen and I take our time as we head to the ballroom where the anniversary party is taking place. We talk about the reactions we're going to receive when our family sees us together ... if anyone notices.

"I'm a little shocked more people haven't picked up on this," Owen says.

I've thought the same thing, but there's been a lot going on. And most of the time my family is much too concerned with their own lives unless it has to do with something they want, like Jackson officially joining the family.

"Of all people to figure it out, Jackson and Brynn," I say. "Evelyn made a few comments, but I thought your mom would've noticed or even asked about us spending the day together."

He raises his eyebrows. "Oh, she definitely suspects something. She was asking about where we went yesterday, but I think she's been distracted with the DeeDee situation and then with Alyssa showing up."

I grit my teeth. This reminds me that I haven't had a chance to tell him I met Alyssa.

"So, I met her when I stopped by your parents' room earlier."

He looks down at the ground. "I'm so sorry, Cora. That must've been weird for you."

I run my hand up and down his arm. "It wasn't bad. She was pleasant, but I could tell she was disappointed with the way things went down here."

Owen gives me an apologetic look even though he shouldn't feel bad. I know it isn't his fault she showed up here.

"Anyway, I know your mom was really upset about you and Alyssa splitting up."

He nods. "She was. My parents did love her, but I think my mom was mostly worried about me. In the end, they want me to be happy."

That sounds awfully familiar. Isn't that why my mother brought Jackson here?

"When she finds out about us, she'll be ecstatic."

Us? I love hearing him say that. Except we still have to discuss what happens next for *us*. I wish we could skip the party and figure this out.

"You've always been very special to my family," he adds. "I know my mother thinks of you as the daughter she never had."

Hearing this warms my heart.

"The feeling is mutual. Alaina and I always had a special relationship. I can't tell you how many times I wished I was a Webber instead of a Fletcher."

I freeze. *Did I just say that out loud?*

Luckily we arrive at the ballroom and face each other.

"Well, here we go. You ready?"

I smile. "I've been ready for a long time."

"Let's have some fun," he says with a gleam in his eye.

He opens the door, and we step inside. As expected, the ballroom is decorated beautifully. The room dividers are closed, making it a smaller, more intimate space. The overhead lights are dimmed, and there are trees with twinkling lights strategically placed around the room. There are a few round tables set up around a small dance floor. The servers are already taking orders, and I hear my father requesting glasses of champagne for a toast.

Shawn is the first to notice Owen and me. He narrows his eyes and flicks Maya on the arm.

"Ow. What the hell, Shawn?" she yells, rubbing her arm.

He points at us.

Maya turns around to face us, and her eyes grow wide.

Owen grasps my hand more firmly as he leads us toward our families.

"Very funny, guys. What's with the handholding?" Shawn asks with a laugh.

Everyone else turns and stares at us. Alaina gasps, and my mother looks confused.

Everyone begins talking at once.

"It's about damn time," Peepaw shouts.

"I know love when I see it," Evelyn says.

"Is there something you want to tell us?" Alaina asks.

"Cora Ann, what's going on?" Mom asks.

"They're messing with us," Shawn exclaims.

"No, they're not," Brynn replies.

Owen asks everyone to quiet down.

"I know this may be a surprise for all of you." He pauses and grins at me. "It's been a surprise to us, even though I think it's been a long time coming. It's been incredible being able to spend time together again after all these years." He gives my parents a grateful look.

"I finally admitted I've had a crush on him since we were kids," I interject. "He even took me on a romantic helicopter ride around the island."

Brynn frowns and looks at Shawn. She's probably going to give him hell for not planning such a romantic excursion.

"I knew you liked him," Shawn yells, as he avoids his wife's glare. "You would always get so nervous when we were hanging out with the Webbers, and you spent hours getting ready."

I scowl even though Owen already knows all of this.

"I had a crush on her, too," Owen admits. "But, I had no idea she had any interest in me."

Everyone begins talking again. The only person who hasn't said anything is Hunter. I know he feels like I hurt and betrayed his best friend.

Jackson gives me a nod, and then I notice him whisper something to Hunter. Maybe he's telling him about our conversation on the beach.

Even Brynn is announcing she knew from day one that we had feelings for each other.

Ashley still looks confused. She's probably thinking about seeing Alyssa going into his room this morning.

Peepaw clears his throat and rises to his feet.

"What a night," he says, raising his voice. "Congratulations to my son and my daughter-in-law for sticking with each other for forty years. You're a good woman, Leann."

Everyone laughs.

"And two childhood friends reconnecting—that's something you only see in the movies."

Owen puts his arm around me.

"Forgive me while I rain on your parade for a few minutes."

My mom gives him a curious look, and for a second I think she might object to another person taking the spotlight off of her tonight. I think it's safe to say she's lost all the attention at the moment. She's still wearing her super tight dress, although I haven't seen her sit down yet.

Peepaw continues talking about losing the love of his life and how painful and lonely it's been for him after my grandmother passed away.

Evelyn takes his hand. This must be the big announcement I overheard them talking about.

"Now for the big news. I've asked Evelyn to be my wife, and since we're all here, we've decided to have a quick ceremony at sunrise tomorrow morning before everyone leaves."

Wow, a sunset vow renewal and a sunrise wedding. The Fletchers don't do anything basic.

Evelyn takes advantage of this moment to stand up. She might as well take the floor, almost everyone else has.

"It has been so lovely getting to know Louie's family. You're all delightful, and I want you to know how much I love and appreciate this man. Louie, thank you for making me feel young again."

Suddenly, the matching leopard lingerie flashes through my mind. I cringe at the memory.

My uncle is the next to stand up.

"Let's toast the happy couples!" he announces, holding his beer high in the air. "How about we make this trip an annual thing, Warner?"

What? Someone needs to cut this man off ASAP.

My dad laughs, but a look of terror spreads across his face. I'm sure he's thinking about the final bill right about now.

Maya takes this opportunity to drag me away from Owen.

"I can't believe you didn't say anything when I asked you if there was something going on," she says.

"I'm sorry," I tell her. "Everything has been happening so fast, and honestly I didn't know how this was going to end. And you've been preoccupied with other things, namely your quest for Jackson and me to get back together."

She scowls.

"And then there was the comment you made about it being weird for us to get together because Owen was like a brother."

She folds her arms and gives me a questioning look. "So, how are you guys planning to do this? You don't exactly live close to each other."

I exhale loudly. "We haven't had a chance to discuss it, but I'm willing to try anything."

Her mouth drops open. "Cora?"

"What?"

"You're in love with him, aren't you?"

I look away. Even though I haven't said it out loud, I'm confident I have very strong feelings for Owen, stronger than anything I've ever felt for anyone before. I know it seems completely ridiculous considering we haven't spent time together in years, but I'm starting to wonder if what I believed was a childhood crush has always been more. Maybe this is why none of my past relationships ever worked out. Maybe I've been carrying a torch for Owen all this time and never got over it.

"I think it's safe to say I've been in love with him for most of my life," I whisper.

She puts her hand over her mouth. "Is that why you didn't go to his wedding?"

I nod. "I didn't want to see him get married." I pause, looking over at Owen, who's now talking to his parents. "I thought I was over my silly childhood crush, but when we were invited, I couldn't bear the thought of going. After the wedding, I accepted he was married and nothing was ever going to happen for us. Then I came here and found out about his divorce. I had no idea because Mom never told me about it."

Maya looks surprised. "Wow. I didn't know you ever felt this way."

I grab her arm and drag her out of the ballroom. "There's something else I have to tell you," I say.

I tell her about Alyssa showing up and how I think Brynn had something to do with it.

"Wait, Alyssa is here? In Hawaii? In this hotel?"

I press my lips together. "She came to talk to Owen about giving their marriage another chance. The interesting thing is Brynn and Alyssa became friends after their wedding. Isn't it convenient that Alyssa randomly decides to come here after seeing a few pictures of Owen's family?"

Maya clenches her jaw. "You think Brynn invited Alyssa to come here?"

I hold my arms up. "I don't think she invited her here, but I have a feeling she had something to do with Alyssa seeing those pictures."

Maya puts her hands on her head and lets out a low scream. "Brynn was trying to sabotage you. What's wrong with her?"

Hah! Where do I start?

"Enough is enough. I'm so over her."

All of a sudden she pulls the door open and stomps into the ballroom before I can stop her.

Crap.

I run after Maya, but I'm too late.

"Brynn, how could you do this?" Maya yells.

Everyone turns and looks at her.

I try to step in and calm her down, but she uses this moment to unleash years of pent up fury on Brynn. My mother is probably going to have a panic attack now.

"You knew Cora and Owen were together, so you called his ex-wife and got her to come out here? I knew you didn't like my sister, but this is low, even for you."

Shawn stands up. "Maya, what the hell are you talking about?"

She looks at him and shakes her head in disgust. "Come on, Shawn. When are you finally going to see the type of person your wife is? She puts on a good act, but we're all catching on."

"Maya, I didn't call or ask Alyssa to come here, I swear," Brynn exclaims, and then she looks at me. "Cora, you have to believe me."

I stand behind Maya and look at Brynn's face. Her usual confident expression is nowhere to be found. The crazy thing is, I think I believe her.

"Hold on. Someone needs to explain what's going on," my father interrupts. "and you're making your mother very upset, so I think you should take this outside. Go."

He's giving us his usual *I'm very disappointed in you* look, which is so much worse than being yelled at. Despite being his *favorite*, even I've been on the other side of this look a few times.

Maya, Shawn, Brynn, and I walk outside.

"First of all, you need to stop accusing my wife of things that aren't true," Shawn says after we exit the ballroom. "Are you girls ever going to stop ganging up on her?"

Maya rolls her eyes. "Are you ever going to get your head out of your ass? Why don't you come clean for once, Brynn?"

Brynn folds her arms. "I didn't think she would come here."

My mouth drops open, and Maya gets a very satisfied look on her face.

Shawn frowns. "Brynn, what are you saying?"

She looks down at the floor. "Babe, you know Alyssa and I became friends after her wedding. We stayed in touch and message every once in a while, even after their divorce."

Wow, I can't wait to tell Fran that Brynn's actually admitting she did something wrong.

"I texted her some pictures of our trip the other day and mentioned the Webbers were here. She asked to see more pictures and then asked how Owen was doing. I told her he seemed to be having fun and was spending time with someone." She pauses and turns toward me. "I never said it was you, Cora. If you remember, Ashley was all over him for the first few days."

I don't respond, and she continues talking.

"Alyssa told me she missed Owen and was thinking about contacting him, but that's it. I didn't know she was coming here; I swear."

Brynn looks completely distraught, and I think she might start crying.

Maya looks at me and raises her eyebrows.

I can't believe I'm saying this, but I believe her. It still doesn't erase the way she treats me or how she's always belittling me. "You may not have convinced Alyssa to come here, but the way you treat me is horrible," I say.

She narrows her eyebrows and glares at me. "The way I treat you? Hah! What about the way you treat me?" she snaps. "I know you didn't want me to marry your brother—I've had to bust my ass to form good relationships in this family. I know what you said about me when Shawn and I got together. How do you think I felt coming into this family knowing everyone already had a negative opinion of me?"

Typical Brynn, she's an expert at playing the victim.

"Okay, I admit I wasn't happy about my brother marrying you of all people, especially after the way you treated me in college. You made my life hell most of the time."

Shawn holds up his hand to stop us both. "Enough. This is Mom and Dad's party, and I'm so over how you two treat each other. You just need to fake it, at least until after tonight."

I fold my arms because he's right—this is not the time or place for us to hash this out. Since when is my brother the voice of reason? "You're right, Shawn," I agree. "We need to put our differences aside for Mom and Dad tonight. Come on, Maya."

I grab her by her elbow and lead her back into the ballroom. When we get inside, I see my mother talking to Alaina and DeeDee, who are obviously being cordial to each other for my mother's sake. I immediately feel guilty. I probably should've held off on telling Maya my suspicions about Alyssa and Brynn.

Maya kneels down and apologizes to our mother for her outburst.

"I'm sorry too, Mom," I say.

I notice Shawn and Brynn come back inside a few seconds later.

My dad waves at a server, and suddenly many servers appear with trays of champagne. I guess now is as good a time as any, and he is good at giving speeches. He's the perfect person to lighten the mood.

He taps his glass with his knife to get everyone's attention. "I think it's safe to say tonight hasn't gone as planned," he announces.

Everyone murmurs in agreement.

"However, I would like to bring it back to the reason we're all here. Because this gorgeous woman agreed to marry me forty years ago. It was love at first sight when I met her, and I'm so grateful she agreed to marry me."

My mom dabs the corner of her eyes with a napkin. I'm not sure whether she's crying over my dad's speech or because her anniversary party has been overshadowed by my grandfather's engagement announcement, Owen and me, and then the blowup at Brynn. Or maybe it's because her dress is too tight? Probably all of the above.

"Despite the disagreements, Leann and I are grateful you're all here tonight, and we hope you enjoy your last night on this beautiful island. Cheers!"

We all hold up our glasses. "Cheers!"

Owen comes up beside me and asks what happened with Brynn.

I motion for him to follow me away from my mother. I don't want to upset her any more tonight. I glance over at Brynn who's continuing her performance of being completely distraught. Shawn is rubbing her back and whispering something in her ear.

"She says she sent some pictures to Alyssa but had no idea she was coming here," I tell him.

He puts his hands on my shoulders. "And do you believe her?"

I sigh. "I' never thought I'd say this, but I do."

Honestly, it doesn't matter anymore. I don't want to spend any more of tonight dealing with Brynn. I want to enjoy the rest of my parents' anniversary party and soak up every second with Owen that I can.

"I don't want to think about her anymore. Let's just enjoy the rest of the evening together."

He rubs my arms. "I agree."

The rest of the party goes off without a hitch. Even DeeDee is on her best behavior. I'm sure she knows one more unexpected outburst might give my mother a heart attack.

Owen and I are sitting with his parents, and as expected the questions are coming.

"So, what's next for you two?" Alaina asks finally.

Owen and I look at each other.

"We haven't had a chance to talk about it yet," he says.

I nod. "As you can see, it's been one thing after another."

She beams. "You know, there was a time many years ago when Leann and I had a discussion about this very thing. I think our families were spending the weekend together and someone mentioned what would happen if you two ended up together." She pauses. "Honestly, we figured our families were too close and you would never feel that way about each other. Obviously we were wrong."

Owen puts his arm around me.

"I thought Owen looked at me like a sister," I admit. "Believe me, I never in a million years expected this would happen."

Alaina gets tears in her eyes and jumps to her feet. "I'm so happy. I love you both so much." She throws her arms around us.

I look over her shoulder to where Shawn and Brynn are still sitting alone. Another wave of guilt comes over me, so I excuse myself and head over to talk to them.

"Can I sit down?"

Shawn waves his hand at the seat.

I take a deep breath. "I just wanted to tell you I'm sorry about how this went down." I pause. "It wasn't the time or the place to have this discussion."

Even though I'm not thrilled about doing this, I need to be the bigger person. I owe it to my parents for the trouble I've caused tonight.

"I accept your apology, and I'm sorry too," Brynn says softly. "I swear I didn't know Alyssa would show up."

"I believe you."

I go to stand up, but she continues talking. "Cora, I'm also sorry for how I treated you back in college. Believe it or not, I've talked to Shawn about it. I was very immature, and I really regret it."

Shawn confirms what she's saying.

"I was planning to make things right with you, until I heard you didn't want Shawn to marry me. I was really hurt, because I love him more than anything."

As rotten as she is, I can see how much she loves my brother.

"I always felt like I had to be on the defensive," she adds. "But, I sincerely would like to try to move on from the past and be friends."

Hmm ... I'm not sure Brynn and I will ever be *friends*, but maybe we can call a truce. I need to be more patient with her because we're family now, and it's obvious she's not going anywhere.

I agree to try and then excuse myself.

I'm walking away from their table, when I feel someone tap me on the shoulder.

"Thanks, Cora," Shawn says. "I appreciate your apology. I know it hasn't been easy for you."

"You're welcome."

He pulls me into a hug. "Love ya, sis."

"Love you, too."

After Shawn returns to his wife's side, I stand back and look around the room at my family. Even though many of our relationships are complicated, I wouldn't trade this family of mine for anything.

Chapter Thirty

*O*h, what a night. My parents' anniversary party ended on a positive note, and we're all looking forward to Peepaw and Evelyn's sunrise wedding ceremony. Although most of the conflicts were resolved, I know it'll be some time before the next Fletcher family reunion, and that's okay.

I'm standing at the waters' edge, when I feel Owen's hands wrap around my waist. He rests his chin on my shoulder and his warm breath tickles my neck.

"I can't believe we're finally alone."

I giggle. "Don't jinx it. Someone could show up at any moment."

"You're right. Sorry."

We're both quiet as we stare out at the ocean. The moon is casting a glow very similar to the first night we were here. I wish I could go back to that night and do things differently. If I could go back, I would've told Owen how I felt as soon as I heard about his divorce.

"I don't want to leave," I say, interrupting the silence.

"I don't either."

I turn around and face him. I still feel like I'm dreaming being in his arms.

He pushes a strand of hair behind my ear.

Neither of us says anything about going to different cities tomorrow. I'm about to mention it when he steps up to the plate.

"We have a lot to figure out."

I bite my lower lip and nod my head. "Yes, we do. I wish I knew where to start."

He opens his mouth to say something, but nothing comes out.

"What is it?" I ask.

"Cora, I want to spend our last night together." He stops and covers his face with his hand. "That came out wrong. Not like that, well, yes, but …" He groans, fumbling over his words. "What I'm trying to say is I want you in my arms tonight. I want to hang out, order pizza from room service, and talk about the future, our future."

I laugh. "I understand what you mean, and I feel the same way."

I take his hand in mine, and we make our way back to the hotel.

"I can't believe you and Maya told Brynn off," Fran shouts excitedly. "Please tell me someone recorded it."

"I don't think so," I say, checking my reflection in the mirror.

"I should've come with you. Tonight alone would've been worth it."

I laugh. I remind her about how many times I begged her to come with me.

"So, you and Owen are hanging out tonight?" she teases. "Don't do anything I wouldn't do."

"Very funny," I reply. "Anyway, he should be here any minute. I'll call you before I take off. Tell Kiwi I'll be home soon."

"Okay, good luck."

I end the call and rush around the room picking things up. After our walk on the beach, Owen went to his room to change. We decide to hang out in my room tonight, since his parents have the adjoining room and his mother is notorious for interruptions.

I change a few times before finally putting on a tank top and a pair of leggings.

My heart begins to race when I hear a knock at the door. I run and fling it open.

Owen is wearing a pair of Nike joggers and a gray T-shirt. He's as good-looking as he was ten years ago, and he has a paper bag in his hand.

"What's in the bag?"

He walks in and places it on the table. "You'll see."

I close the door, and when I turn around, he pulls me into his arms, lifts me off the ground, and kisses me. I wrap my legs tightly around him. I wonder if this feeling will ever go away. He carries me into the room and sets me down gently. My eyes are still closed when we stop kissing.

"You okay?" he asks.

I open my eyes and can feel my face turning red, yet again. How does this man still have this kind of power over me?

"Mmm ... I'm good."

He runs his hand through his hair. "I've been meaning to ask you what it's like to finally kiss me. Is it everything you thought it was going to be?"

I giggle. "Oh, it's better than I ever imagined."

He punches the air in excitement.

I grab the bag off the table and sit down on the couch. Inside the bag I find a package of my favorite snack, caramel popcorn. I give him a confused look.

"How did you know I like caramel popcorn?"

He smiles. "You probably don't remember, but I owe you a bag of popcorn."

I quickly flip through my memories, and then something pops into my head. "Are you kidding? You remember that?"

He nods. "We were at your parents' house for someone's birthday, and it was really late after Shawn and I had an epic battle on the pool table. I was hungry, and Shawn told me to get whatever I wanted out of the pantry. I grabbed a bag of caramel popcorn and plowed through it."

All of a sudden that night flashes through my mind. "I remember, and when I went looking for it, it was gone. I stormed into Shawn's room and yelled at him for eating my favorite snack, again."

He laughs. "And when I apologized for eating it, you said it was okay because I was a guest."

I shake my head. "I can't believe you remember that."

He sits down on the bed and pulls me onto his lap, wrapping his arms around me.

"You'd be surprised what I remember." He stops talking, and a thoughtful look spreads across his face. "Ever since I saw you again, I haven't been able to stop thinking about you, and all these memories are flooding back to me, like the popcorn."

"Even I totally forgot that night," I say.

We're both quiet.

"I've been trying to think of ways for us to be together. Work is finally settling down for me, and I have some free weekends coming up, and if I don't have to be in court, I can work remotely..."

Although weekends only aren't ideal, this may be the only way for us to be together right now. I'm sure my boss will understand when I tell her about Owen. She made such a big deal about the importance of me taking this trip.

"I've been doing the same thing. We have a few big events coming up with important clients, but after that I'll have more free time. And I have plenty of vacation time I haven't used. My boss practically kicked me out of the office and put me on the plane herself. I haven't taken a trip in years."

He gives me a confused look.

"I know it's strange, but I told you my job has been my life for as long as I can remember."

He lifts my chin with his finger.

"I hope that's changed."

My pulse picks up, and I can almost hear my own heartbeat.

"It has."

"Cora, I meant what I said earlier. I want to give this a chance and see where things go."

I take a deep breath. "You know I feel the same way."

He cradles me in his arms, and any ounce of doubt I was feeling has vanished. I'm not going to let Alyssa or distance come between Owen and me. He's walked back into my life after a very long time, and I'm going to do whatever I have to so we can be together.

I open my eyes and see Owen lying next to me. I'm not dreaming, Owen is really here by my side. It's still dark outside, but we need to be on the beach before the sun rises for my grandfather and Evelyn's wedding ceremony. I slide over and rest my head on Owen's chest. I close my eyes and listen to his heart beating. He begins to stir, and I feel his arms tighten around me.

As amazing as this feels to be lying here with him, a dreadful feeling is looming. Knowing later today we're going our separate ways makes me want to cry.

He kisses me on the top of my head. "Good morning."

"Morning," I say.

We've only been asleep for a few hours. I'm not sure what time we drifted off, but after he arrived, we ordered room service and talked until we fell asleep. We had many years to catch up on since the last time we saw each other. Each time I was sure I told him everything, I thought of something else.

I know I need to get dressed, but I don't want to move from this spot.

"I should get back to my room and change," he says finally. "And you need to get ready. You've got another ceremony to attend."

"I know, but I don't want to get up."

I lift my head off his chest and rest it on the pillow facing him.

"Your family never does anything small, do they?" he asks, clearing his throat.

I snort. "You should know this by now. Everything has to be a big production. Why do you think I don't fit in?"

He pushes my hair off my face. "You stand out."

I make a face. "Yeah, I stand out all right."

"You do to me."

I rest my chin on my hand, and then I realize my breath probably smells like death. I jump up and run to the bathroom.

"You okay?" he calls.

"Brushing my teeth," I mumble with my mouth full of toothpaste. Not that it matters because it's time to get ready for the wedding. Thankfully, Peepaw told us to show up in casual attire.

When I come out of the bathroom, Owen is sitting on the edge of the bed. I sit down next to him and rest my head on his shoulder.

"I guess I need to do the walk of shame back to my room."

I start to laugh. "It's good material for everyone to discuss this morning, not that they haven't had enough gossip to talk about."

I walk Owen to the door. He takes my face in his hands and gently kisses me. Every time this man kisses me, I fall into a trance.

"I wish we could get some breakfast before the ceremony," I mumble.

He laughs and kisses me on the forehead. "Me, too."

"I'll see you soon," I say, holding the door open for him.

"Yes, you will."

consider wearing my tank top and leggings to Peepaw's sunrise service. He said we should dress casual, but this is my sweet grandfather's wedding. I put on a flowing floral-printed maxi dress and pile my hair into a top knot.

As usual I'm the first to arrive on the beach, and I find Peepaw sitting alone on a chair. I appreciate the moments I've had alone with him.

"Good morning, Peepaw," I say, giving him a kiss on the cheek. "Are you excited for your big day?"

He looks up and smiles. "You bet I am."

I close my eyes and smile. The weather is perfect right now.

"Have a good night, did ya?" he asks with a wink.

I feel heat spread through my cheeks.

He laughs. "I recognize that shade of crimson. I've made a few ladies turn that color in my time."

His statement causes me to blush even more. My grandfather must've been a total player in his time.

"It's not like that," I tell him. I know he's assuming Owen and I slept together. And although we fell asleep in the same bed, we didn't take our relationship to the next level. Not that we didn't want to, but it's only been a few days since we reconnected. We agreed to doing this the right way, despite our intense level of attraction to one another.

"I don't care what you did. It's your business," he says.

I let out a sigh of relief. I'd rather not have the sex conversation with my eighty-nine-year-old grandfather.

"Remember you're a Fletcher. If you're going to do it, you better do it well."

I force a smile, but I really want to find a hole to crawl into. Maybe I should start digging in the sand right now.

"I used to tell your father the same thing, and I have no worries about him and Leann. The fire is still there for the two of them."

And now we're talking about my parents' sex life. *Mayday!* This conversation is going south very quickly.

For the love of all that is holy, I need to change the subject. It's a good thing the rest of the family shows up because I was about to fall ill very quickly. Anything to get me out of this conversation.

"Anyway, let's talk about your big day. Are you excited or nervous?" I ask. "You're getting married in a few minutes."

The same minister that performed my parents' vow renewal last night is performing the wedding ceremony. He interrupts our conversation, and I sneak away to find my seat.

When Owen arrives, he sits down next to me and leans over to kiss me. Everyone is here except for Jackson, and I don't blame him one bit. I think it's safe to say he's over this family reunion.

"You okay?" Owen asks.

Maybe my red face has turned green with nausea.

"Oh sure, I'm good, other than discussing the sex lives of various members of the Fletcher family with my grandfather."

He bursts out laughing. "Your family is one of a kind."

I make a gagging sound. "Yes, they are."

My thoughts are interrupted by music. I turn around to see a violin player walking down the path toward the beach where we are sitting. My grandfather joins Evelyn where she is waiting. She's wearing a long white linen dress, a lei around her neck, and is holding a single pink rose in her hand. The violinist continues to play as Peepaw and Evelyn follow him along the path together. They stand in front of us, and the service begins.

As I listen to them talk about companionship and someone to grow old with, I get choked up. Like clockwork, Owen produces a tissue for me. I look over at my parents, who are both smiling because they know Peepaw has found happiness, even after loss.

This is what it's all about, and why I needed to come on this trip. As frustrating as my family can be, they come together to support and celebrate each other. Yes, it was a bonus to have an all-expense-paid trip to Hawaii, but celebrating my parents is ultimately why we're all here.

Peepaw and Evelyn say their vows as the sun rises on the horizon.

I'm in awe of these last few days. Being able to witness our final sunset and sunrise while here is something I'll never forget.

Owen takes my hand in his, and I know everything is going to be okay.

The minister pronounces them husband and wife, and we all stand and cheer.

Peepaw thanks everyone for coming and announces that we'll have a big breakfast to celebrate.

"That's what I'm talking about," Owen says excitedly.

I grin.

He puts his arm around me, and we head to the hotel to have our last family breakfast.

Ashley is the first to leave. We're still eating breakfast when she runs around saying good-bye to everyone. When she comes to me and Owen, she gives me a tight hug.

"I'm happy for you, Cora. And take my advice, don't rush your relationship. Take your time. After breaking off my engagement, I realize this. Four days wasn't long enough to get to know a person."

Four days? Wow, that might be a new record, at least for her.

"Thanks, Ashley."

She looks at Owen. "You take care of my cousin, and don't propose until you're sure you're ready."

I cringe. We're definitely not ready to talk about getting engaged. We don't even live in the same city.

After breakfast I return to my hotel room to pack. I walk out onto the balcony and look out over the Pacific Ocean. I'm really going to miss this view. One thing's for sure, I have every intention of returning to Hawaii.

"It's kind of a bummer we can't have this view every day, huh?"

I look over at the next balcony and see Jackson holding a cup of coffee. His hair is a mess, and he looks like he just woke up.

"Good morning."

He asks me about Peepaw's wedding service.

"Why didn't you go?"

He sighs. "I think I've crashed enough of the family activities on this trip."

I press my lips together and think about the dreaded family photo session. Is it bad to hope none of those photos turn out?

"You didn't crash. You were invited. Your participation in that nightmare photo session is admirable."

He laughs. "Oh well, I got to visit Hawaii and tackle some items on my bucket list. It was totally worth it."

We both grow quiet.

"So, what's next for you?" he asks. I already know he's referring to Owen and me.

I clear my throat. "Back to real life and to work. I'm excited to see Kiwi."

He grits his teeth. "Ah yes, the cat who hated me."

I giggle. "She didn't hate you." I'm lying. She totally hated him.

"Yes, she did. But it's okay." He clears his throat. "Cora, I sincerely hope everything works out with you and Owen."

"Thank you, Jackson."

"And hey, maybe I'll see ya at the next family reunion," he says, with a laugh.

I shake my head. "I think I need a break from family fun for a while. Anyway, I need to get back to packing. I'll see you later."

I stare out and soak up one more look at this unforgettable view.

Mahalo, Hawaii, you've been amazing.

Chapter Thirty-Two

---

*I*t's definitely not as fun leaving a vacation as it is arriving. And to make matters worse, everyone is in a bad mood. Perhaps it's the fact that we all woke up before dawn, or maybe it's because we're leaving Hawaii, or it could be we're all sick of each other. My vote is the latter.

Peepaw and Evelyn have decided to stay a few more days and celebrate their marriage with a proper honeymoon. Or as he put it, a few days without the drama. We all know he's referring to the rest of us, and it's a valid point.

If I could stay in Hawaii longer without everyone else I would. Crap— maybe I should've extended my trip?

"Just think about it, Warner," my uncle says, pounding my father on the back. I'm pretty sure he's propositioning him about another family reunion, expenses paid, of course. Figures.

I'm surprised when I see Aunt DeeDee give Alaina a hug good-bye. Of course, she's completely sober, so that could be the reason. She makes her rounds with tears in her eyes.

"You promise to come visit me, sugar," she says, squeezing me tightly.

"I will," I say into her neck. At least she doesn't reek of alcohol today.

Alaina and Ken are the next to leave. Alaina pulls me aside, giving me a long hug.

"So, we'll be seeing you in a few weeks? I'm so glad Owen is taking more time off from work. You've already been so good for him. I don't know how to thank you."

Owen and I have already made plans to visit his parents at the end of the month. Apparently he hasn't been home in months due to his work schedule. I'm looking forward to spending some time with the Webbers without other distractions.

Owen's flight isn't until later today, so we take a walk before my shuttle arrives.

It's taking every bit of my self-control not to completely lose it.

He takes my hands in his and faces me. "Well ..."

I look away because I'm about to burst into tears.

"Call me when you land," he says softly.

I nod as I try to swallow the lump in my throat.

He puts his arms around me. "I don't want you to be sad. This is just the beginning for us."

I rest my head on his chest and close my eyes as I fight back my tears. I breathe in his scent because I don't want to forget it. Neither of us pulls away, and I wish I could to stay in this moment forever. This is what I hoped for as long as I can remember. I can't help but be afraid to lose him already.

"Cora, it's time to go," Maya yells.

Owen lifts my chin and kisses me passionately.

He walks me to the bus where they're loading our luggage. Owen says good-bye to everyone and kisses me on the forehead one more time.

"Safe travels."

We all pile into the bus, and Brynn slides in next to me. I force a smile and wave out the window before we drive away. Everyone is quiet, and I'm giving myself an internal lecture not to cry or make a scene in front of my family. All of a sudden I feel an arm around my shoulders. I glance at Brynn, who's fixated on her phone. Her arm is around my shoulders, and she gives me a comforting squeeze.

She gives me a sympathetic nod, and I give her a grateful smile in return. Neither of us says a word, and I doubt this moment will ever be mentioned again.

As we drive to the Honolulu airport, I think about everything that's happened over the last few days. As difficult as it is to say good-bye to Owen, I know he's right. It's just the beginning for us.

As soon as I walk in the door, Kiwi is waiting for me. I drop my stuff, scoop her up into my arms and give her a long hug. I know some people say cats aren't affectionate, but Kiwi definitely is with me.

I sit down on the couch and run my hand over her soft fur.

The flight home was totally uneventful, unlike the flight to Hawaii. I sat next to my dad, who snored loudly most of time. Thank goodness for noise-cancelling headphones. Before taking off I got a text from Owen wishing me a safe flight and telling me he missed me already.

I tried to sleep, but I stared out the window for most of the time.

Owen should be on his flight right now, but I send him a text letting him know I'm home and can't wait to talk to him.

I sigh loudly. I know I can do this. Long distance relationships aren't ideal, but it's worth it so we can be together.

Fran isn't home yet, so I begin the daunting task of unpacking and doing laundry. At the bottom of my suitcase I find the coconut bra and cheap grass skirt. I dramatically chuck them into the trash can. I have to beg my mother not to use that photo on her Christmas card or splash it across social media, especially the pictures where I'm standing with Jackson.

When I hear the door open, I run to Fran, throwing my arms around her. I begin to sob. I'm proud of myself for holding my tears in for as long as I have.

"It's going to be okay," she says softly.

I continue to cry without saying a word, and she lets me, because she's an awesome friend.

When I finally calm down, we sit on the couch and I tell her about my final hours with Owen.

"So, did you guys ever see Alyssa again?"

I shake my head. "Owen's mom said she stayed for one day and then took a flight home."

Fran looks shocked. "So she flew all the way there for only one day?"

I shrug. "She only went for Owen. I guess after he rejected her, she had no reason to stay."

"And what about Brynn?"

I tell her about our moment on the bus on the way to the airport.

"I'm not surprised. I think Brynn is really insecure, but I don't think she's completely evil."

I sigh. "Who knows? I definitely learned a lot on this trip."

"So, when will you see Owen again?"

I frown. "In two weeks. He's working through this weekend to catch up after being gone. We're getting together the weekend after next and then going to his parents' house at the end of the month."

She nods. "Two weeks. You okay with that?"

"I don't have a choice, do I?" I say. "We have our careers and our own lives. This is the way it has to be for now."

Fran leans over and gives me a hug. "I told you something big was going to happen for you on this trip. I think Owen was the guy in my dream."

I laugh. "And as usual, you were right. I'll never doubt you again."

"I'm glad you're back," she says, "and so is Kiwi."

"Thanks, Fran." I wish I could say the same. I'm glad to see them, but I would be lying if I said I was happy to be here.

We spend the remainder of the evening talking. I tell all about the events of the Fletcher family reunion, we laugh about the family picture, and she starts calling me Cara. As hard as it is to be away from Owen, hanging out with my best friend certainly makes it more bearable.

~

I open my eyes, and for a second I forget where I am. I look around at my pale gray walls and remember I'm home in my own room. A feeling of sadness washes over me.

I look at my phone, it's two o'clock in the morning. *Ugh*, my internal clock is so messed up. I've heard adjusting to the time change can be brutal.

I see a missed a call from Owen two hours ago.

I send him a text letting him know that I'm glad he's home safely and I would talk to him in the morning.

A few seconds later my phone buzzes.

ARE YOU AWAKE?

My heart starts to beat quicker as if Owen was right here next to me.

YES. JUST WOKE UP.

A few seconds later my phone rings, and I answer it on the first ring.

"I assume the time change is messing with you, too."

I smile. "Yes. I fell asleep for a few hours. How was your flight?"

He groans. "It was terrible. I was stuck in the middle seat with a mother and a baby on one side and a larger man on the other. The baby kept screaming and projectile vomited all over the arm rest. And that was before we even took off."

I laugh. "I'm sorry."

"It was the worst flight ever," he wails. "And to make matters worse, the larger man was sweating profusely and his leg was pressed against mine the whole flight."

I apologize for laughing.

"Oh, and it gets worse," he exclaims. "After the flight from hell, I come home, and you're not here. Being in this lonely house is miserable."

I stop laughing, and tears well up in my eyes. I'm grateful Fran's here with me. I don't know what I'd do if I had to come home to an empty house.

"I miss you so much, Cora."

I start to blush, but at least he's not here to see it.

"I miss you, too."

"I'm actually looking forward to going to work," I tell him. "I think it'll be easier being away from you if I'm busy."

He agrees and tells me he may go back to working longer days so he can take more time off for us. We discuss the things we're going to do together, and after an hour on the phone, I feel my eyes getting heavy. After we hang up, I feel less sad than when I first got home.

I know I can do this distance thing, and I think it'll make our time together even more special. I'm feeling very hopeful about what the future will bring for us.

Chapter Thirty-Three

First day back at work, and it's bittersweet.

It's a good thing I enjoy my job, otherwise coming back after vacation would be utterly miserable. My email box is loaded, so I'll be spending the morning responding to messages.

"Welcome back, Cora," Lydia says as she comes into my office. She sits down across from my desk. "Did you fall in love with Hawaii?"

A smile spreads across my face, and she raises her eyebrows.

"Ah … I'm guessing you fell in love with more than just the island. Tell me all about it."

"I will. But first I have to give you these." I reach into my bag and pull out two boxes of chocolate covered pineapple.

Her eyes light up. "Thank you so much. You're the best."

She immediately opens one of the boxes and offers it to me.

I tell her all about reconnecting with Owen. And then about my mother and sister inviting Jackson to come along.

She practically picks her jaw up off the floor. "So, you were there with your ex-boyfriend and your childhood love interest? And your mother actually put you in a hotel room next to your ex? Now I understand why you were so hesitant to go on this family vacation."

I nod as I munch on a piece of chocolate.

"That's just the beginning." I go on to tell her about the family photo session.

"No!" she exclaims.

"Oh, yes. We were all standing there on the public beach in coconut bras, grass skirts, and loincloths. And my mother insisted Jackson and I stand together. Apparently this picture is going on her Christmas cards."

Lydia shakes her head in disbelief as I give her more details.

"The trip started with my father holding an exercise class in the middle of the airport terminal, and then I found out about Jackson."

She listens intently as I continue.

"My aunt was drunk most of the time and started a big fight with Owen's mother. My cousins decided they wanted some companionship for the week, so they started flirting with Jackson and Owen."

"No they didn't!" she shouts.

"They sure did," I reply. "Oh, and my mom got drunk at her anniversary bachelorette party and vomited all over the place."

Lydia holds up her hand to stop me. "What's an anniversary bachelorette party?"

I shrug. "Who knows? And then there was a shotgun vow renewal at sunset and wedding ceremony at sunrise."

She laughs. "Sorry I'm laughing, but your family sounds like something out of a movie."

I crack a smile. "Oh, and the best part is Owen's ex-wife showed up after my sister-in-law sent her pictures."

Her eyes grow wide. "The sister-in-law you told me about?"

"Yep."

Lydia's eating the chocolate like it's popcorn as she listens to the sordid details of my week.

"So, what about you and this Owen?" she asks, leaning into me. "When do I get to meet him?"

A familiar feeling of sadness comes over me. "Unfortunately, that's the only downside. He lives in San Diego."

She purses her lips together. "I guess it's a good thing you have a lot of vacation time available."

This is why Lydia is the best boss ever.

"I was hoping you'd say that, and I promise I won't let this affect my work."

She holds up her hands. "I have complete faith in you."

Lydia's phone rings, and she excuses herself to take the call.

As the day goes on, I'm grateful for my job. This is the distraction I need to keep me from missing Owen. I text him a few times throughout the day, but he doesn't respond. I try not to be discouraged. He's also busy getting back into the swing of life.

～

I finally get home after a very long day and a stop at the grocery store. That's another thing I miss about Hawaii—I could definitely get used to having someone prepare all my meals.

"Fran, I'm home," I call.

"Hey. I'm in the kitchen."

I walk in and drop my bags on the floor. Fran is sitting at the table, but she's not alone.

"Owen."

He smiles. "Surprise."

I jump into his arms. He lifts me off the ground, kissing me like we haven't seen each other in weeks instead of twenty-four hours.

"I'll be back after a while," Fran says, hurrying out of the kitchen.

After Owen places me back down on the ground, I put my hands on his cheeks. He's here, in the middle of my kitchen. I feel like I should pinch myself. Maybe this is some strange dream caused by extreme jet lag.

"I can't believe you're here. Is this really happening?"

He kisses me again.

"Shouldn't you be back at work?" I ask, not letting go of him.

He points to his laptop sitting on the counter. "I went into the office this morning, and I worked on the flight here."

We go into the living room and sit on the couch. Owen pulls me into his lap and runs his fingers through my hair.

"I could hardly sleep last night. I knew I needed to see you as soon as possible so I called your mom early this morning to get your address. I booked the first flight out of San Diego."

I cover my face with my hands because I don't know what to say.

"I know we talked about seeing each other next weekend, but that seemed too long." He sighs. "I can't fly up here every day, and there will be weeks we won't see each other, but I needed to show you I'm committed to this, to us."

Kiwi casually jumps on the couch and curls up next to Owen.

He looks down at her. "I guess I have Kiwi's approval."

I've always known she was a great judge of character, and she obviously has no issues with him. If that's not a good sign, I don't know what is.

My eyes fill with tears. Owen wipes one away and kisses me. I don't think I've ever been this happy, which reminds me that I have to make a phone call. But for tonight I'm going to enjoy my time with Owen.

"Good morning, Cora Ann."

"Hi, Mom."

"I'm glad you called," she says. "I wanted to let you know I got the proofs back from the photo session."

I was afraid of this. "Oh, how did they turn out?"

Please say they were blurry and they can't be used.

"They're nice, but I won't be using any of the photos of our immediate family and Jackson. Honey, I'm so sorry. I was way out of line, I should've never made you and Jackson stand together like you were a couple."

This is somewhat of a relief, although there's still the big family photo with everyone and all that skin.

"Thanks, Mom, I appreciate that." I clear my throat. "Anyway, the reason I'm calling is to apologize to you, too."

"Oh, honey, you had every right to feel the way you did. We certainly don't make things easy on you."

I laugh. At least she finally admits it. "I owe you and Dad so much right now. If you hadn't chosen to spend your anniversary with all of us, Owen and I may never have reconnected after all these years."

I hear her sniff, and I know she's crying.

"You're so welcome. Owen called me and asked for your address. I suspect he's planning a surprise visit."

I smile. "Yes, Mom, he's actually here right now."

She gasps and begs to talk to him.

I raise my eyebrows. "Hang on."

"She wants to talk to you," I say, holding the phone out to Owen.

He takes the phone from me.

"Hi, Leann," he says cheerfully. "Yes, it's good to talk to you."

He's quiet for a few minutes which means she has plenty to say. At some point he's going to have to cut her off, or she'll monopolize the short amount of time I have with him.

"Of course. Thank you for inviting me and for being such a good friend to my parents."

He grows quiet again.

"That would be great. I'd love to see you next time I'm in town."

She wants to see him? Here we go. I expect we'll be spending quite a bit of time at my parents' house, and that's okay.

He says good-bye and hands the phone back to me.

"Hey, Mom."

"Oh, honey, you and Owen," she cries. "This is so wonderful. I thought you wouldn't find love after Jackson. How did I not see this? I should've told you Owen was available the second I found out about the divorce."

"Mom, it's okay," I assure her.

"Well, you're together now. Better late than never."

Owen's now typing on his laptop.

"Exactly."

"I love you, Cora Ann."

"Love you too, Mom. Give Dad a hug from his favorite girl," I say, with a giggle.

"I will."

A few seconds later, we hang up. I know we've taken a huge step in our relationship, and I'm happy about it. For the first time in a while, I'm proud to be a Fletcher. My family is quirky and complicated, but I wouldn't trade them for anything. I'm sorry it took me so long to realize it.

"Everything all right?"

I look up at Owen and nod. "Yes, you ready?"

He sighs. "Yep, but we have enough time to make a stop before heading to the airport."

I lean my head to the side. "Where?"

He gets a gleam in his eye. "Breakfast, of course." He kisses my hand.

"Perfect."

Chapter Thirty-Four

*a*s soon as I arrive home from work, I sit down on the couch and close my eyes. Kiwi saunters over and lies down beside me.

It's been a week since I arrived home from Hawaii and Owen's surprise visit, and I'm exhausted. I think I'm still recovering from the time difference, and my long late-night conversations with Owen aren't helping. I've made it a week being away from him, and so far so good. Only one more week to go until we see each other again.

I'm about to force myself to get up and make some dinner, when I hear my phone buzzing from my bag. I stare at the screen for a few seconds before answering it.

"Hello."

"Hi, Cora. It's Brynn."

Well, this is a surprise. Brynn and my brother have been married for a few years now, and I don't think she's ever called me before tonight.

"Hey." I try to hide my surprise that she's on the other end of the phone.

"Don't sound so shocked to hear from me," she says with an irritated tone.

Ah, I guess I didn't hide it very well, but what does she expect?

I try to laugh it off and ask her what I can do for her.

"Well, I'm calling for a few reasons. First of all, Shawn and I were talking last night, and we were wondering how you were doing, you know, with being home. We know how hard it was for you to leave Hawaii."

I know she means being home and away from Owen.

"I'm doing okay," I tell her. "Owen and I are planning to see each other next weekend. We're making the best of our situation."

"Good for you guys," she says, sounding a bit surprised.

Maybe she was thinking Owen and I were just having a vacation fling and nothing would come from it. For a second the thought crosses my mind that she could be calling to get information for Alyssa. I hate to be skeptical, but considering everything that's happened, it's a valid question.

"Thanks for checking in on me," I say gratefully. I need to try with her for my brother's sake. It probably hasn't been easy for him being stuck in the middle.

"You said you called for a few reasons. What else can I do for you?"

I get to the point because the fact is, Brynn and I haven't had much to say to each other, ever. Even though we're making small strides in our relationship, I don't think we're to the point of having slumber parties and braiding each other's hair.

"Oh yes, the other reason I called is … I wanted to do something for your parents as a thank you for the vacation. I was thinking of putting together a photo book and was wondering if you could send me some pictures you took. I've already left messages for everyone, so hopefully we'll have some great shots for a beautiful memory book. Or if you can think of any other ideas…"

Wow. Brynn is actually asking *me* for ideas. That's a huge step for her. Maybe she's really trying.

"Um, sure. A photo book sounds great. Mom will love that."

We both grow silent.

"Cora, I know this is weird."

Yes, it is.

"Shawn and I have talked a lot about our situation since we got home from Hawaii, and I promised him I'd make an effort with you, so that's what I'm trying to do."

I knew my brother was behind this gesture, but it's a start. And I need to do my part.

"I owe it to Shawn to try," I tell her. "I love my brother, and I know you do, too."

"I really do, Cora," she insists.

I chew on my lip while going back and forth about addressing the Alyssa situation. Since we're both making an effort to improve our relationship, we should be upfront about things. I think when we hold things in, they fester and become bigger issues.

"Brynn, can I ask you something? And please don't take this wrong."

"Okay," she replies. I can sense some discomfort in her voice.

"Have you talked to Alyssa since we've been home?"

There's silence on the other end of the phone, and I think that answers my question.

"Yes, I have. She texted me," she says finally.

"And."

"And she asked me who Owen had fallen in love with."

My mouth drops open. Owen and I have been honest about having feelings for each other, but we haven't said the *L* word yet.

"Oh?"

"She told me Owen said they'd never have another chance and he'd fallen in love with someone else."

My heart is racing.

"Obviously he was talking about you, Cora."

Owen loves me. I mean, I suspected it, but hearing someone say it out loud is completely different.

"Anyway, I told her I was sorry if I made it seem like she should come to Hawaii. We haven't texted since then."

Fran walks in, and I hold up my hand to her.

"Cora, if you don't want me to communicate with her, I won't. It's not like we're close friends or anything."

It's not my business who Brynn is friends with, even my boyfriend's ex-wife. I'm not thrilled about it, but with this family it's not unusual.

"That's not up to me, Brynn."

Fran's eyes grow wide, and she mouths Brynn, and I nod at her.

"Thank you for being honest, though. I'll try to come up with some ideas for Mom and Dad. In the meantime, I'll send you those pictures."

"Thanks, Cora. It was nice talking to you."

"You, too."

I end the call and look at Fran.

"What was that about?"

I tell her about our conversation and how Brynn says she wants us to try to be friends.

"I know she's just doing this for Shawn," I add.

Fran shrugs. "I don't know. I think people can change. Maybe she's being sincere."

I lean my head back against the couch and stare at the ceiling while I replay our conversation in my mind.

"Brynn said Owen told Alyssa he was in love with me."

She jumps up from the couch. "Cora, that's amazing. I mean, I already knew he was in love with you."

I laugh. Fran loves being right.

"You know I still wish that you and Shawn had ended up together."

She waves her hand. "I know you do. But it's like your situation with Jackson. Your family wanted you to end up together, but it wasn't meant to be. And now look. You've found someone even better. That means that I'm going to meet someone even greater than Shawn."

I lean over and hug her. "You will Fran. I know it."

Chapter Thirty-Five

*A*s soon as I walk into Owen's parents' house, I'm flooded with memories of my childhood. They've done some renovations, but otherwise not much has changed. Alaina's window seat is still there, which was my favorite reading spot (other than watching Owen, of course). I sit down and run my hands over the blue cushion.

"Everything looks the same," I tell Owen as he puts our bags down near the bottom of the stairs.

He nods. "I know. Mom and Dad are very nostalgic, so I'm sure a lot of things will be familiar to you."

Alaina runs into the living room and throws her arms around Owen and then me.

"It's so good to see you."

"She's been talking about this visit for days," Ken adds, squeezing Owen's shoulders.

Alaina tells us they've ordered dinner from their favorite Mexican restaurant, and she sends Owen and Ken to pick up the food, giving us some time to talk.

"I can't believe I'm back here," I say as I look out over the Webbers' sprawling backyard and smile. When I close my eyes, I imagine being sixteen again, sitting right here on this deck, pretending not to be watching my brother and Owen playing baseball.

"Here you go," Alaina says, handing me a glass of her famous strawberry lemonade. I take a sip and smile.

"Oh, it's so good."

Alaina laughs. "It was always your favorite. You would ask for it every time you came over."

She sits down in the chair next to me.

"I've really been looking forward to this weekend."

She reaches over and puts her hand on mine. "We have, too. As nice as Hawaii was, it was also a little overwhelming."

Yeah, that's one way of putting it.

"I'm still trying to convince Leann not to use those pictures for anything. Poor Ken about died when he saw the proofs."

"Don't remind me," I say with a groan. "Thankfully, she told me she wouldn't use the picture of our immediate family and Jackson. Now if only something would happen to the entire file, we would be in good shape."

She wipes the side of her glass. "The picture from the vow ceremony turned out lovely. I think I almost have her convinced to use that one for her cards."

If Alaina can pull that off, it'll be a miracle.

"So, before the boys get back, tell me how things are going," she asks excitedly. "Owen has been so busy with work we haven't had a chance to talk."

I smile widely, because that's what happens to me when I talk about Owen. I tell her about the last few weeks and only being able to see each other twice.

"It's difficult, but we're making it work," I say. We don't have a choice right now anyway.

I leave out that we still haven't admitted we love each other yet. There are some things I probably shouldn't discuss with his mother.

"I don't think I've ever seen my son this happy," she exclaims. "Even when I thought he was happy it was nothing like he's been since he saw you again."

I feel tears well up in my eyes, and she leans over to give me a hug. If she only knew how happy I was right in this moment and how much I love being back in this house with the three of them. Although things aren't perfect and we're trying to navigate the distance and time apart, I think it's making us appreciate each other even more.

"Don't cry, or you'll make me cry," she insists, patting me on the back.

I laugh through my tears. "I'm sorry."

She fans her face. "Wait until we get together with your parents. That's when you'll really see the tears."

I press my lips together.

"Leann told me you had a good conversation."

"We did. Things are a lot better. Probably better than they've been in a long time."

She squeezes my hand. "Your mother loves you very much. I know how she can be, but her heart is always in the right place."

We hear the kitchen door open. "We're back," Ken calls.

Owen comes outside with two large shopping bags. He gives me a funny look as I dab the corner of my eyes. "Everything okay out here?"

"Everything is fine," Alaina says, jumping up from her chair. "Just girl talk."

He puts the bags down on the table and kisses me on the top of my head.

I'm quiet as I watch Alaina buzz around the kitchen, getting plates and silverware out. Owen begins to unload the Mexican food, which smells divine. A few minutes later we sit down to eat, and the Fletcher family reunion is the first topic of conversation.

"I never understood why DeeDee pulls out the fake Southern accent," Ken says, dipping his chip in the guacamole.

"Honey, she's done that since the day we met her," Alaina reminds him. "I still remember that night like it was yesterday. Warner and Leann invited us over for dinner, and they were already there by the time we arrived. DeeDee had already had a few drinks."

"No way," I say sarcastically.

Everyone laughs.

"Yes, really," she says, giggling. "Anyway, she was in rare form that night, flirting nonstop with Ken."

Ken nods and munches on his chip. "I think the real reason she doesn't like Alaina is because she has a crush on me."

"Dad," Owen exclaims.

"It's possible," Alaina insists. "She was calling him baby and sugar for most of the night."

Owen looks at me and shakes his head.

I sigh. "I'm sorry for the way DeeDee treated you in Hawaii. She can be a handful, but I never expected her to act like that. I don't think my parents did either."

"I could've handled things better, too," Alaina says. "Leann is my best friend in the whole world. Screaming at her sister-in-law in the middle of a crowded luau wasn't my finest moment."

"DeeDee was trying to push your buttons," Owen interjects. "She wanted to get a rise out of you, and she succeeded."

"But you handled it very well after that night. Aunt DeeDee was still being nasty, and you stayed because you knew it meant a lot to my parents and you're a good friend." I glance at Owen who smiles back at me.

"I'm so glad you didn't leave early," I add.

"So are we," Alaina agrees. "I owe that to you. If you hadn't sat and talked with me at breakfast, we probably would've left. I don't know if Leann would've forgiven us."

After dinner we sit outside around the fire pit, reminiscing about the all the time our families have spent together.

"Our best memories include your family," Alaina says. "And look at everyone now."

Owen tightens his arms around me, leaning his chin against my head.

"Speaking of that, it's time for us to say good night," Ken says, his eyes twinkling.

I blush, feeling grateful the darkness hides the color in my cheeks.

"I'm not tired," Alaina says.

Ken clears his throat motioning toward Owen and me.

"Oh, right," she says, taking his hint.

They hug us and hurry to bed.

A little while later Owen and I are alone in the Webbers' loft, the very place we saw each other for the last time all those years ago. It's weird because it feels like so much time has passed, but at the same time as if it were yesterday.

My head is on his shoulder, and his arm is around me.

"What are you thinking about?" he asks, tracing circles on my hand with his finger.

I exhale slowly. "I was thinking about how good it feels to be here again. What about you?"

When he doesn't answer, I sit up.

Looking into my eyes, he takes a deep breath. "I was also thinking about the last time we were sitting on this couch together. I know I've already said this, but I wish I could go back to that night," he says, moving his face closer to mine. "If I could go back, I never would let you go."

Keep it together, Cora.

He kisses me, while pulling me on top of him. I run my fingers through his hair, and my heart begins to race faster and faster as his hands move from my hair to my back and down to my waist.

"Cora," he whispers between our breathless kisses.

"What?"

"I love you."

We stop kissing, and I pull back an inch.

He cups my chin in his hand. "I think I've always loved you."

I try to swallow the lump in my throat as tears well up in my eyes. "I love you, Owen. I'm pretty sure I've loved you since we picked weeds in the backyard."

He smiles, wrapping his arms tightly around me. This is it. Finally. I'm home.

Chapter Thirty-Six

*W*hen I open my eyes, I immediately smell bacon and pancakes. I smile as I look at the familiar walls of Alaina's guest room. I stretch out and think about the events of last night.

After Owen and I admitted we loved each other, we talked more about our plans for the future. I don't think this smile has left my face since then, and it probably never will. Any doubts I had were washed away the second he said those words. The fears of losing him again are gone, and although I know there will be bumps along the way, I'm confident things will be okay.

I pick up my phone from the nightstand and text Fran.

LOTS TO TELL YOU. I'LL BE HOME TONIGHT.

As I scroll though my messages, I notice an email from my mom, which I ignore. My weekend is going so well, I'd rather not take a chance reading it. I'll wait until I get home, and hopefully Kiwi will park herself on my laptop so I can't open it.

I finally drag myself out of bed, brush my teeth, and shower. As I'm getting dressed, I look out the window. Owen and his dad are playing catch in the backyard. It's possible this view is better than the one from my balcony in Hawaii.

When I get downstairs, Alaina is in the kitchen flipping pancakes.

"Good morning. How did you sleep?"

I stretch my arms above my head. "Better than I ever have before."

She gives me a coy smile. "That's funny, because my son said something very similar to that."

Heat fills my cheeks.

I walk to the french doors and watch Owen and his father throw the ball back and forth.

"Come on, old man, put some more muscle behind these throws," Owen yells. "I can't believe you're getting soft."

Ken holds the ball and points at his son. "You sure you want a piece of this, boy? Don't make me pull out my old tricks."

I laugh. "They're cute together," I say as Alaina hands me a cup of coffee.

"They are, aren't they?" she says, taking a sip from her cup. "Owen woke up this morning and asked his dad to throw the ball. He hasn't done that in years."

I pour creamer into my coffee and stir it.

"Normally he'd get up and spend the morning pounding away on his laptop," she adds. "You've done wonders for him. I feel like I have my son back again."

I love hearing this, but it also makes me wonder about how Owen was with his family during his marriage. I know how much his parents loved Alyssa.

"I hope I'm not overstepping by asking this, but what about when Owen and Alyssa were together? Didn't they ever spend time here?"

She shakes her head. "You're not overstepping. Honestly, when he was with Alyssa, they'd both be in here on their laptops. I never realized it until today."

Interesting. Owen has told me repeatedly that they rushed into their marriage, but I don't know the specific details yet.

"I guess that's what Owen meant when he said he felt like something was missing in their marriage." She continues, "I know they loved each other, but there's something different about him now. Maybe he worked so much because he was constantly searching for something more."

She looks out the back doors at her husband and son and then back at me. "I think he's finally found what he's been looking for."

Tears fill my eyes as I smile.

"That's it, folks. The old man has still got it," Owen yells and starts clapping loudly.

Alaina clears her throat. "How about some pancakes?"

"You don't have to ask me twice." I load my plate with all the delicious breakfast food and sit down at the table. I'm happily digging in when Owen and Ken come inside.

Owen walks over and pulls me to my feet. Without a word he lifts me off the ground and kisses me fiercely.

Ken and Alaina whisper to each other.

"Morning, beautiful," he says in my ear.

Owen obviously doesn't mind showing how he feels in front of his parents, and while I'd normally be embarrassed by this, I'm not.

"Your mother is spoiling me again," I tell him.

"I have a lot of years to make up for," she interjects.

Owen piles several pancakes onto his plate. "So do I," he adds. "And I can't wait to get started."

After spending a wonderful weekend with the Webbers, I'm in the guest room packing my stuff when Owen pops his head into the room.

"You almost ready?"

I sit on the edge of the bed and nod sadly. "Unfortunately."

He sits next to me.

"What's wrong?"

I look around the room and sigh. I thought I was handling this well, but I'm struggling. Owen will be back in San Diego tomorrow, and I'll be home. I know it's going to get harder to leave each other as time goes on.

"This has been the best weekend ... I guess I'm sad we're leaving."

Once again I'm fighting to hold back my tears. For someone so happy, I'm crying a lot.

He kisses my hand. "Hey, do you remember what I told you before we left Hawaii?"

I press my lips together as I continue to choke back tears.

"I told you I didn't want you to be sad because this is just the beginning for us."

"I know it is, and I'm really trying," I say, my voice shaking.

"We have so much to look forward to, and I've already met your family. That's one of the hardest parts of a new relationship," he adds playfully.

I throw my head back in laughter. "That's true. My mother made you wear a loincloth, and you're still here."

He smiles. "That's what I'm talking about."

He kisses my hand. "We're going to have a lot more weekends like this, and eventually we're never going to be apart."

I put my arms around his neck. "I can't wait. We've already spent too many years apart."

He pulls me to my feet, engulfing me in his arms.

"I'm never letting you go again, Cora Fletcher."

I look out the window at the Webbers' backyard and smile. I've waited for this my whole life, and as hard as it's been, some things are totally worth the wait.

Epilogue

I sigh as I read the first of three messages from my mother. Even though we're in a good place, I still haven't learned my lesson about opening these emails.

I look over at Kiwi, who's sitting on the back of the couch. She's really been letting me down lately. This time the email includes an invitation to a gender reveal party for Brynn and Shawn. Apparently, my brother was right and he and Brynn were extremely productive while in Hawaii. They are now expecting the first Fletcher grandchild. My parents are over the moon, and as expected, Maya and I are already over a pregnant Brynn and soon-to-be grandmother Leann.

You'd think Brynn is the first woman to be pregnant, judging by her outlandish demands. Not that any of us are surprised.

It's been five months since our epic family reunion. My mother is in full party-planning mode, and as usual, the Fletchers don't do anything small. There is a dress code, but thankfully it doesn't include any Hawaiian attire.

Things between Brynn and me have been better since the vacation, and she even invited Owen and me over for dinner. This hasn't happened yet, but we accepted her invitation.

I've been extremely busy with my job and spending most of my weekends with Owen. We've managed to make the long-distance thing work for this long, but it's getting more difficult each time to leave one another, almost unbearable.

I've talked to Lydia a few times about working remotely if I were to move to San Diego, which is the most viable option because of Owen's career. For now, we're doing what we can, but we're both ready to make a change.

Fran has been very supportive, despite the fact that I might be moving out. Her massage therapy business is really picking up, but I know she's ready to find someone and settle down. I could see the disappointment in her face when I told her Brynn and Shawn were expecting a baby. I think it finally hit her that there wouldn't be a chance for them even though she claims she's known this for a long time.

In another shocking turn of events, Jackson and Tara did go skydiving together, and according to Maya, they are spending a lot more time with one another because Tara has had some time off. Supposedly they've also been to Mexico together. They tell everyone they're friends, but Maya fears they might become more. Maybe my mother will get her wish and Jackson will officially become part of the family.

Speaking of my cousins, Ashley is engaged again—to a man she met on the plane coming home from Hawaii. He's a pilot and, according to my aunt, a very nice guy. I hope he knows what he's getting himself into. It's only been a few months, so we'll see what happens—hopefully they don't take any trips apart between now and their big day.

Aunt DeeDee has already recruited my mother to help with wedding plans, and apparently wants to do a Southern ball theme with an open bar. Big surprise! According to my mother, Ashley isn't onboard with this idea, but everyone is holding their breath to see if this big wedding actually happens.

Peepaw and Evelyn are loving life as newlyweds and have been traveling a lot. They also spent some time with her son and his family. The last time I spoke to them, Evelyn was still calling me Cara. I've given up on her calling me by my real name, and now it's become a family joke. Everyone in my family except my mother calls me Cara. She of course still calls me Cora Ann.

Owen and I are planning a trip with his parents to—where else, Hawaii —and I can't wait. We try to spend at least one weekend a month with them, and Owen never opens his laptop while we are there.

My mother is also planning a big family Christmas to celebrate her becoming a grandmother, and everyone has been invited, including Owen's parents, but not Jackson. It wouldn't be the holidays without some good old-fashioned family dysfunction.

I've learned it's okay to be different than my family members—that's what makes us who we are. I'll continue to embrace our differences and enjoy the chaos.

You can't pick your family, and as crazy as the Fletcher family is, I don't think I would pick a different one.

The End

Dear Reader

I hope you enjoyed *Love and Ohana Drama*. Please take a few minutes to leave a review on Amazon. Watch for Fran's story coming in 2020!

Love my books? Join my reader group on Facebook!

Visit my website for updates, and stay tuned for my next book coming soon.

AuthorMelissaBaldwin.com

Acknowledgments

To my wonderful readers! You're the best! I hope my stories continue to bring joy to your lives.

To my awesome editor Wendi Baker, thank you for your patience and time. Have you memorized this book yet? ☺

To Sue Traynor, thank you for another dazzling cover! I can't wait to see the next one! ☺

To Karan Eleni, thank you for your knowledge and willingness to help.

To Paula Bothwell, thank you for your support and advice. Stay tuned for Fran's story.

To the fabulous author Aven Ellis, thank you for your insight and friendship! 2020 is going to be amazing.

To my husband and my daughter. I couldn't do this without you. I love you.

About the Author

Melissa Baldwin is planner-obsessed Disney fan who still watches Beverly Hills 90210 reruns and General Hospital.

She's a wife, mother, and journal keeper, who finally decided to write the book she talked about for years. She took her dream to the next level, and is now an award-winning, bestselling author of seventeen Romantic Comedy and Cozy Mystery novels and novellas. Melissa writes about charming, ambitious, and real women, and she considers these leading ladies to be part of her tribe.

When she isn't deep in the writing zone, this multitasking master organizer keeps busy by spending time with her family, chauffeuring her daughter, traveling, attempting yoga poses, and going on rides at Disney World.

Connect with Melissa at
authormelissabaldwin.com

Made in the USA
Coppell, TX
14 July 2020